Unholy Desire

Sinful Natures 3

Lynn Burke

Unholy Desire

As an overseas missionary who leads lost souls toward salvation, it's imperative I live a godly existence, even in the midst of life-shattering grief.

Returning to the States brings about a trial worse than the loss of love, and I'm faced with desire for someone forbidden to me by my church and the word of God.

Aaron Weston.

My best friend's son who is no longer a gangly teen. He makes me want things no newly widowed man should.

His presence fills the emptiness in my life, but my sinful nature longs for more. Every inch of him—in my heart, in my body, making me feel whole again.

Giving into the hunger of the flesh will take us down a path of immorality, one that goes against my strive for holiness.

I lost my wife from focusing on promised riches in glory.

And if I make the same mistake, I fear responsibility for the ruination of another soul.

Chapter 1

Ezra

The plane's speaker crackled to life, announcing our descent into Philadelphia's airport.

The woman in the cramped seat beside me shifted awake, rousing another waft of strongly-scented rose perfume to clog my throat. Grimacing, I blinked at the sand in my eyes, my focus coming to rest on my worn loafers cramped beneath the seat in front of me.

No matter my exhaustion from the twenty-plus hour flight to the States from the Ukraine, adrenaline had kept me wide awake.

I would touch American soil for the first time in fifteen years. I would get to sit in church and rest, to soak in sermons I hadn't studied to preach. I would see the people I'd left behind in my drive to fulfill the Lord's calling on my life and serve Him.

I hadn't meant to emotionally distance from loved ones and family back home, but after meeting Sofiy, falling madly in love—

Cutting the thoughts off that had sagged my shoulders and left my face haggard since her death, I focused on my future.

My best friend since childhood, Phillip Weston, had offered me his spare bedroom until I decided what my next step in life would be. He'd been diagnosed with Parkinson's close to eight years earlier, but the previous three had shown a serious decline in his health.

Guilt twisted my stomach over not being there to help and support Phillip, but even worse, his son Aaron had moved back home to care for him.

The memory of the leggy boy who had tagged along at my heels once he'd learned to walk always brought a smile to my face. And he'd been the reason for the steady release of excitement through my blood since having the freedom to return home.

Aaron had been nothing but skin and bones last I'd seen him. At twenty-nine, I expected—hoped for his sake—he'd grown a bit. I also hoped once high school had ended the bullies he'd seemed to attract no longer attempted to make his life hell.

He'd never shared why he got beat up or why he'd come to hate school and his peers.

But he had his dad, he had me, and the three of us had spent more time together than not. And summers? They held some of my best memories of fishing, hiking, and camping in the woods of northern Pennsylvania.

I wondered if he remembered the life we had together once upon a time, if his own smile made an appearance with the fond recollections.

I'd lost touch with my friends due to Sofiy's selfishness, only sharing a call with Phillip for the first time in years after she'd passed. The regret of allowing her control over my life for so long pained my heart—especially given his poor health.

A flight attendant walked past my aisle seat with a plastic trash bag, and I dropped in my emptied water bottle with a forced smile and "Thank you."

Letting out a shuddered sigh, I tipped my head back and rested my eyelids once she shuffled past.

Returning home a newly widowed man, I should have been wallowing in grief, not looking forward to living without restraint like I'd done due to Sofiy's depression and manipulative ways.

The crumpled note in the back pocket of my chinos burned clear through to my skin, radiating an ache bone-deep that caused my head to hang whenever I thought too long on my dead wife.

Longing to escape the shame of the words she'd scripted in shaking ink always made me cower wherever I went, but I couldn't go without its presence —reminding me of my failure. The need to do better. The many questions her words had roused in my head.

Ones concerning my dogmatism and drive.

Ones of eternity.

Ones of *life*.

The plane's wheels jolted on the ground, making for another burst of adrenaline through my system.

Phillip. Aaron.

God had gifted me new beginning, and we would be the three musketeers again.

Once the plane taxied and the passengers exited ahead of me, I slung my old bag's long strap over my head and shoulder, leaving it to cross my chest. I'd kept my passport, a few books and other papers, as well as my Bible inside, only packing two large suitcases with everything I didn't want to leave behind in the Ukraine since I had no plans to return.

The Bible I had yet to open since I'd seen Sofiy pale and cold on our bed a few weeks earlier. I used to find my peace and comfort inside its thin pages where passage after passage had been underlined and highlighted.

But no longer. I didn't understand why—and the Holy Spirit I trusted to intervene for me at my lowest didn't give me peace either.

I stepped off the plane, sending up an automatic prayer of thankfulness to God for seeing me safely across land and ocean.

Home.

Since Phillip was wheelchair bound due to his disorder, he'd said Aaron would pick me up.

The first sense of life bubbled up inside me after too many days to count. Would he see me as an old man since my hair and beard had taken a liking to gray? Would he notice the lines around my eyes, the fact the shoulders he used to perch atop weren't as wide and strong as they once had been?

Heaviness descended over me again, and I trudged on tired legs with the other passengers into the baggage claim area. The clack of moving belts, the murmurs of voices filled my ears.

Phillip had said Aaron would meet me there, and I scanned the area, looking for messy brown hair and big blue eyes hidden behind glasses, but didn't see him.

I followed the other passengers toward our conveyor, hanging back a bit since everyone else crowded in their rush to claim bags and escape the airport.

Tingles slid over my left cheek like a brush of a dove's feather, and I turned, knowing who watched me before my eyes found him.

Aaron Weston.

Without glasses and sporting a short-clipped beard of his own...far from the young boy I imagined when thinking of him.

My facial muscles remembered how to full-out grin, how to crinkle the lines around my eyes in happiness all thanks to how the sight of him buoyed my heart.

He held my gaze and strode toward me as though on a mission, his sure steps causing my feet to do the same.

Both our arms extended as one, and we fell into each other, laughter wanting to rise up inside me.

He'd grown close to six feet, putting us almost eye to eye, but the feel of Aaron beneath my arms and hands...

All man, he'd filled out with hard muscle and plenty of it.

The sense of actually being at home returned with force, and I clung to him, eyes clenched shut as the scent of soap and dryer sheets I remembered all too well expanded my lungs.

For the first time in countless years, someone held me, their arms seeming to cherish me for *me*—Ezra the man, not a pastor, missionary, or man of God.

My throat threatened to swell shut, and I forced myself to pull back the slightest bit. I kept my hands on his shoulder and neck, needing to know Aaron stood in front of me for real.

"Aaron," I whispered and leaned in to kiss his forehead as I'd done hundreds of times in the past.

His slow exhale ghosted hot over my throat, sending an unnerving, strange shiver down my spine.

I dropped my hands from him and stepped away fully. "You look good, young man."

He grinned, those blue eyes lighting up with a mischievous glint I'd often thought about—and had missed. "It's great to finally see you again, Ezra."

And with that one sentence, the reason for my return slapped me across the face in harsh reality.

"I'm sorry for your loss," Aaron stated quietly as though he knew why my happiness at seeing him had dimmed.

"Thank you," I murmured, flicking my focus toward the conveyor and readjusting my bag's strap across my chest. Most of the crowd had dissipated.

Aaron cleared his throat and moved closer to the carousel, and I pointed out my two bags. He slung them off the belt as though they weighed less than a sack of groceries, and my eyebrows lifted. I'd packed them both full, paying the extra fee for them being overweight.

Another smile tempted my lips upward.

"What?" he asked, side-eyeing me with that twinkle in his eyes again.

I shook my head. "You've changed."

"My growth spurt hit not long after you left." Aaron pulled up the first case's handle while I did the same with the second. "I packed on a little muscle weight in college too."

I glanced down over his wide shoulders, the tapered V of his waist, and the bulging thighs beneath his shorts. Even his calves appeared like he enjoyed his spinach a ton more than he had as a kid. One of my eyebrows raised. "A little?"

He chuckled and led the way toward the glass door, leaving me to follow.

The slider opened ahead of him, letting in a blast of hot summer air and bringing the scent of his soap to my nose once more.

That same shiver licked at my spine, and I frowned, wondering at my body's reaction to him.

Not exactly comfort like it should have been...and definitely not peaceful.

Perhaps I'd gone too long without physical touch and his hug had cracked open a need inside me I had smothered for many years. Sure the strange feelings would subside once I got used to affection again, I strode ahead to walk beside him.

We traversed the path toward the parking garage, my face once more tingling. Glancing over, I found him peering at me, the warmth in his eyes smoothing my frown. More than mere happiness resided in his blue orbs, something I couldn't name, but...

Suddenly parched, I flicked my tongue over my lower lips looking for moisture, and Aaron's focus dropped to my mouth.

Want—beyond platonic friendship.

That was the feeling prickling to life inside me, what filled his eyes.

Unsure how to pray or what to say, I turned my attention forward, falling back a step in order to follow Aaron again.

I'd never felt drawn to a man before, never once considered studying the body of the same sex to find attraction.

But young Aaron Weston had definitely woken up something inside me I didn't know what to do with, some unholy desire.

I needed to put a stopper on whatever it was he'd brought to the surface of my old sinful nature, or I would find more trouble for myself than the truth of Sofiy's final attempts at manipulation in my pocket.

Chapter 2

Aaron

The natural scent of Ezra—fresh fallen leaves after a rain storm—swarmed the inside of my old SUV within seconds of us being shut in together. A blast of frigid air conditioning didn't lessen the longing from the memory of drawing him deep into my lungs even as a kid.

Add in my body's awareness of him being in close proximity, and I once again thanked myself for thinking *briefs* when dressing to pick Ezra up at the airport.

I asked about his flight, hoping senseless chatter would get my mind off the need that had slammed into me when our gazes had met in the baggage claim area. All those teenage hormones I hadn't understood at fourteen had come back with the force of a hurricane, swirling inside me like rushing wind.

Ezra had been one of my best friends, even though he'd been Dad's first. My protector, my shoulder to lean on, my hero.

In my mind, he'd been my and Dad's third musketeer, and we'd been inseparable until he'd left for the Ukraine as a missionary in order to lead lost souls to Christ.

Then he'd married the woman who'd kept him away from us, and the connection he'd had to the US lessened with each passing year.

"How's your dad doing?" Ezra asked after brushing off a conversation about his too-long flight over the Atlantic.

Since Ezra would see for himself within twenty minutes, I didn't bother holding back the truth. "Parkinson's has turned him into a miserable bastard."

Ezra didn't admonish me like he'd have done if I were a fourteen-year-old boy.

"But I understand why," I continued. "He's bound to a wheelchair. Losing his mind." I turned onto the highway leading us home. "Knowing that doesn't make it any easier to deal with him."

"How are you holding up?" Ezra's soft voice always soothed me as a kid, and I found myself smiling at how effortlessly he set me at ease.

"I'm hanging in there." Barely, some days, but what choice did I have? I couldn't afford to put Dad in a home, not that I would even if we had the money. Doing so would harshly point out my weakness I'd fought for years to turn to strength.

"Do you get out much? Make time for yourself?" Ezra sat still, his hands on his thighs which I forced myself to not focus on but failed. Wide palms I wanted on my skin. Strong fingers my body ached to feel inside.

My dick pressed against its prison.

I cleared my throat. "I hit the gym every morning long before he wakes up, work there for a few hours too. Church is my other two hours of freedom." The latter because Dad could watch the service livestream at home which freed me up to escape the house.

As for the church destination for those precious moments without responsibility...I wasn't sure where

God's and my relationship stood, but the worship brought me a sense of comfort. And hearing Pastor Welker's sermons gave me and Dad something to discuss for the rest of the day since he would be jolly and talkative for a change—even if I didn't believe much of the drivel shared from the pulpit.

"It appears you know what you're doing at the gym," Ezra said, and I caught a hint of a smile in his voice.

He appreciated my body. Fuck, did that thought flood me with a shot of adrenaline.

"I might have an addiction," I admitted, finding it hard to keep my voice level.

"Is that because you were bullied in high school?"

He'd guessed half of the reason I worked out until exhausted six days of the week. Having been seen as a weak kid, I'd focused on becoming stronger. The other reason for my intense workouts the previous three years came about from a need for release—from pent-up anger toward my dad and not being allowed a life.

Or much of anything else for that matter.

A stockpile of bills sat on Dad's desk at home, ones I struggled to keep us from drowning beneath, so even if

I had the freedom to go out once in a while, I couldn't afford to.

"Yeah." I agreed to the bullying suggestion as I took an exit to grab some KFC, Dad's favorite food. Sitting down to fried chicken for dinner would make him happy for the rest of the evening, and leftovers for lunch the following day assured that mood would stay. "Thanks for coming into the high school when Drew first kicked my ass," I repeated what I'd already said dozens of times before but couldn't help revisit.

It was the day Ezra went from friend to hero since Dad hadn't been able to leave work.

Fucking Drew Bradley had called me a fag even though I hadn't been aware of my own sexuality at that point. Between him and his two buddies, I'd ended up with a broken nose, arm, and three ribs.

And the asshole, being from money and the principal's nephew, hadn't even gotten suspended.

Ezra clasped my shoulder, sending shots of electrical currents through my entire body, jerking my dick inside its prison. "I wish I could have done more."

I hadn't told him why I'd gotten my skinny ass handed to me—or spoke of the times afterward when Drew used me as a punching bag, but twice more before Ezra went to the Ukraine, he'd seen the bruises on my body.

"You never shared why that boy hated you so much." He removed his hand from my shoulder, a sense of loss and coolness rising.

"It's been so long, I don't even remember," I lied. No one except for my good friend Zeke had known, and even then, he'd guessed at my sexual orientation—and I hadn't confirmed.

As far as our church believed, desiring a man led to the pits of hell. Bad enough or even forbidden in more accepting eyes because he was Dad's best friend and had a few years on me. Not that *I* gave a shit. But like my religious dad, Ezra would see me as an abomination, nothing but a perversion.

Or would he? The look I'd given him while walking to the parking garage...the flick of his tongue over this lower lip...did Ezra have secrets of his own?

My heart thumped a little harder as I pulled up to the drive through and placed my order.

"He's still a sucker for KFC, huh?"

I grinned, finally glancing over at Ezra while waiting for our bucket of chicken. The lines of grief around his eyes remained smoothed out, and I found myself wanting to keep him that way. "I would get it for him every night if it wasn't so damn bad for his heart."

"And expensive." Ezra eyed me as though he knew about Dad's and my situation. "Phillip told me you're struggling to make ends meet." His lips downturned fully again, and I inwardly cursed my dad.

"Things are tight, yeah, but nothing I can't handle."

A lie with only being able to work three hours a day. But I couldn't have Ezra thinking I was deficient in any area.

"I insisted on paying rent for the next three months, so hopefully those funds will help you get caught up."

I doubted as much but wasn't about to state the truth. "Thanks, Ezzie."

Ezra barked out a laugh, and my heart squeezed in my chest over his rich baritone chuckle. "I haven't heard that nickname in—"

"Fifteen years," we said at the same time, mine sounding more like a question.

His laughter died away along with my smile as we stared across the console at one another. Hazel eyes flicked over my face, settling on my mouth for a heartbeat longer than was appropriate for a man of God.

And I would know. I'd sown my so-called wild oats.

Perhaps I am *wrong about his thoughts on homosexuality aligning with the church—*

A horn blared from behind us, igniting another shot of adrenaline to rush through my blood. I let off the brakes and pulled up to the drive through window.

Two minutes later, a record for Dad's favorite restaurant getting my order into my hands, I took a right out of their parking lot.

"Dad's not the same man from fifteen years ago," I told Ezra, needing to prepare him for what he would find when we arrived at home.

"I could hear the difference in his voice. Softer rather than boisterous like I remember. It's been a while since we spoke on the phone."

Three years.

And I didn't have to wonder why. Ezra had always been a driven man, hell-bent on being a missionary, winning souls from the pits of hell, and receiving his crown in glory.

He'd put God first, leaving everything behind, including his best friend and the young teen who'd adored him.

I still do.

Even though he'd abandoned me and stopped calling once he'd married. My love and desire for Ezra wouldn't ever change no matter the twinge I sometimes felt over his departure from our lives.

I glanced over again, loving the silver in his beard and hair. He'd been handsome before he'd left for the Ukraine, and the years had only aged him like a fine wine.

My mouth watered.

Tightening my grip on the steering wheel, I turned back toward the road. "The decreased facial expressions will be the biggest physical change you'll see—outside of the wheelchair and loss of muscle weight," I said. "He can't stand very well by himself, definitely can't live alone. Mornings are the worst. Lots of stiffness. Rigidity."

"And you take care of him all on your own?"

I nodded, looking both ways before crossing the intersection into our neighborhood.

"You truly have a servant's heart."

Ezra didn't know my innermost thoughts—and I wouldn't ever share what would out me as the spineless, selfish asshole I was.

"The woman who lives next door to us comes and sits with him if I need to head out for an extended period of time, but that's rare," I said, staying away from his misconception of what kind of person resided inside me.

"And how is his mental health?"

"He's irritated a lot. Depressed, but understandably."

"I can imagine I would be in a constant state of prayer to do what you do."

"I've found the best way to handle his aggressive behavior is to remain calm. Reading scripture to him helps lessen his aggravation."

"He's always been a fervent soul." Ezra's tone suggested respect and love.

"Same as you," I pointed out.

He turned his focus out the passenger window and didn't reply.

I assumed part of the grieving process Ezra went through included questioning God, but I would have no such thoughts when it came time for Dad. The day he breathed his last, *I* would get the chance to breathe again.

Sacrificing oneself, especially at a young age, didn't inspire joyful emotions. The Bible commanded people to serve each other in love, but obeying that one was no easy task. I hated how my life had changed when I'd become a caretaker, even though Dad had been my friend as much as my father. I could admit to myself the truth of feeling overwhelmed. Oftentimes depressed. But no one else would ever learn I was anything less than the steady, selfless rock that I portrayed myself to be.

Yes, I loved Dad—but I also wouldn't be completely heartbroken when he passed.

The pit of my stomach hollowed out as it always did when I thought of the near future. With how quickly Dad's health had declined due to Parkinson's, his doctor didn't expect him to live out the year which would put me pretty much on my own since I'd lost touch with old friends—and Zeke had moved back to Boston. It'd been Dad and me for three years...so yeah, I would miss him.

I pulled into the driveway and filled my lungs with one last deep inhale of Ezra's warm scent to rid my mind of Dad's outburst at his last doctor's appointment when we'd been given the dire news. It had been a dark day for him, and his mood had remained sour until learning of Ezra's return.

"Ready?" I asked, pulling Ezra's gaze off the front of our house that hadn't changed much in the years he'd been gone.

"Yes." His firm conviction came through in the single worded answer...but I wondered what all he'd meant beyond meeting Dad.

Because his tone invoked so much more.

Unable to help myself, I grabbed hold of his knee and nodded. Letting him know I was ready too.

Chapter 3

Ezra

Phillip had always been a strapping man, brutish in strength and thick through the chest. The man slumped in the wheelchair who greeted me with a half-smile and slurred words of welcome was nothing more than a mere shell of my memory.

Regret like I'd never known slammed into me. Sofiy had stolen years from me—from us, and a feeling of heaviness settled over my shoulders beyond what her death had caused.

"I'm sorry I left." I struggled to apologize without shedding a tear.

"You gained your place in glory," Phillip slowly got the words out, but his smile remained.

Throat tight, I bent to hug him, taking care of the frail bones beneath sagging skin. He didn't smell of the outdoors and Old Spice like I remembered but of age and sickness.

Or perhaps my senses betrayed me in recognizing my oldest and best friend didn't have much time left.

My stomach knotted from a swell of emotions that I couldn't begin to number. I should have been there for Phillip, been available for him to vent or console when he'd been diagnosed with Parkinson's.

I'd failed him, same as I'd failed Sofiy.

The note burned through to my skin, but I forced the previous couple of weeks from my mind and focused on the reality of my life.

The here and now.

I would make up for all we'd lost out on and redeem myself with the second chance God had given me.

Glenda, the neighbor lady who'd stayed with Phillip while Aaron retrieved me from the airport, declined the invitation to join for dinner, so the three of us sat down to dine on fried chicken and the instant potatoes and gravy I hadn't tasted in fifteen years.

And the warm biscuits…smothered in melted butter.

"So good," I said and licked crumbs off my fingers.

Phillip made a grunt of agreement, but my face burned.

I glanced at Aaron to find his focus on my mouth rather than the half-eaten chicken thigh in his fingers.

Swallowing hard, I turned my attention back to my plate.

Whatever strangeness had come to life between us at the airport remained, and I couldn't figure out my thoughts. I seemed to be…drawn to him in unhealthy ways, but I didn't sense conviction from the Holy Spirit over such feelings.

Exhaustion had to weigh in on my tumbling emotions. Chances were, his hug had opened a floodgate of longing for all I'd been denied for ten years from my frigid wife.

Clinging to that hope, I pushed against the memory of his hand on my knee before entering the house. I'd wanted to pull his touch higher to the part of me that hadn't known a loving caress from another human for much too long.

Forced celibacy due to Sofiy's issues should have given me an opportunity to somehow glorify God, but I'd never found how. Our lack of intimacy had only intensified my bitterness toward her.

And now she's dead because of me. Better I'd never left Phillip and went on the mission field.

My appetite waned, and I pushed the plastic spork through the coleslaw rather than eating it, fighting off the demons in my head.

"You must be tired." Phillip's slow words escaped as barely more than a mumble.

I forced a half-smile. "I am."

The sun had begun to sink in the window behind him. Not late enough to go to bed, and it had been too long since I'd spent time with my friend.

"But I'm not ready to sleep just yet," I added.

"Why don't you wheel Dad into the living room," Aaron suggested what I'd been thinking, "and I'll clean up our mess."

Unable to look at Aaron's face, I nodded. "Phillip?"

My friend grunted an affirmative, and I pushed up from the table.

Backside tingling, I wheeled Phillip from the kitchen, and the sense of being watched ceased the second we turned the corner, away from the kitchen and Aaron's view.

Aaron had taken down a few walls to open up the space for his dad's wheelchair and cleared a spot alongside the couch for Phillip. I parked him beside the end table, angled a bit toward the couch.

"Can I get you anything?" I asked.

"No."

I settled on the couch cushion closest to him, sitting somewhat sideways to make discussion easier. "How are you?" I asked quietly, giving him the opportunity to open up without his son hearing.

"Dying," he bit out.

Gathering his wrinkled hand in mine, I studied the veins along the back...the thinness of his wrist, the lack of muscle beneath the sleeve of his T-shirt. "God blessed us with a lot of good memories, my friend."

"Not enough."

Pale and sunken, his face was void of expression even though his words suggested anger and regret. His hand shook slightly in mine.

My fault. "Well, I'm here now," I managed to whisper, "and we're going to make the best of our time together." Since I hadn't done so with Sofiy.

Another hard swallow had me shifting my attention toward the TV on its stand.

"Grief is for the birds," Phillip muttered, "and not my favorite chirping ones."

He'd lost his wife too—but because she'd run off with another man, leaving him and Aaron alone. Death of a different sort but hurt all the same, and I'd been there to help him pick up the pieces.

My heart longed to pour out my shame to Phillip, my fingers to pull the note from my back pocket. Of all the people in my life, he was the only one I could trust with my deepest secret.

But my friend faced a depression of his own, and I wouldn't add to his burden by unveiling mine.

Forcing another smile, I turned my focus back on him. "You're blessed to have Aaron."

Phillip's body twitched as though annoyed even though his expression stayed neutral. "He's a good boy."

Not a boy.

A shiver rippled through me as the image of him striding toward me in the airport flashed through my memory, and I closed my eyes, wanting to bask in the strange desire he'd roused—and rid it from my mind.

"Okay?" Phillip asked me, and I nodded. "Time will lessen the hurt," he murmured, taking care to form each word.

But it wasn't the pain of loss I dealt with at that moment. The feeling shifting over my skin, through my body was desire, plain and simple.

For affection, I assured myself. *Nothing sexual.*

I squeezed Phillip's hand gently, hoping to alleviate my wayward state of dealing with the lack of physical touch.

No strange vibe filled me from the thin hand in mine. No shiver of need. No prickling awareness like the one causing the hair on the nape of my neck to rise.

I turned to find Aaron in the living room's doorway. Our eyes locked on one another, and for the first time since I'd caught sight of Sofiy all those years ago, my lungs refused to pull in oxygen.

Aaron's gaze flitted over my face but not as though tracking how I'd changed from the man he'd known before. No, his focus seemed on taking me in, on memorizing the newer version—and the soft smile lifting his lips made me think he appreciated what he saw.

In more ways than was proper for a man and his father's best friend.

My body tightened, but Aaron shifted his attention toward Phillip, allowing me to breathe again. "You okay, Dad?" he asked, noting our clasped hands.

Phillip grunted an affirmative, and Aaron rounded the couch to sit beside me. He sprawled rather than perching on the cushion, angling toward me. Inches separated his pulled-up knee from my thigh, and I stared at the distance, wishing to lessen it.

Knowing I shouldn't.

"Remember our last camping trip?" Aaron asked, his tone happier than I'd heard all afternoon. "That black bear that got into our cooler?"

"He stole the bacon," Phillip mumbled.

"And you chased him off by banging two pots together and howling like a banshee," I tacked on, chuckling at the memory I hadn't thought on in years. "In your boxers—and you woke up the neighboring campers."

"I swear they fried up bacon and ate it in front of us on purpose that morning to get me back for waking them up." Phillip's long sentence took a while to make it past his lips, but his blue eyes Aaron had inherited twinkled with a bit of life.

"The bastards," I murmured, leaning toward him like we shared in our unkind, ungodly thoughts toward those folks.

If Phillip could have laughed, I knew he would have with the deep rumble that used to give me such a sense of camaraderie.

My smile faded as I realized again all the years Sofiy had stolen from me—time I had allowed her to take.

Heaviness settled over my chest and lingered as the three of us continued to reminisce even though neither of them seemed to hold any bitterness over my having left them with silence for so many years. Still, I smiled rather than revealing my regrets outwardly, soaking in the feeling of home, of belonging I'd always felt with Phillip and his son.

But the sense of *more* rested in the back of my head that I couldn't shake, and it kept me on edge. Tense and unsettled inside.

Eventually, darkness claimed the windows, and Aaron wheeled Phillip back to the dining room he'd converted into a first-floor bedroom to settle him into bed for the night.

Given the reprieve of privacy, I filled my lungs fully and climbed the stairs, focusing on what needed to be done rather than the unrest inside my soul.

I'd been once again gifted my old bedroom on the second floor and set to unpacking my things into the bureau and bookshelf Aaron had emptied for me. I shoved the two suitcases through the pull-down into the attic, and a quick shower washed the weariness of travel from my body. Although exhaustion weighed my shoulders, I knew I wouldn't sleep.

Aaron sat watching TV when I meandered back downstairs against my better judgement.

"Did you have any problems getting him into bed?" I asked, collapsing in the seat I'd vacated an hour earlier.

"No. We have a pretty set routine." Aaron shifted on the couch, once more turning my way. He lifted his knee up onto the cushion beside me again, stretching his shorts tight over bulging thighs. Dark hair on sculpted calves—

I tore my wandering focus off him to fiddle with the edge of my T-shirt.

"And he's on an emotional high after all those memories and laughter," Aaron continued on as though he hadn't noticed me looking at his legs.

"He seems well, all things considered," I agreed, glancing up at his face.

"Because you're here." Aaron's smile warmed my heart. "Once that newness wears off, you'll see him in all his negative, complaining glory. For someone who claims to love the Lord as much as he does, you'd think he would be a little more filled with the Spirit." His lips clamped closed as though he'd said too much

I noted the hint of bitterness in Aaron's voice that crept in at the end of his vocalized observance but wasn't about to admonish him. Not having lived in his shoes, I couldn't begin to imagine his thoughts and feelings.

It didn't appear as though he'd be forthcoming with them either, but perhaps he needed a little encouragement to release some of his bottled-up emotions.

"How are you really doing, Aaron?" I asked, allowing myself to look him full in the face. Last I'd done so was when I'd turned to find him behind me while Phillip and I had our quiet time together, my body zapping like a live wire.

"Good." He lied to some extent, but his smile didn't.

"I can imagine you feel as though you're missing out on life right now. At your age, it must be tough to be in the situation you're in."

"I have my moments." Aaron's gaze slid down over my face, lingering on my beard, my neck, and my shoulders.

I turned my focus on my hands rather than dealing with the strangeness the want in his eyes inspired. Tingles raced down my spine, settling in my balls, but I refused to allow a foothold to such desires.

"You're lucky to still have your loved one," I stated quietly, and suddenly I needed to feel his arms again—compassion and comfort.

The affirmation of being loved that came from physical touch.

But I feared I wouldn't be able to keep from taking advantage of what I expected Aaron wished to give.

Chapter 4
Aaron

More than anything, I wanted to hug Ezra tight against my chest, hold him, and offer him what his stooped shoulders claimed he needed, same as he'd done for me countless times when I'd come home from school bruised and crying.

But knowing him as I did, I felt sure he would prefer scripture, assurance that God had his best interest in heart. That his loss in some way would bring glory to the Lord.

I couldn't do that either.

"Tell me about her," I decided to say, not that I wanted to hear about the woman who'd kept him from returning to us. Speaking of loss often helped those grieving to move forward though, and there wasn't anything I wouldn't do for my father's best friend.

Ezra let out a heavy sigh and rested his head back against the couch, his focus on the ceiling. "She loved the Lord. Loved serving others in our tiny church. She had beautiful blonde hair she wore long as the Bible suggested a woman ought to do. I would have loved her even if she'd cut it short." His throat worked as though he swallowed against rising sadness. A lone tear slipped down his cheek, and I clenched my hands to stop myself from wiping it away.

The droplet fell to his shoulder, darkening a round spot on his gray T-shirt that appeared soft as butter.

"We didn't always get along," Ezra admitted, seeming to sink deep into the old cushions beneath his body.

"I can't imagine relationships are easy." Mom had left Dad, which Ezra had witnessed. It had been the reason he'd originally moved in with us when I was a young kid—and ended up staying until he travelled to the Ukraine.

First Mom, then Ezra...and Dad would leave me before long.

Talk about fucking abandonment issues.

But Ezra's back, and maybe he'll stay this time.

"Relationships are not easy," Ezra stated quietly while I clung to the hope of my thought. "Are you in one?" He rolled his head, finally giving me his eyes that held pain and emotions far beyond I'd ever experienced in my years.

"A relationship?" I asked.

He nodded.

"I've never met anyone who tempted me into more than a fling."

"Fling, huh?"

I nodded, wanting to bite back a smirk rather than feel embarrassment over the truth I'd done a few things he wouldn't approve of.

"So my little Aaron isn't an angel anymore."

My little Aaron.

I huffed a snort over the life I'd lived before returning home to care for Dad, choosing to ignore how Ezra had called me his. "Far from it."

"Do all the ladies throw themselves at your feet?"

I shrugged his question off, not about to tell him I preferred when men propositioned me.

"Don't be humble." His tone had lightened.

"There've been a few."

Ezra lifted his head and used his shoulder to dry his cheek. "I can imagine."

His words held more meaning than an off-handed assumption which thrilled me right down to my core.

"It's the women in the church who are the worst, though," I said, giving him the honest-to-God's truth. "They're not out for just a piece of me—they want it all. Ring. White picket fence. Walk-in closet." I shuddered at the thought of sharing my life with a woman. Cloying perfume, heels, and soft flesh draped over mine.

My hands itched for hardened skin, muscle, and bone like the man beside me.

Ezra turned toward me, mirroring my pose.

Our knees brushed together, but he didn't pull away as most men would with a muttered apology. Energy slid up my leg straight to my groin, but a sense of comfort also came from the slight touch.

My hand found his knee without thought, the slight intake of air into his lungs not lost to me. "I'm glad you're staying with us again, Ezzie." I could have gone on to number the many reasons why, but doubted he would appreciate being called silver fox eye candy or jerk-off fodder atop the sense of rightness I felt from having him in our lives again.

His fingers shifted where his hand rested on his thigh above mine, and I willed him to reach out. Take my hand. Thread our fingers together and show me that he experienced even a fraction of what I could swear brewed between us.

"I've never apologized for not calling you or your father more while I was in the Ukraine," he stated quietly.

"Water under the bridge, Ezzie." I verbally waved off his apology even though he'd abandoned me same as Mom had done when I'd been a kid. It'd hurt like hell, but Ezra had returned, and that's all that mattered to me.

The future.

"Still," he insisted, his voice low, "I'm terribly sorry, and I hope you'll someday be able to forgive me."

I squeezed his knee where my fingers still lingered. "Already done, Ezzie. Honestly."

"All things considered," he said while eyeing my hand, "I can say I'm glad to be here, Aaron."

Silence ruled for a few tense seconds between us as we studied one another's faces. My dick continued to stir to life, and my pulse kicked up a notch as I allowed a brief caress of my thumb along the side of his knee.

Ezra's lips parted slightly like he too felt the connection of something tangible as fuck between us.

"I'm off to bed," he finally said, his tone ragged as though winded from running a 5k.

Unable to voice anything beyond begging for him to stay there with me, to allow me to touch—to taste him —I nodded.

He slid from beneath my gentle hold and walked off, his lounge pants cradling an ass I wanted to squeeze until bruised while pleasuring him. Or wrap my ankles around while he thrust balls-deep into my body. Vers as fuck, I'd gladly give or accept whatever the hell he desired.

My breath left in a rush as he disappeared up the stairs, each creak of his tread taking him further away from me and my tension-strung body.

"Fuck." I rubbed over my face and shifted on the couch to adjust my uncomfortable bulge. Adjusting didn't ease the ache, so I got up and turned off the lights before heading up the stairs to relieve my hard-on.

I passed by Ezra's shut bedroom door, the image of him stripped down and under clean sheets sending another jolt to my groin.

Biting back a groan, I locked myself in my own room, yanked off my clothes in record time, and laid back atop my quilt, leaking dick in hand. Pre-cum eased my tugs, and I focused on the image of Ezra's mouth in my head. Parted lips opening wider. Tongue extending. Gifting me a place to shoot my cum.

"Ung." I grunted with the first ribbon of spunk erupting from my dick, fisting myself harder, faster, biting my tongue to keep from hollering. Groaning out his name with every spurt ejaculated up over my abs and chest.

My nostrils flared with each inhale, and I slumped back against my bed once spent. Tingles raced over my skin, settling in my toes and fingertips. I closed my eyes and soaked up that feeling of release, knowing the need for it would return sooner than normal thanks to our new house guest.

* * *

I skipped out on the gym the next morning. Took off work too since it was Ezra's first day back with us. He came down the stairs in shorts and a T-shirt, eyes all sleepy and hair sticking up.

Sexy as fuck.

And my dick noticed enough that I didn't get up from where I sat at the table nursing my second cup of coffee.

"You're awake earlier than I expected," I told him as he shuffled to the coffee pot.

"I passed out before my head hit the pillow," he replied with his rich baritone while filling the mug I'd set out for him, "and I don't even remember dreaming."

Two sugars and milk found its way into his cup—same as always, I noted with a smile.

He let out a groan while sitting across from me, his focus on the steam rising beneath his nose.

I watched his lips as he sipped, his low murmur of appreciation like a shot of lust to my balls. "Good stuff, huh?"

"When did you start?" he asked, motioning with his chin toward the mug I held.

"This morning at four-thirty like always—but my freshman year in college when I partied too hard and needed to wake up for class."

"So you *did* sow your wild oats."

I shrugged, spinning the almost empty cup in my hand. "My fair share, I suppose."

"And you never fell in love?" His voice hinted at teasing.

I considered the older guy I'd given my virginity to when I'd still been a scrawny freshman, but that had been more a crush than anything. After him, it'd been nothing but hook ups. Once I moved home to care for

Dad, all thoughts of the guys I could meet on apps had diminished.

"Nah." I finally answered the truth and swallowed down the last of my coffee, wondering if going without being dicked down for three years had anything to do with how badly I wanted Ezra.

"What did you earn your degree in?"

Sore subject, enough to relax my groin, but I wasn't about to let him in on that weakness of mine either. "I had to drop out after my sophomore year due to money problems. I worked for a while and managed to tuck away enough to go back." I stated facts he would learn about eventually, trying to keep the bitterness from my tone.

"But you never finished?"

"No," I replied without a hint of how I felt inside about that truth. "I had to come home and take care of Dad."

Not bothering to tack on that I'd only had two semesters left, I got up to refill my cup—not that I needed more caffeine either. My muscles missed the workout that morning, and the excess energy left me *bouncy* as Dad would call it. Lying also didn't help my inability to rest.

"Hungry?" I asked, taking out the eggs and bread rather than sitting again where discussion might become too deep.

"Starved." Ezra got up and helped me. "Still like your eggs over easy?" he asked, pulling the frying pan from the same place we'd always stored it.

"You still like your toast black?" I shot back with a grin.

He chuckled and grabbed the butter from the fridge.

The next ten minutes filled my mind up with memories of us working alongside each other in the kitchen before he'd left me and Dad. I'd been devastated, and having the chance to soak in his presence again lightened my chest. Both smiling, we settled at the table for breakfast—and Dad rang the bell I kept beside his bed.

A good two hours earlier than usual.

Guess he'd woken up due to the excitement of having Ezra back home.

My happiness faded a bit, and I took a minute to shovel some food into my mouth before hopping up.

Once I had Dad ready for the day and wheeled into the kitchen for his own breakfast, mine had gone cold.

But I squashed my annoyance as always and zipped my lips.

Ezra had cleaned up the dishes and dressed, and once more sat at the table with another cup of coffee. "Good morning, Phillip," he said, pushing up from his chair. "If it's alright with you, I'm going to make your breakfast this morning. Give Aaron a break and the two of us some time together to reminisce over our younger years." He winked at me, and my stomach bottomed out at the smirk on his lips—and the gracious gift he offered.

Freedom.

Although I would have loved to hang out with Ezra, I expected the two best friends wanted to be alone. Taking that back seat didn't hurt nearly as bad as I'd expected, and I went upstairs to shower.

"Heading out?" Ezra asked when I came back downstairs later and found him and Dad still at the table.

"Figured I'd grab some groceries if you don't mind watching over Dad?"

Dad grunted his annoyance at my word choice.

"Of course I don't mind *helping* if he needs me," Ezra said, having picked up on Dad's unspoken thoughts. "Here." He pulled some money from his pocket, dropping a folded piece of paper in the process.

I bent to retrieve it, but he snatched it from my hand before I fully stood back up.

"Sorry," he muttered, tucking it away and shoving a few twenties at me. "Why don't you get a nice pot roast and I'll make us some dinner."

"Mashed potatoes and roasted carrots too?" I asked, grinning at the thought of my favorite meal he hadn't cooked for us in too damn long.

"You got it, kid."

Kid. *Goddamnit.*

Even though he'd mentioned how I changed, he still saw me as a youngster, which for me, meant vulnerable and weak. Two things I wouldn't be. Hell, it was why I was so steadfast in caring for Dad. Crumbling beneath the responsibility would be nothing but cowardice.

And I refused to be seen as anything but strong.

My smile faded and my shoulders rounded a bit, the excitement over an Ezra-made dinner waning.

But I took his cash and headed out to the store, determined like fuck to enjoy a hard-earned reprieve from the damned drudgery.

Chapter 5

Ezra

Sunday morning, the congregation at Simply Grace Church welcomed me with open arms, some tears, and hundreds of condolences. While I appreciated people's words, I quickly grew tired of murmuring my thanks.

I didn't want to think about Sofiy and the loss of her life. I had no desire to be reminded I'd unexpectedly become a widow at the age of forty-nine or that my future lay in shadows of gray.

Even Pastor Welker sidelined me after the service, asking if I would be interested in a position at the church while on furlough in order to keep my brain occupied, my grief at bay. Knowing I had no plans to return to the Ukraine and the small church I'd built from the ground up didn't give me any clear answers.

I politely declined—*for now*, I told him.

Hindsight made me overanalyze and question every decision I'd made overseas, and the self-doubt Sofiy's passing inflicted on my soul only created more of a haze in my mind about moving forward.

I imagined a fish flopping around on dry land having swallowed a steel hook, knowing it needed to return to water yet couldn't—and I identified with the poor creature.

Enough I actually considered never casting a lure again for all of three or so minutes before remembering the joy fishing had once brought me.

My whole life, I'd followed in the ways of my older parents' footsteps and served God first. I'd obeyed His word, His commandments.

And my existence had turned over because I'd been *too* focused on that calling.

So much so that my wife had chosen death over her husband.

And no one but me knew the truth.

No longer having my job of winning lost souls to Christ, I found a deep neediness in me, some part that hadn't ever been fulfilled—but I couldn't put a title on it. Couldn't even pinpoint exactly what my heart longed for beyond companionship and affection.

The hugs of Pastor Welker's flock, even the people I'd known in my prior life who still attended, didn't fill the void. Every gentle embrace and every firm handshake fell short.

Aaron stayed by my side the entire service and afterward, patiently waiting to drive me back home. Strangely, I felt more comfort once in the privacy of his SUV when we headed home to Phillip than I had in my old place of worship.

"Thank you," I murmured, resting my head back and closing my eyes once he pulled from the parking lot.

"For?"

"Standing by me. Your faithfulness. You're a good friend, Aaron." My voice choked up a bit, and I fisted my hands to keep from squeezing his thigh or grabbing hold of his shoulder.

"I'll always be here for you, Ezzie. No matter when, no matter what you need."

Assurance filled his tone, but that strangeness settled between us as my mind wondered over the *what* he'd implied.

Unable to deal with such thoughts and emotions, I turned on the radio to an oldies station we used to listen to. *Stand by Me*, of all songs, played moments later—and we both belted out the lyrics.

Same as we'd done all those years ago whenever King's voice came on the radio.

As Aaron had told me, Phillip stayed in a good mood most of that day and the next. By Tuesday, however, he showed signs of the man Aaron had warned me about.

Aggressive behavior, snapping at his son for doing something wrong. Finding fault in almost everything from his toast in the morning to his prune juice at night not being cold enough.

Not once did Aaron speak up. Like a doormat, he let Phillip walk all over him, and like a slave, he allowed the sick man to order him about.

I recognized the stoop of Aaron's shoulders by Tuesday night. I understood the bleakness in his eyes. The hands shoved in his pockets when he left for the gym each morning.

Because I'd missed the signs in my own wife—and had dismissed them, encouraging her to just trust God.

Depression wasn't so easily lifted, I'd learned.

And my heart ached even while I quietly and often praised Aaron for his selflessness and dedication to caring for his dad because I couldn't stand the idea of him falling so deep he searched for a way out.

I'd screwed up once, and I wouldn't again.

Aaron had always considered himself to be weak—I expected he hated that about himself the most—and yet I'd never seen a stronger man. His self-control was beyond commendable. His patience top-notch maturity. A fierce protective nature dwelled inside him and wouldn't allow any chance of injury to his dad.

He showed himself to be responsible and resourceful in the midst of money trouble.

While I wasn't rich by any means, I'd invested my inheritance after my father died. My much younger sister who served the Lord with her husband and two kids out in Oklahoma had done the same. Neither of us hurt for cash, and we'd chosen a life of servitude, using those means to support our work.

Although she lived in the States, I still considered them missionaries, soul winners for Christ.

"I was thinking about taking Dad out for the fundraiser tonight," Aaron said while walking into the living room. He'd put Phillip down for a nap—the man seemed to sleep during the day as much as he did the night.

"I'm sure he would love to go."

Aaron collapsed onto the couch, head tipped back and eyes closed. He wore a threadbare T-shirt and ratty gym shorts, but he smelled like dryer sheets and soap.

I filled my lungs with his scent, allowing myself a moment to actually enjoy the strange shivers his nearness always brought rather than pushing them away.

"He might be too embarrassed," Aaron said, and I watched his lips move. Thin upper lip, fuller on the bottom...

I tore my focus off his mouth and cleared my throat. "He always was a prideful man when it came to his looks," I stated the truth we both knew all too well. God forbid he didn't have his hair slicked down and face cleanly shaven when going to church. Freshly-starched shirts and pristine suits had been a must.

"I'll ask him when he wakes up," I offered, thinking we might be more apt to get him out of the house if I wanted it rather than if Aaron suggested it. "When's the last time he went outdoors and socialized since being diagnosed with Parkinson's?"

"Doctor's appointment a few weeks ago."

"Before that?"

"A month."

"Maybe it'll boost his spirits again."

"Wouldn't that be nice," Aaron muttered and clamped his lips tight as though annoyed with himself for his sarcastic tone.

"You're an amazing man, Aaron. I'm so damn proud of who you've become." I clasped his shoulder without thought, the heat of hard muscle beneath my hold radiating up my arm and into my chest.

His head lifted, those blue eyes finding mine and giving me a jolt to my core, the kind I hadn't felt in years. Instinctive response—a sexual awakening that swelled blood into my ignored dick.

I blinked, unsure what to make of my body's reaction to his gaze.

Fish out of water...

His lips twitched as a mischievous glint lit his eyes. "You swore, Ezzie."

"I'm no angel," I rasped out, all too aware of that truth.

One of his eyebrows rose in question, interest warming his gaze even more, flooding my face with warmth. "Don't be embarrassed for being human," he said quietly. "Life is too short...and sometimes living it up a little can take the darkness away."

I squeezed his shoulder and let go, pushing up to my feet and immediately angling away to hide what touching him had done to my groin. "I'm going to shower and spend some time in prayer before tonight," I forced out, already planning to sin in the only way I could allow between us.

He didn't speak, but I felt his stare on me until I disappeared from sight.

Minutes later, hot water beat on my back, and I stared at my erection sticking straight out. Leaking. Throbbing.

I'd gone months without giving myself release—it'd been years since my wife had offered or agreed to my initiations.

But I couldn't be bothered with thoughts of her, for she had nothing to do with the state of my roused-from-the-grave libido.

All Aaron...he'd somehow taken me to a place I'd never been before even though he was Phillip's young son. My balls ached, and unable to help myself, I wrapped my fist around my girth, moaning at my firm grasp. I'd forgotten how good the physical attention felt.

Lord, forgive me.

I didn't have the strength to choose right. Aaron's hooded gaze flashed in my mind, his lips I longed to taste. My eyelids shot open at the image of him dropping to his knees before me.

"God," I groaned—and erupted countless geysers of cum. Every snap of my hips thrust my length through my fist, sending sprays of sticky white all over the shower wall. My legs shook and breath sawed in and out as copious amounts of ejaculate continued to ooze from my slit. I gasped for breath until finished.

Sagging forward, I pressed my heated forehead against the cool tile.

Euphoria rushed through my blood, endorphins I wished I could bathe in and hang onto for hours to come.

Guilt came crawling into the back of my mind, but I pushed it away, needing something for myself for just a little while longer.

* * *

Simply Grace's new assistant pastor greeted me and Aaron at the door, his dark hair appearing almost black beneath the gymnasium lights. Jedidiah Simpson couldn't have been more than five-foot-six at the most and looked a lot younger than thirty-two with his clean-shaven cheeks. He shook my hand warmly between both of his, leaning in with a smile rather than pity on his handsome face.

"Welcome home. Sorry I missed you on Sunday," he stated simply, flashing pearly white teeth, and I hoped his kindness set the stage for the evening ahead. "There's too many baked goods to be healthy, and Mrs. Astbury made her famous chili if you're hungry."

I remembered the dish she'd always brought to potluck dinners at the church, and my mouth flooded with drool.

"Have you heard from Zeke?" Jedidiah asked Aaron, his voice dropped to a near whisper, his dark eyes filled with concern.

"He's doing well in Boston."

"And Levi?" Jedidiah's tone lowered even further.

"Couldn't be happier," Aaron answered, a hint of envy in his words.

I glanced around while the two men caught up.

The Astburys and Townsons had been in charge of the fundraiser, and over a dozen tables were set up around the gymnasium floor with food, wares for sale, and games for the children.

Phillip had chosen to stay at home, and no amount of persuasion on our end had changed his mind.

Stubborn mule refused to be seen as an invalid.

Thank goodness their kind neighbor had agreed to sit with him while us boys enjoyed our so-called night on the town.

I'd have liked a quiet dinner at a restaurant or settling down into a dark theatre to lose myself in a movie, but church it was.

At least I had Aaron at my side while moving farther into the gym, same as Sunday morning when people offered condolences and pitying gazes. A few times while making our rounds and greeting others, our shoulders brushed, and the desire to lean into him, to let him be my rock, swept over me.

I hummed King's song once when we had a moment of somewhat quiet, and what a smirk it earned me. Twinkling blue eyes held mine captive before I remembered where we stood.

Aaron's presence filled the emptiness in my life, but after allowing myself release that afternoon, my sinful nature longed for more. I wanted every inch of him—in my heart, in my body, making me feel complete again.

Forget fish out of water. I'd become a damn swordfish caught on a massive hook. Swallowed whole. Captured and seemingly powerless against the force of nature named Aaron Weston.

But giving into the hunger of the flesh would take us down a path of immorality, one that went against my goal of holiness, one that would condemn us both.

I refused to allow such a thing to happen to someone I loved.

He walked beside me, shoulders still stooped a bit, but he held people's gazes when speaking to them, showing a deep confidence that didn't make itself known in any other way. But I recognized the little boy inside his old soul. I knew the self-esteem issues he still struggled with.

And I desired nothing more than to wrap him in my arms and tell him how much I appreciated and respected him.

Mr. Townson approached, a welcoming smile on his face. His firm grasp on my hand and the pull-in for a quick back-slapping hug made me want to put distance between us again.

"I saw your wife earlier. Your son isn't here?" I asked, remembering the child who had always followed behind him like a meek little lamb, head down and hands clasped in front of him.

A storm cloud rolled over Mr. Townson's face, his lips pressing into a thin line as he glanced at Aaron beside me. "My son has fallen into perversion and left the church."

"I'm sorry to hear that," I replied on autopilot, aware of Aaron stiffening beside me.

"He moved to Boston to be with a *man*." Disgust filled Mr. Townson's voice, enough venom I cringed—and I realized that was the Levi that Jedidiah had asked Aaron about. "He had been engaged to Lily Astbury and gave up that gift to live a life of sin."

Unsure what to say, I kept my mouth shut, shifting on my feet and wanting to get the hell out of his presence.

While the Bible called homosexuality a perversion, I'd never once preached or ranted against it. Part of me had always thought people ought to be free to love—and seeing the obvious homophobic reaction from Mr. Townson sickened my stomach.

That wasn't showing God's love even if the Bible taught otherwise.

My thoughts toward Aaron were nothing more than sinful urges left at the throne of God, I believed, but I seemed unable to banish them from my mind, the longing from my heart.

"I'm going to get some cider," Aaron muttered. "Want some?"

"Yes, please."

The second he meandered away with his hands shoved in his jeans' pockets, I felt vulnerable. Unsheltered and open to attack.

And Mr. Townson didn't hesitate to degrade his only son. At least he kept his voice down, but I expected more from him than embarrassment over his son's supposed failings and how it might reflect on him.

Had I been gifted a child, I would have loved them unconditionally. Never would I turn my back against them or call them names. Tell others of their sins and how their choices were nothing more than a disappointment.

I made my excuses the second Mr. Towson paused for air and hurried after the way Aaron had fled, my inner self raw as though my skin had been flayed off like a fish's scales.

He stood in line for cider, and I sidled up to him, bumping against him so I could breathe easier. "You okay?" he asked quietly, and I shook my head. "Ready to get out of here?"

"I do, but being the guest of honor, I can't leave after an hour of mingling."

Unfortunately.

Aaron wrapped his arm around my shoulders and pulled me in tight for a brotherly hug. Weakness plagued my knees, and I wanted to sink into him, hide away. Lose myself in him.

Were it not for my faith, I would have eagerly given in to the lust Aaron's presence filled me with.

I pulled from his hold, straightening my spine and lifting my chin. I'd chosen to live a godly existence, even in the midst of grief and life-shattering shame, and I would gain those riches in glory. A moment of sin with Aaron, were he to offer more than heated glances, would ruin my friendship with Phillip. It would ensure the severing of a father/son relationship--and my fall from grace.

None of which I could imagine doing no matter how strong my desire for him.

After a bowl of chili, we got our cider and found a quieter corner to stand in while the chatter and children running around laughing filled the echoing chamber.

"Who is Zeke?" I asked, watching Levi's father as he smiled and spoke with Pastor Welker.

"He used to be one of the church's counselors—but it's a long story." Aaron kept his voice low.

"I'm assuming he fell in love with Levi and they were found out?"

"That's the gist of it." He sipped his cider, a furrow deeply embedded between his eyebrows.

"He was your friend." I didn't ask a question. The pain etched into his face declared as much.

"Is," Aaron corrected me, turning toward me. A challenge glinted in his eyes.

"Unconditional love is one of God's greatest teachings." I spoke with sure conviction.

"And so is his stance on sexual perversion."

I tore my focus off Aaron's eyes, needing to escape the want, the longing to agree with him even though sarcasm laced his tone.

"Still," I finally stated quietly, about to spill God's greatest command, "we are to love one another."

But I no longer felt sure where to draw the line between platonic and physical.

Chapter 6
Aaron

After two weeks of putting up with Dad's shit, I talked Ezra into going to the gym with me to blow off some of the steam that simmered to life every time we were in close proximity.

Namely at night after I put Dad to bed and sexual tension settled over the living room.

We hopped on the assault bikes to loosen up at five in the morning, and as usual, a couple girls in tiny shorts and sports bras ran on the treadmills in front of us, offering a view of jiggling asses and bouncing tits.

Neither did a damn thing for me. A few covert glances let me know Ezra didn't watch them either. He seemed to have picked a spot on the floor in front of us to focus on, but his thinned lips eventually gave way to parted as his body warmed up.

We hit the weights next, and we finished up with a few bench press sets. Standing over him to spot put his head too damn close to my groin and yet not close enough.

Laying as he did on the bench draped the material of his gym shorts over his bulge, and goddamn what a sight it was. A clear outline of a thick cock made my mouth water, and my hole clenched repeatedly as I imagined him sinking into my body. Stretching me. Filling me.

I had to take a goddamn bathroom break to quickly milk one out of my balls so I could finish our workout without walking around with a jutting hard on.

Ezra, at forty-nine, was probably the oldest guy in the gym that morning, but he was by far the hottest. Other beefcakes strutting their shit around us being ogled by the women didn't draw my gaze or my focus.

Just Ezzie.

I wanted him to be mine.

Cursing his faith, I hit a new personal record, gritting my teeth to keep from hollering my frustration while shaking to push the barbell away from my chest.

"Amazing, Aaron," Ezra said once I sat up.

"Thanks," I muttered, slumped over and catching my breath.

"You must enjoy all the attention you get. I can imagine being looked upon with lust and envy alike feeds your self-esteem."

"I couldn't give two shits." I stood and tipped my head toward the locker room.

"You don't want a girlfriend?" Ezra asked, grabbing a hand towel off the rack where he'd flung it.

I'd rather have you.

I shrugged when he caught my gaze. "You're still young too," I told him. "A sexy silver fox. You could find another woman."

His eyes went from glinting at being called sexy to closed off. "I don't want another woman."

How about a man?

I kept that question to myself.

I hadn't pushed him too hard in our workout, but sweat still dripped from his face and soaked his shirt. Hot as hell…I yearned to lick the droplet off his cheek. Bury my face in his balls and breathe in his musk—fucking sweat and all.

Sporting another chub, I headed toward the locker room, cursing my fucking life. Who the hell in their right mind fell for their father's best friend—a missionary for God to boot?

A moron, that's who.

But wanting and loving Ezra wasn't a choice. He just *was* the attention of my mind and body. Every bit of both.

"I appreciate you investing in my life, Aaron," he said once we collapsed on a bench.

We both chugged water, and I lifted my shirt to wipe my face off.

Ezra's gaze dropped to my abs and quickly jerked away. His hand trembled as he drank more water.

"Did you enjoy yourself?" I asked rather than diving into a conversation that would result in me being brokenhearted and without doubt prompt him to move out sooner than agreed upon.

Fuck knew I couldn't deal with his leaving me again after how he'd shattered my heart the first time.

"I did—but I'll be cursing my choice to come here when I try to crawl out of bed tomorrow," he muttered, turning to retrieve his bag from a locker.

I wasn't nearby to hear if Ezra groaned getting up the next morning, but he cursed a mild word while sitting down at the kitchen table for coffee. He refused to give in to old bones, he called them, and continued to visit the gym with me on the regular, waking at four-thirty and then using my old SUV to head home at six until I got off work at nine when he'd pick me back up.

Usually after work, I went straight home and helped Dad out of bed, but a few times, Ezra came back for me, letting me know Dad already had eaten and sat watching TV.

One day, he skipped the gym, and I returned home after my few extra hours of work to find him walking Dad up the sidewalk.

I pulled into the driveway, grinning at the color in Dad's cheeks and the slight tilt to his lips.

"Looking good, Dad!" I called as Ezra wheeled him closer.

I lifted my focus to Ezra and held his gaze, dipping my head and hoping he could read the appreciation in my eyes.

Having him there made life easier, but with each passing day, my desire for more than companionship and conversation intensified. I offered to do his laundry with mine and Dad's just so I could hold his dirty shirts and shorts to my nose, filling my lungs with his fallen leaves and musk scent.

One morning when he and Dad sat outside, I buried my face in a pair of his silk boxers and sniffed like a total perv. My dick had already hopped on board with the idea of doing so, and I groaned at the richness of Ezra in my nose.

I palmed myself over my shorts and squeezed the base of my dick, but trying to stave off my erection was pointless. Heeling the door shut behind me, I pulled out my dick and wrapped the soft material of his boxers around my length.

"Oh fuck." I watched the leaking head of my dick peek through navy silk, tugging with just enough friction to drive me insane. *Shit...so good...so good.*

I breathed hard through my nose, my hips starting to snap forward into my fist. Giving over to the fantasy fully in my head, I imagined burying into Ezra's tight, untried hole—and shuddered as my climax barreled through me.

"Christ." I gasped, milking one last spurt to coat his boxers. White spunk smeared across the material, and I wiped myself clean, letting out one last heavy exhale before tossing the soiled clothing into the washing machine.

Knowing I'd found my new favorite pastime, I settled on doing laundry at least twice a week.

And I enjoyed the fuck out of each and every jerk off session, once doing it while Ezra and Dad watched TV just down the hallway. I bit my lip on that one to keep quiet, fantasizing over Ezra walking into the laundry room to find me jacking off into his dirty clothes.

Made me a sick piece of shit, but it kept me from getting too handsy with his body like I'd have preferred.

Every night after Dad went to bed, we sprawled on the couch beside each other to watch movies or binge free shows available on cable. Ezra had missed out on dozens of good movies during his years in the Ukraine, so he insisted on getting a Netflix subscription for us.

And every night after going our separate ways, I fantasized over the "chill" part of Netflix-ing that I never got to experience.

We sat together in church, our shoulders broad enough that brushing against each other couldn't be helped. Neither of us pulled away. Eventually, the couch seemed to shorten, and if he half-laid down, his head on the far arm, knees somewhat drawn up to his chest —his feet rested on my thigh.

Friday, a month into Ezra's stay, Dad had a rough day, hardly napped, and I insisted he go to bed early.

Ezra had already curled up on the couch, and I threw myself at his feet, not bothering to put as much space between us as usual. He poked me with his big toe.

"Everything okay?" he asked as I grabbed up the remote and flicked on the TV.

I needed noise. Fucking release of some sort from all the shit Dad had pulled throughout the day. Nothing I'd done was good enough. His oatmeal had been too cold. His coffee too hot. The soup I fed him for lunch was too fucking dry.

Bastard.

Not for the first time, I imagined lowering his casket into the grave with a sigh of relief even though I knew my heart would hurt with loss.

"Fine," I bit out at Ezra and immediately felt like an asshole. I grabbed hold of his foot and gave it a squeeze-type hug. "Sorry."

He didn't pull away—so I kept my hand lying atop his ankle bone. "You don't have to apologize. I can imagine most people would get tired some days."

I nodded and started up the movie we'd already agreed upon before he went up to shower while I'd gotten Dad to bed.

My hand stayed put on his ankle, and my attention didn't waver from the warmth of his skin beneath my palm. The tickle of hair along my pinkie. While touching any part of Ezra turned me on, in that moment I took comfort in his nearness more than the amped up sexual energy. Weariness slowly leaked from my system, and I slouched down a bit and let out a heavy sigh.

"Switch spots with me," Ezra said, sliding his legs to the floor. "Give me your feet."

I didn't hesitate at the offer—laid on my back and set my aching feet right in the hands he held open with a silent *thank fuck* in my head.

Jesus washed his disciples' feet, but Ezra rubbed mine, his fingers strong and digging into my arch and pressure points. He kept his focus on the TV, and I watched his face while soaking in his touch.

"You used to do this when I was a kid." I suddenly remembered—I'd been young.

"Yeah," Ezra murmured, his gaze glued to the screen. "You weren't ticklish, no matter how hard I tried. It started out as a joke until you decided you liked my hands on you."

Fuck.

"On your feet," Ezra hastened to correct and swallowed, his Adam's apple bobbing. Still, he wouldn't look at me.

Blood flooded my groin, but I didn't move as Ezra eventually massaged up my ankle to my calf.

I fought not to tense up, but with every caress of his fingertips, the energy between us intensified.

No way in hell he didn't feel the connection. No way in hell it didn't affect him.

And if he hated it, found it wrong as a sin or due to my being his best friend's son, he would have stopped. Fled. Moved out weeks earlier.

He worked my right foot, so I shifted my left along his thigh the slightest to test him a bit. Ezra feigned watching the show, but his chest barely rose and fell.

Another shift of restlessness placed my foot higher. The pulse in his neck thumped in time with my racing heart, but still he didn't react.

Leave it or push for more?

Fuck, my aching groin wanted it—wanted to know if I made his dick as hard as he did mine.

Fuck it.

One more slight movement rested the outside of my left ankle against his groin.

He bit back a gasp but didn't move.

His dick was hard. As. Fuck.

Christ.

I clenched my jaw and closed my eyes, my hands fisting at my sides as he ignored the intimate touch, his hands still flexing and kneading around my right foot.

"Ezzie," I choked out, unable to not say or do something.

He slid from beneath me without a word and slipped from the living room on near silent feet. The stairs creaked as he ascended toward the bedrooms.

He hadn't apologized. Called me out for my forward action.

But he hadn't offered an invitation to follow him, not even a glance in my direction.

Was he leaving the next step to me, or had he fled out of fear and shame?

I squeezed the base of my dick, unsure and fucking baffled, never mind horny as fuck. "Damnit." I sat up and turned the TV off. A quick check on Dad showed him sleeping.

Skipping every other stair, I hurried up to the landing, needing an answer.

Ezra's door was shut, and I stared for a few seconds, worrying the inside of my lip. Knock and see if he was all right? Let myself in and pray he'd allow me make him feel good, show him how to live again?

My hand found the door handle before I made a conscious decision, but a quiet twist proved fruitless.

Ezra had locked me out.

Fuck.

Releasing an inward groan over the sense of loss in my chest, I forced my feet away and crawled into my own bed—leaving my damn door cracked open in case he had a change of heart.

He didn't.

And when I woke up in the morning, bleary-eyed as hell, I picked up all the tissues I'd used to clean up my spunk I'd made a mess with while trying to wear my ass out the night before waiting on him.

Ezra didn't come down stairs by the time I had to leave for the gym and work. No noise sounded from behind his bedroom door.

Realizing he probably dealt with a shit ton of guilt, I didn't force the issue because I didn't want him taking off on us again.

I went to the gym and worked out by myself—and had never felt so alone.

Chapter 7
Ezra

I could barely choke down my burnt toast as Phillip struggled with his oatmeal. What a pair of old men we were.

But nothing about my body felt old. I'd come alive the night before while massaging Aaron's feet. Showing him attention, touching his skin had turned me on like I used to get as a teenager. Hot and horny. Heavy balls that ached for relief.

And when he'd brushed against my obvious erection, he stole my breath—and slapped my face with reality.

Sin.

Phillip's son...almost incestuous considering how close we'd all been once upon a time.

We couldn't go there, no matter how I longed to do so—I loved him too much to bring shame and damnation down on his head.

As for my own...the temptation proved ripe. Intoxicating. And strangely fulfilling.

"Do you want some help?" I asked Phillip, forcing my mind off the night before.

"No," he slurred the word, his shaking hand slipping more of the oatmeal from the spoon than landed in his mouth. "Parkin...son's...sucks."

As an ordained pastor, I should have had the words to bring him comfort, a verse or two in hopes of easing his despondency that seemed to intensify with every day. At least Phillip didn't hold anything in like Sofiy had done. Her misery had been hidden deep within her mind, her soul, and the darkness had eaten her from the inside out.

I recognized Phillip's mood for what it was and cursed myself for not having the answers.

Aaron said they couldn't afford a therapist.

But I could.

"Would you like to have someone come over once a week for counseling? I can spare the money if that's what would help you."

"I don't need a shrink, Ezra. I need to fucking live." It took quite some time for Phillip to get the words out, and I sat stunned to hear my friend use such language.

"Perhaps Pastor Welker would—"

"No."

"Phillip." I rested my hand atop his, stilling his attempts to spoon up more oatmeal.

"Just let me live out these final days in peace!" His speech halted, slurred, but his tone tightened enough to bark out the final word like the Phillip I remembered.

My throat swelled, and my eyes welled. I patted his hand and went back to my breakfast. "Okay, Phillip. Okay."

An hour later, we skipped our daily walk thanks to the downpour outside, and I went upstairs while Phillip watched a show on TV.

Aaron's bedroom door stood open, and I paused on the threshold, taking in his room I hadn't yet seen. The baby blue from his childhood had been painted over with a light gray. An old patchwork quilt I recognized covered his double bed.

He'd snuggled beneath the blanket I'd kept in the back of my truck forever, the one he'd often curled up in while we sat by the campfires up north. I'd wondered what happened to that quilt.

I found myself beside his mattress, fingering the different blues of the fabric, eyeing the pillow he'd plumped after making his bed.

Letting out a shuddered exhale, I closed my eyes, allowing my thoughts to drift to what I'd attempted to avoid all morning long.

Aaron's feet in my lap. A massage, for crying out loud—an intimate touch I shouldn't have initiated. He'd just been so exhausted, so beaten down by Phillip's negativity all day that I'd yearned to give him relief and set his body at rest.

My mind reminiscing how he'd loved his feet held as a child, I'd acted on instinct, only remembering as I caressed his skin and ran my fingertips over bone and muscle that Aaron was no longer a child.

Hairy ankles gave way to a bulging calf muscle, and I hadn't been able to keep from kneading and pressing, telling myself I did so in hopes of easing his tension.

I'd created one ten times worse, and unable to look at him, I had barely exhaled as my ears strained for his heightened breaths. The one hint of a moan that passed his lips had swelled my groin with blood.

The second time he shifted his ankle closest to my torso and farther up my thigh, I knew he did so on purpose. Not thrusting forward to close the distance between his ankle and my aching length proved my most difficult choice in life.

I had choked on my own gasp when he did the deed himself.

Desire like I'd never known had made me light-headed, thundered my pulse throughout my entire body.

Flooded my mind with shame.

Without a word, I'd escaped on shaking legs, fleeing from the face of sin, the unholy urge to touch another man in a sexual manner.

Perversion.

I snapped my eyelids open and realized I held Aaron's pillow in a tight grip. My face had buried in the softness on its own.

Worrying over my ability to follow God's law, I let myself out of a room I never should have entered, quietly closing the door behind me with a click I solidified as final in my mind.

And the only way I knew to stay on the godly path of a true Christian was to avoid being alone with Aaron.

I managed to do so until Sunday morning when we climbed into the SUV together to head to church.

So many unvoiced words sat between us, heavy as a boulder on my shoulders. Knowing I ought to apologize didn't make the words come though—I wasn't sorry for offering him the comfort and affection he craved as much as I did.

Tension strung me tight throughout the quiet ride until I couldn't handle the stifling silence.

"Aaron." I rasped out his name like he'd done my nickname that night but lost sight of all I needed to say when he gave me his attention for a brief clash of gazes.

Pain and desire filled the depths of his blue orbs, but I didn't get the chance to delve deeper before he turned his focus on the road once more.

"We're good, Ezzie," he nearly whispered. "It's all good."

It was—therein lay the problem.

Shit. I exhaled slowly, hoping to lessen the adrenaline rushing my heart rate.

No more words passed between us, and I forced a smile to greet other members of Simply Grace Church while making my way toward Aaron's usual row. He'd told me the week before that I'd inherited Zeke's seat since his friend had found happiness in New England.

I settled beside Aaron, and as always, our shoulders brushed. Pressed tight on purpose. We eventually stood for praise and worship. Sat during announcements delivered by a smiling Pastor Jedidiah. Stood once more along with everyone else to clap for the choir's rendition of *When the Saints Go Marching In*.

And every time we took our seats, the distance between us seemed to close. The heat of Aaron's body distracted me from Pastor Welker's message, and I cursed the devil for attacking me with lustful thoughts while I trudged through the lowest point of my existence.

Exploring the attraction between us would require a sacrifice of my beliefs, my past, in order to start a new life—one I wasn't even sure Aaron wanted beyond a mutual giving of relief.

But I did.

Desperately.

Pastor Welker's voice rose, drawing me back to the service, but one word in particular captured my focus.

Homosexuality.

I gave him my attention, listening as he listed the texts often cited by those of our faith to condemn such sins. Noah and Ham, Sodom and Gomorrah, along with the other Levitical laws, letters from Paul to the Romans, and a few other verses in the New Testament.

Aaron shifted beside me, and I wondered over his state of mind. Did he think of his friend Zeke and Levi?

Did he worry about his own soul and the sinful desires that radiated with vivid light between us?

Numbness crept into my heart, same as it always had whenever the topic of homosexuality arose when I'd served the Lord in the Ukraine. I'd chosen to focus my sermons on love, forgiveness, and grace instead.

But homophobia lived in Simply Grace Church. Mr. Townson had shown evidence of such sentiment on the night of the fundraiser, and Pastor Welker's words drew many head nods, grimaces, and hollered *Amens* from his flock.

I struggled to sit still as he riled up the congregation into a strange frenzy—as though one of hate rather than loving the sinner and drawing them into the light as the Bible commanded.

Escape couldn't come fast enough, and the second we stepped outside into the cooling late summer air, Aaron and I both made quick strides toward his SUV as though of the same mind. I loosened my tie that seemed to choke me.

The second we shut ourselves into the quiet interior, Aaron let out a heavy exhale. "Glenda is bringing lunch over today," he reminded me, and I sagged into the seat, thankful he chose such a topic. "Feel like grabbing cheesesteaks instead?"

A rush of warmth flooded through my soul at our earlier tension lessening. "I'd love that."

He called Glenda, asking if she wouldn't mind sitting with Phillip for an hour, and her assurance it was no problem reached my ears through his cell. The heaviness on my heart lightened up even more.

A few minutes later, he pulled into the sandwich shop we'd frequented before I'd gone overseas.

"I can't believe this place is still open," I said, rounding the hood of his vehicle to walk alongside him. The building's facade appeared the same—worn and broken down. Dilapidated, like a building from the 1800s.

"Best cheesesteaks in Philly." He shoved his hands into his pockets and led the way, shoulders slumped as always.

Ignoring the itch in my fingers, I followed him into the small shop, the scent of fried onions and steak making my mouth water. We both ordered and settled into the booth farthest from the front door to wait for our food.

Our gazes locked over the table.

His foot brushed against mine—and I didn't shift away from the intentional show of affection.

Bubbles swelled inside my chest, enticing my lips to smile.

So I did.

And Aaron's blue eyes lit with the same life, causing my throat to thicken.

I loved him, and while I always had, the platonic had given way to more, and I longed to share it with him.

Awareness of the note in my pocket, the reminder of my greatest shame, shifted into play inside my brain, bursting some of those bubbles. My smile faded, and I studied my clasped hands atop the table.

Perhaps telling Aaron the truth of Sofiy's death would change his heart toward me, making the decision to keep our friendship platonic easier. But I couldn't bear the thought of Aaron losing his hero.

He'd suffered enough the previous three years.

And he was the one who stood beside me and allowed me to lean on him. The one I'd begun to see as substance to my soul like food did my body.

I couldn't go without the steady rock he'd become in my life.

Chapter 8

Aaron

"Talk to me, Ezzie."

Ezra kept his focus on his white-knuckled hands on the table between us, and I slid my foot more firmly alongside his.

His chest slowly rose as though steeling himself to share what had dulled his eyes.

"I've striven my whole life to gain those golden crowns in glory," he stated quietly, a furrow deeply denting his brow. "I focused so hard and so long on those selfish goals that my marriage suffered. Fourteen years together, countless hours of serving the Lord and chasing heavenly riches together in the Ukraine...and Sofiy swallowed a few too many sleeping pills."

I'd heard through church about her accidental overdose and couldn't imagine how he'd suffered from finding her cold body in their bed.

I waited for him to expound, my hands itching to hold his, but Ezra thinned his lips and slightly shook his head. He had no intention of uncovering more of his supposed shortcomings.

"You don't have to strive for anything, in my opinion," I told him when he didn't say anything else. "You've always stuck by your convictions. Showed love to those in need. Compassion and acceptance. If there really is a mansion in glory for the good and faithful servants, your name is definitely engraved front and center on the biggest on the block."

I remembered him always handing money to those begging on street corners. He even gave a shivering man the coat off his back. Never once did he offer to pray with those in need—it was always something physical. A tangible gift even if it left him without.

"You're the personification of a true Christian, Ezra."

He closed his eyes and let out a heavy exhale.

"Order for Aaron!" One of the staff called, and I got up to retrieve our lunch.

Ezra had gathered himself by the time I returned, his face once more free of angst, hazel eyes warmer than they'd been for days.

We ate in silence, our feet finding their way alongside the other's.

"What will you do when you're no longer able to care for your father?" Ezra asked, and I took a few seconds to consider what I'd thought of countless times.

"I'm hoping he just passes in his sleep before that happens." A coward's way out, but I didn't mind admitting it to Ezra, because who wouldn't wish that for their loved ones?

"And if he doesn't?"

I wiped my mouth with a napkin and settled back in my seat, hands on my thighs and focus on his face.

Genuine concern and love radiated from his eyes, tightening my chest.

"Dad refuses to go into a home, not that we could afford one, but I can't pay for in-house care either. I'm expecting that by the time I need help, it'll be hospice rather than something more."

Ezra studied my face, and I wondered if he knew how my mind worked, the insecurities I faced, and how I chose to deal with them. If anyone besides Dad did, it would be him.

I might have changed physically in the fifteen years he'd been gone, but my inner self still cowered like the scrawny, timid shit I'd been back then.

"Have you spoken to him about his future?" Ezra asked. "How you're handling the stress of looking after him?"

"He's my father."

"And you're a selfless man who deserves to be treated with gratefulness, not badgering and constant ridicule."

"It's my job to care for him."

Ezra sat back too, his head tipping to the side. "And you need to prove to yourself it can be done."

He didn't ask a question.

My throat swelled shut, but I didn't nod to let him know he'd put my feelings into words either.

"Being vulnerable, being honest about your emotions, isn't weakness, Aaron," he said quietly, his rich, low tone easing through my heart, attempting to make everything better like he always did. "It takes balls to speak up. It saves lives." Ezra's voice broke, and he finally looked away.

I considered what he'd said, remembering how I had encouraged Levi to take another chance on Zeke. And because he found the guts to do so, travelled out of state without evidence of a clear outcome, he'd found happiness. They both had.

And my heart envied what they shared.

My cell rang, and seeing Glenda called, I answered.

"Phillip is really upset," she said.

I could hear muttering in the background—a few curse words.

"We'll be there in ten," I said and hung up.

Ezra stood as I did, gathering our trash. "Your dad?"

"Sounds like he's giving Glenda shit."

We didn't speak again until we walked into the house.

Red-faced, Glenda nodded and made a quick escape past us in the foyer.

"We were supposed to have dinner together!" Dad slurred when I strode into the kitchen. Red splotches tinted his cheeks as he wheeled himself forward and back with shaking hands as though wishing he could pace. I steeled myself for the hell to come that Glenda's red face promised. "You take Ezra from me every morning!"

I didn't bother placating or arguing but set about cleaning up the mess he'd made while trying to feed himself, the stubborn bastard.

"I'm always back here before you're even awake," Ezra stated quietly behind me.

"You stay up late together." Dad's grumbled voice lowered a bit. "You laugh out in the living room while I'm in bed wasting away."

My throat tightened as I tried to see things from his point of view. Ezra and I had somewhat normal lives, enjoying each other's company while he faced imminent death.

But Dad continued to throw out accusations left and right, his narcissistic tendencies rising to the surface.

"You want his company more than mine because I'm a miserable prick," he said to Ezra who portrayed the patience of a saint while letting Dad slowly spill shit from his lips. "Well, you would be one too if your body didn't cooperate with your brain. If your mouth refused to move right and allow you get out the words racing through your mind. Imagine having to let someone else feed you!"

Dad heaved an exhale and slumped in his wheelchair after his speech that had taken a long as fuck five minutes to complete.

"Let's go for a walk," Ezra suggested, heading to the coat closet for Dad's sweatshirt.

Dad didn't mutter another word as his best friend bowed into his tantrum by giving him all of his attention.

Score a point for the miserable prick.

I remained in the kitchen, cleaning, telling myself being jealous was no different emotionally than how my father had behaved when I'd stolen Ezra away for a half-hour to enjoy lunch.

And that night, Dad remained in the living room with us, falling asleep in his wheelchair before half the movie played. He grumbled about being woken up when I wheeled him into his bedroom, but I didn't shoot back that he'd made it clear earlier in the day he'd wanted to stay up with us.

Ezra waited for me when I returned to the living room twenty minutes later.

As usual, I slumped down on the couch, hands on my thighs.

"I was thinking about delaying my hunt for a place of my own," Ezra said, and I rolled my head along the back of the couch to face him. My pulse picked up a bit at the thought of Ezra staying in our house indefinitely—same as it'd been when I was a kid.

"You could use the help," he added.

So it was a pity offer rather than his desire to be near me.

Dad.

I picked up the clicker, my stomach falling even though the thought of his sticking around soothed another part of my mind. The idea of him living with us again pleased me beyond anything in my life, but I wasn't about to admit to needing the help. If that meant turning him away, then I would—so he could find his new path in life.

I swallowed hard, my chest going heavy.

Loving someone meant letting them go. The saying sucked ass, and although I had abandonment issues, I longed for Ezra to be happy, not slugging through daily living laying down his life for someone who didn't appreciate the effort.

I loved him too much for that.

"I've got it under control," I muttered, my heart torn. "You should move on in your freedom, Ezzie, not hang out here in limbo with my asshole of a father."

"Do you *want* me to stay, Aaron?"

Self-sacrificing as always—and the thought of him leaving me alone with Dad again twisted my insides up tight as hell.

Selfishness took control for a moment.

"Yes." I gave him all my attention, let him see exactly what I desired in my eyes. He hadn't shied away but that one time, but brushing against his dick had probably been a bit forward.

"Then I'll stay," he murmured, clasping my shoulder to connect us which he seemed fond of doing.

Had he glanced at my mouth, licked his lower lip—had he tugged even the slightest bit, I would have leaned in and tasted the lips I'd been dreaming about since laying eyes on him in the airport.

Ezra dropped his hold after a quick squeeze. He cleared his throat.

I guessed the evidence in my eyes I hadn't bothered to shield didn't go unnoticed.

"Tell me this guy gets the shit kicked out of him," he said about the character frozen in pause on the TV screen.

I bit back my smirk at Ezra's curse word. Little by little, he seemed to be falling my way when it came to his faith, and while that probably would make me look like an asshole to those who knew my inner workings, I didn't care.

How long until he gives in to the obvious desire between us?

If he did, it wouldn't be soon enough.

Tuesday after the gym, I gathered the laundry, ready to relieve the ache in my balls from watching Ezra in his gym shorts with that luscious-looking bulge, listening to his grunts while lifting.

He did me in every time, and it only seemed fair I empty my balls in his dirty clothing.

Dad and Ezra sat in the living room watching a show instead of taking their after-lunch walk due to another rainstorm, so I bit my lower lip to keep quiet rather than groaning with every silken glide of his boxers over my leaking dick. Still, his name hissed from my lips while I spurted my release.

And I gulped oxygen while cleaning myself up.

I grabbed the rest of his clothes from the bottom of his basket to toss into the washer atop the soiled underwear, and something fluttered out of his jeans' pocket to the floor.

Once I got the load started, I bent to retrieve the crumpled piece of paper.

Shaky handwriting scripted in ink drew my focus...

I blinked, reading the three lines again, sure I misread, misunderstood. A fourth assured me I didn't.

Sofiy had left her husband a note—she hadn't accidentally overdosed.

And Ezra hadn't corrected everyone's assumptions.

"Fuck." I swallowed hard, her accusation of loving the church more than her clenching my bowels up tight as fuck.

How the fuck dare she? Ezra was one of the most giving men I knew, and for her to accuse him of selfishness, of ignoring her in her need...

Ezra would never do such a thing.

Jaw tight, I refolded the piece of paper, tempted to toss the lies into the trash where they belonged—but it also belonged to Ezra, and he'd obviously hung on to it for a reason.

It must have been in one of his pockets.

I listened to the TV's muted buzz, my heart heavy.

Was it any wonder he grieved how he did? I couldn't begin to imagine how her words had hit him, doubtless continuing to haunt his mind. Perhaps it was the note rather than her death that left his eyes haggard, his shoulders slumped so often.

An intense desire to confront him, rail about her bullshit, and assure him he was the best man to walk the face of the earth rolled over me with staggering intensity.

I wanted him in my arms. I needed him to understand that I would never judge him for whatever he believed happened in their marriage.

Because I knew better.

And I also expected Ezra wouldn't be ready to face my truth with how he carried around the reminder of his supposed failures.

I'll show him in the small things. I'll rebuild what she tore down.

Same as I'd told Zeke all those months ago when he offered condolences for my friend's loss, I told myself *I* wasn't sorry.

She hadn't deserved him—but I did, and I would do anything in my power to make him see he was a good man.

And worthy of a second chance at love.

Two hours later, I folded his laundry, putting the note back where it'd fallen from.

I would let him have his shame.

But helping him overcome it lay first on my to-do list.

Chapter 9

Ezra

Summer's heat remained even as August drew to a close. Aaron took on a few more morning hours at the gym every week, and I used part of the money gifted to me from the fundraiser to purchase a nice chair for Phillip to sit in while watching TV with us at night.

I pushed for his company in the evenings to avoid temptation, oftentimes being the one to put the sleepy, grumbling man to bed after he passed out in the living room. A part-time job—also in the evening—became my next mission, and even though I could tell Aaron didn't like the idea of me working, he agreed to let me use his old SUV to deliver pizzas since there was only one vehicle between the three of us.

Forty-nine, and I drove around our neighborhood in a borrowed car to avoid my friend's affectionate son, dropping off takeout three nights a week. The tips were nice, even if I didn't need them as much as I did respite from being in close proximity to Aaron.

He'd become even more handsy at home, and I allowed more touches than was probably appropriate. And his edification, his words of praise and appreciation for all I did in helping him and his dad filled my soul with happiness and peace.

We didn't go out to lunch after church again and always went straight home to keep Phillip happy. I spent the bulk of my day with him, walking unless it rained, reading scripture, and sometimes just talking while I cooked for the three of us.

I'd taken over the household chores, only leaving the laundry for Aaron who insisted on keeping that one for himself.

Since I felt better physically and mentally after working out, I continued to go to the gym every morning with Aaron, and my chest swelled over seeing a difference in my physique. I'd always been on the muscular side and couldn't be more pleased to see definition once more taking shape like I'd had in my late thirties.

But I would never reach Aaron's level of cut. Sculpted like a Greek god, he drew gazes left and right while working out, and he never paid attention to anyone but me.

The way his gym shorts hugged his behind ensnared my stare whenever he turned his back too. When I spotted for him, grunts and groans escaped his parted lips and jolted electrical currents straight to my groin.

And with each passing day, the awful reminder I continued to carry around on my person lessened its burn through my clothing and the ability to make me feel like a failure. As though I'd been given a chance to redeem myself, I found satisfaction in caring for Phillip, in noting his mood swings and helping him to manage them. Contentment filled me whenever I crawled into bed at night knowing I'd chosen to be aware of others' thoughts and emotions rather than keeping my focus on eternity like I'd done with Sofiy.

On the three-month anniversary of her death, I fell asleep with that same contentment, a sense of pride in my chest over battling and seemingly finding peace in my grief.

But my deceased wife came to me in my sleep, her face as white as heavenly garments, black eye sockets as empty and cold as the grave.

You left me, she mouthed the silently screamed words, but I heard the accusation ring in my mind.

"I didn't," I told her, my heart racing. "You chose death over me."

Her mouth gaped open, jaw cracking like a demon in a horror film, and I scrambled backward through thickening fog, stumbling in my haste to escape her.

Floating white material gave way to black shrouds around her skeletal frame as she moved like the breeze, drawing ever closer. *Selfish, horrible man...you loved God more than your wife. You couldn't see how I withered away, how I suffered because of you!*

"I'm so sorry, Sofiy...so sorry. I hadn't known—you never shared your pain with me!" I whisper-hollered.

You didn't love me as Christ loves the church. She moved forward, ever relentless rather than a meek mouse who didn't share a peep.

My back came to rest against a solid wall.

No escape.

And as my wife closed the distance between us, jaw ever-widening with a shriek, the skin melted on her bones, dripping burning black onto my bare legs.

"Fuck!" I hollered and jolted upright on my bed, pulse pounding and chest heaving for oxygen. "Not real. Hell." I grasped my head in my hands. "Not real. She's dead. Gone."

Gulping, I slid my legs to the side, holding onto the mattress for a few seconds until I knew my heart wouldn't stutter to a stop and I had enough strength to stand.

Just a dream, I told myself over and over while slipping from my bedroom and sneaking down the stairs on shaking legs.

I got myself a glass of water and stood at the kitchen sink, one hand gripping tight to the counter to try easing my trembling. Shoulders rounded and head bowed, I fought off the images flashing in my head, the horrific memory of Sofiy's empty eyes, her hissing voice stating the truth she'd written in her note.

Her scrawled words ate at my insides, the kind of disappointment in myself I had no wish to share with anyone.

Not any spiritual leader in my life.

Not even my best friend Phillip.

I'd neglected Sofiy's emotional troubles and paid the highest price.

And if anyone found out the truth about her death, I would be seen as a failure rather than a godly man.

A sense of disgrace already hovered over my mind like a shroud, and I didn't know how to erase the self-blame that occupied my thoughts more than the grief a newly widowed man ought to experience.

Yet another truth to be ashamed of.

A shudder rippled through me, almost taking me to my knees.

The stairs creaked, but I kept my focus straight ahead while placing my empty glass in the sink with a slow exhale.

"Ezzie?"

"Sorry if I woke you," I croaked out to Aaron without turning. Even though the kitchen remained warm from the daylight hours, shivers raised goosebumps along my skin.

I could feel Aaron approach on silent feet, and I whimpered at the soft touch of his hand through my T-shirt on my lower back. As though he knew I needed physical touch, he caressed back and forth, the solidity of his palm easing my mind—but bringing my body to life in a whole different way.

"Are you okay?" he murmured too damn close to my ear, the warmth of his breath teasing along my neck.

All thoughts of my dream ripped from my mind as the heat of his body radiated through the distance between us.

I swallowed hard and shook my head.

Aaron slid closer and wrapped his arms around me.

Hugged me.

His chin on my shoulder, every inch of hard muscle pressed along me.

I should have pushed him away, should have pointed out the inappropriateness of the solace his actions brought.

"Let me," he murmured as though hearing my thoughts, his voice a deep rumble against my back.

A shudder rippled over me, and blood swelled my dick, tenting my sleep pants.

Comfort flooded through me along with physical desire, and I couldn't flee temptation, the rightness I felt at being held by the younger man even if he was Phillip's son. I sank into his arms, allowing him to keep me upright.

Tears slid down my cheeks before I recognized the burn in my eyes, the thickness in my throat. A sob choked from me, and I clasped at Aaron's hands on my stomach.

"It's okay," he whispered against my ear what I'd told him so many times when he'd been a kid, and I finally allowed the pent-up emotion to flow.

As though his affection opened the floodgates, I gave into the release, but my heart didn't ache like when I'd first found Sofiy. Perhaps it was the sturdy support of someone holding me. Perhaps it was simply the fact someone showed their empathy beyond mere words.

I tipped my head back against his shoulder, gulping through my tears when I'd thought I'd beaten grief's sorrow. Clinging to his hands, I allowed my feelings their necessary moment I hadn't before, telling myself it would be the final goodbye to the woman who'd chosen death rather than our marriage.

She'd accused me of leaving her—which I had, emotionally.

And now it's time to let her go for good.

The tears lessened, and a sense of freedom erased the accusations from my mind.

Aaron's lips ghosted over my neck, rubbing lightly along the whiskers of my jawline, arousing me once more.

Within a matter of seconds, I realized with certainty Aaron felt the same as I did for him, the thickness of him hardening against my backside. My hole clenched at having him so close, and my lingering tears quickly gave way to the lust brought on by a simple hug meant to offer peace.

Tension of a different sort returned to my body, stiffening me in his hold, but I didn't pull away—and Aaron didn't release me.

"Ezzie," he murmured against my ear, his hot breath sending a shiver down my spine and straight to my balls.

I couldn't speak, couldn't open my eyes for fear—hope, perhaps—I still dreamed so loving on him wouldn't be a sin. Immorality lay upon the path ahead of us, and while I didn't dread the ruination of my own soul, I loved Aaron too much to hurt him.

"Aaron," I said, readying my body to turn and leave.

He grasped my chin and angled my face toward him.

I gasped an inhale—and he licked over my lower lip and slid his tongue into my mouth in an unholy kiss.

Lust hit my groin, and I moaned as my knees went weak. A rush of wind filled my ears, and I once more sagged against him, submitting to his control, to the sensual way he glided his tongue along mine.

"Mmm," he moaned a deep rumble.

I realized I kissed him back—became ravenous for more hint of the wintergreen he exhaled into my mouth, for the soft whimpers and deep-throated groans. The noises from him...I'd never heard such ball-tingling sounds.

Delicious.

Addictive.

My hand slanted his head to better reach his luscious mouth. I wanted to turn into him, plaster our bodies together, and rub my aching dick against his, but he held me firm with one banded arm around my core keeping me in place.

"Fuck, Ezzie." He swept his tongue into my mouth, licking, tasting me.

And his hard length...he ground against my backside in time with his tongue, swiveling his hips in a sensual dance that heated my blood to combustion. Gentle thrusts in and out of my mouth, he mimicked what I'd never tasted before but craved.

To feel physical love like I knew he longed to show me. Filled—

Perversion.

The Holy Spirit's whisper broke through the lust controlling my mind, and I moved my head away from Aaron's hungry mouth.

"Aaron," I managed to choke out, leaning my torso forward to escape him even though he'd pressed me against the counter.

He licked my neck—dragged his tongue from my clavicle to my whiskers and made another rumbling noise—sending another shudder through me hard enough to leak fluid from my aching dick.

"You taste good, Ezzie." His hot breath ghosted over my ear, and he flicked his tongue inside. "So good."

"I-I can't," I gasped, grabbing hold of my length to stop from ejaculating in my boxers.

"You sure about that?" He tightened his arm banded around me and pressed his length against the crack of my ass, which made my head spin and caused my eyes to roll back.

"Yes," I spoke truth even though my sinful nature screamed the opposite.

I wanted Aaron. His mouth on mine, his naked body moving over me, his dick sliding balls deep into my body.

Lord.

Squeezing harder on the base of my dick barely kept me from tumbling headlong into sin.

"Please," I gasped out.

"Please what?" His rumble shivered over my skin again.

I paused before answering what I desired—what I shouldn't want. "Let me go," I barely managed to whisper the lie.

Aaron hesitated while releasing a heavy exhale, but he stepped away, giving me space.

Cold slid down over my back at the loss of his body heat, and I once more gripped the kitchen sink, too turned on, too shaky to move.

"Ezzie."

Fuck. Teeth clenched, unable to feel guilty over the curse ringing in my mind, I forced myself to face him.

"Why won't you let me love you?" The black of his pupils had swelled, leaving nothing more than a ring of blue, and delicious tension rose between us as he studied my face, every inch of him seeming to tremble with desire, same as me.

Nothing I could say would make any difference. I believed what took place between us was wrong even if he didn't. Telling him we couldn't would be laughable since we already had. Never again would be a lie, because as long as we lived beneath the same roof, I wouldn't be able to say no if he initiated what my soul, what my heart longed for.

A smirk curled the corner of his lip as though he heard the thoughts whispering in my head, and that damn glint that lit butterflies in my belly flashed in his eyes. "I'll wait." He turned and slipped away before I could tell him not to, before I could spout off bullshit we both knew wasn't true.

I should have dropped to my knees and begged God's forgiveness, asked him to fill me with the Holy Spirit's help in making godly decisions. For more than half of my life, I'd dedicated my all to living a pure existence.

But the hands, the tongue of one young man caught me up in whirlwind of desire I couldn't escape—and in the deepest reaches of my soul, I didn't want to.

Chapter 10

Aaron

Hearing Ezra holler had jerked my eyelids open, and I'd held my breath, listening as he'd gone downstairs.

I'd crawled out of bed and followed, not having any intention of touching or putting my lips on him.

But the slump of his shoulders, the droop of his head had demanded I offer comfort, and I'd done so without ulterior motives, knowing the thoughts that must have haunted him thanks to that damned note.

Ezra had let loose, crying like I'd never heard before, damn near breaking my heart with how he leaned against me, accepting my strength.

He made me feel like an oak, unwavering and sturdy, a place for him to rest. Like he saw me as someone he could trust to help him carry his burdens even if he didn't speak them out loud. Same as I'd believed of him when I'd been a kid.

He'd been my hero, and I wanted to be that for him in return.

I thrived off the sense of power, and my self-esteem rose to the choking level I'd only ever dreamed of.

The scent of him had flooded my nose, and I'd slid my lips over his skin without thought, loving how his whiskers tickled my face.

His tears had stopped, and I'd pushed to bring to fruition the lust that simmered between us.

Never had I been swept up in a kiss before, my body trembling with the desire for intimacy.

That moment with Ezra had been right.

Fucking perfection.

Damn delicious, better than I'd fantasized about. Slick and warm, his mouth had encouraged my neediness, his tongue exploring as much as mine had.

And my dick continued to leak, my mind buzzing long after I left him—but not before letting him know my availability, my desire for him, wouldn't end.

With languid strokes, I slickened pre-cum down my length and listened as Ezra came back up the stairs and shut himself in his bedroom. Ears straining, I hoped to hear him do the same as I did.

Because no way in hell could we share a kiss like that and him not get hard as fuck like he'd been against my ankle from a mere foot rub.

I imagined his hand wrapping around his girth.

Did he leak pre-cum as much as I did? Bite back a groan that held the whisper of a name?

Ezra.

I came with a grunt, ropes of watery white gushing up over my contracting abs. Every spurt pulled a deep moan from my chest, and my breath left in a rush as I slumped onto my bed, spent.

My hand was a sticky mess.

Tingles settled in my bones.

A smile curved my lips.

Ezra wanted me with the same intensity as I did him. No doubt. And I could be patient for him to accept the truth of what tangibly lived between us.

Because the end result would be better than anything he'd known before. I would stand by him, be his immovable rock, and he would eventually be able to leave behind the grief that kept him from accepting my love.

* * *

Ezra skipped working out the next morning and appeared haggard when I returned from the gym after work at noon. Dark circles rested beneath his eyes, letting me know he hadn't gotten much rest for himself the night before—while I'd slept like the dead, waking with the smile still on my face.

Dad's lips downturned slightly upon my walking into the kitchen while he attempted to eat lunch. He stared at me with eyes almost void of expression as usual, but his aggravation came through clearly.

"My favorite sweatpants aren't clean," he muttered while I sat my water bottle on the counter and pulled open the fridge to seek out some leftovers for my own lunch.

Prior to Parkinson's, Dad only ever wore slacks and ironed jeans—God forbid he lazed around in something so...blue collar even though that's what we'd always been.

Fuck, I missed the man he used to be.

"I did laundry yesterday, Dad," I said, grabbing the container of rice and chicken Ezra had made the night before. I'd also jerked off all over Ezra's shorts he'd worn to the gym while switching it too.

"Sweatpants," Dad grunted, refusing to be put off.

I didn't remember seeing the black cotton ones he wanted to wear all the time.

"I couldn't find them," Ezra stated quietly, moving past me toward the sink with his empty plate.

"You didn't look hard enough!" Dad attempted to holler but merely slurred and mumbled.

I shot him a glare while gently touching Ezra's lower back. He shivered but didn't step away from me. "I'll get them."

Putting aside my hunger for food and to devour Ezra's lips again, I headed into Dad's bedroom because I knew him and he wouldn't relent until he wore them.

The sweatpants had been shoved beneath his bed and had gotten missed when I'd gathered up the laundry the day before.

"They were under your bed!" I called while heading to the laundry room. "They're filthy too, so I'm throwing them in the wash!"

Dad's muttering reached my ears, but I thankfully couldn't make out his words.

I put the washer on small load and went back to the kitchen.

"You're a walking disaster."

Ezra caught my gaze at Dad's words hurled my way, his lips pressed tight, his eyes encouraging me to stand up for myself.

Turning away, I did as I always did—ignored my father's grumbling—and heated up my lunch, telling myself his hurtful bullshit meant nothing. But my cringe inside stated otherwise.

"Ezra does a better job than you."

My frown escaped.

Why Dad felt the need to put me down, I had no fucking clue. Three goddamn years of sacrificing my life for him, and not once had I heard a thank you.

"Selfish," Dad slurred, and I slammed the microwave door shut a little too hard. "Always thinking about yourself."

"Phillip," Ezra snipped while I swallowed the damn bitter pill. "That's enough."

My throat tightened at Ezra's support.

"Aaron has given up everything the past few years to look after you, and you treat him no better than a slave," Ezra continued on in a stern voice.

"His duty," Dad muttered.

"He could have put you in a home and left you to the care of strangers." Ezra took the remainder of Dad's lunch off the table while I waited for mine to finish heating through.

His shoulder touched mine as he stood at the sink, his hand finding my shoulder seconds later.

I wanted to lean into his touch, let him be the oak when I needed emotional support, but I wouldn't allow such weakness. "Just ignore him," I stated quietly enough Dad wouldn't hear. "He's a miserable bastard."

"It's okay to hurt, Aaron."

I met Ezra's steady gaze, wanting to tell him it was okay to let the past go, to love again and chase after the things your heart and body desired.

His focus shifted to the floor as he moved away from me. "It's almost time for your show," he told Dad, and I listened as Ezra wheeled him into the living room even though Dad could have made the short distance himself.

I sat and ate my lunch, thankful as fuck to have help in dealing with Dad when he got moody. Fuck knew, some days I almost reached a breaking point.

Ezra returned, walking past me and ruffling my hair in an awkward display of his affection from when I'd been a kid. Life stirred in my dick, but he went to the sink to fill Dad's water bottle.

"Treating me like I'm still a child won't change what's growing between us." I gave him the brutal truth, my attention on my chicken and rice.

He let out a heavy exhale, the silence almost stifling. "I know."

"Or your body's desire for mine."

"My wife was frigid."

I lifted my focus off my lunch to find Ezra propped against the counter, his arms crossed.

And she'd accused him in that note of ignoring *her* needs.

Fucking bitch.

"I've been starved for physical touch for years," he continued when I didn't respond due to my clenched jaw. "Desperate for a loving caress, a connection of tenderness. That's what made me respond to you last night."

Even though pissed, I bit back the sarcastic snort wanting to explode over his bullshit line.

"This *connection* between us is more than just a hunger for physical touch, Ezzie." I called him out rather than offering apologies for the woman who'd kept him from me and hadn't given him what *he* needed.

I leaned onto the table to better peer at him. "Your dick gets hard for me," I stated the truth quietly enough Dad wouldn't hear. "And frigid isn't a part of me when it comes to you, Ezzie."

He dropped his gaze to the floor and tightened his arms around his torso, stretching his T-shirt tight to pecs that had taken on more definition since coming home. "You know my thoughts on this matter, Aaron."

I could guess at them quite clearly, but I would find a way to break down those ideals, those so-called morals all thanks to a book he saw as truth.

Arguing theology with Ezra would have me shutting down in a matter of minutes from all his schooling. But honey drew flies, just like he'd stated countless times before leaving for the Ukraine that showing kindness and unconditional love brought hurting souls to Christ.

I decided to go that simple route because loving and edifying him came easily. I would be what he needed, *whenever* he needed, knowing he would eventually fall again.

Into my arms. Hopefully my bed.

"Tell me your limits—" he flitted his focus back to my face as I spoke "—because we *are* affectionate with one another. Always have been—and I'm desperate for it too, Ezzie. I'm just as starved for affirmation as you are. Words and touching."

Our gazes held for a few seconds in my vulnerability, but the tension between us lacked the desire he considered sinful.

My breath hitched, and I waited, my heart beating heavy in my chest.

"I don't know," he finally admitted.

"It doesn't have to be sexual between us," I assured him even though my mind whispered *yet*. "But I won't keep from giving you what you need because people will look at us funny or because some old writings declare two guys hugging is wrong. We're connected by history, by friendship"—*and a hell of a lot more you won't admit to*—"and nothing is going to change that."

He nodded slowly.

"How about we just continue on as we used to?" I suggested when he still didn't give me a definite answer like I hoped for before we could move forward. "And if it becomes too much, you let me know? I promise to respect your boundaries."

Ezra's gaze dropped to my mouth and quickly jerked away. "Okay."

Grinning, my heart lighter than it'd been in months, I went back to my lunch, shoving a forkful into my mouth. "So damn good," I said around my food, still grinning.

A slight smile lifted his lips.

"You're like the male version of...who's that English woman known for basting chickens?"

"Julia?"

"Yeah. Her. She's got nothing on you." I filled my mouth again.

His smile widened—Dad's bell rang, erasing some of the happiness in his eyes. "I'll go see what he wants." Ezra ruffled my hair on his way past, and I grabbed hold of his wrist before he could leave the kitchen. Tingles swept up my arm from the contact.

"I appreciate you, Ezzie," I said while staring up at him and breathing in his scent that twitched my dick with interest.

"I appreciate you too," he rasped out and glanced toward the living room. "Does your dad know about…"

"My preferring dick?"

He swallowed hard and nodded.

I decided to allow vulnerability in the chance he would do the same with me.

"No," I answered. "He would be disappointed in me, and with Parkinson's robbing him of a quality life, I decided he doesn't need anything else to be depressed about. Telling him the truth would get me kicked out of his house—who would care for him then?"

Dad hadn't been anything but my friend for years, and we'd had too good of a relationship to just throw away because his body failed him along with his mind. Admitting I was gay wasn't a weakness, but it would keep me from doing my duty and doubtless break his heart.

Ezra studied my face for a silent moment. "You're a good man, Aaron Weston," he whispered what he'd told me before and I wanted to believe.

"So are you, Ezzie," I said, just as adamant. "One of the best."

He tugged from my grasp, and I let him go, a sense of peace settling over me.

His agreeing to the usual affection, not ordering me to keep my hands to myself even after all but outright telling him I'd gladly offer up my body for his use, had instilled hope in my heart.

Nothing would stop me from giving him love.

Chapter 11

Ezra

Aaron and I had always been a bit handsy with each other, but after sharing that kiss in the middle of the night, he'd definitely become more insistent in showing physical appreciation.

And I didn't push him away. My body craved his touch, the pads of his fingertips trailing over my forearm. The heat of his palm on my lower back.

The brush of his entire body while leaning over me to reach into the cabinet when a simple excuse me would have worked. Those were the best encounters with temptation—Aaron's hard, muscular form along my backside. Riotous feelings erupted to life inside me.

Every. Single. Time.

And I craved it, salivated for another taste of his mouth while he thrust his hard length against me.

I didn't bother trying to limit how often I gave myself relief, taking my dick into hand every night after two hours of ball-aching agony of sitting on the couch together when I wasn't out delivering pizzas.

Once, when my eyes drooped, he'd tugged me down onto the couch, putting my head on his thigh. The thought of sleep swept away as I breathed in the scent of his bodywash, the skin of his bare thigh two inches from my lips.

He'd run his fingers through my hair, rubbing against my scalp and neck until I relaxed. A shift of his backside beneath us eased my head closer to his groin, and I rolled off the couch, quietly offering him a good night. He didn't mention my tented sleep pants or how quickly I fled his presence.

And with every soft touch, every lingering press of fingers or his palm, my desire for unholiness heightened.

Sunday morning while I poured myself a cup of coffee, he snuck into the kitchen behind me, pressing his bare chest against my back, his hands on my hips.

He ran his nose over my neck, releasing a sigh—and brushed his lips over the top of my spine.

My morning wood returned with full force, and teeth clenched, I slid sideways.

Aaron let me go without a fight, backing off. "Too much?" His deep, sleep-filled voice rumbled through me, and I shuddered.

Never enough.

I nodded, not trusting my voice, and focused on sweetening my coffee, the clink of the spoon on the mug's side loud in my ears.

He poured himself a cup. One sip of black brew, and another ball-tingling noise escaped his throat. "Delicious." Aaron stated the word quietly, his tone inflecting he spoke of more than the bitterness on his tongue.

Eyes clenching shut, I offered an automatic silent prayer for strength like I did countless times a day.

Aaron's hand settled on my lower back, and I sucked in a quick breath at the heat sweeping over me. "Thanks for making the coffee, Ezzie."

I held my breath, hoping for another kiss on my neck or cheek, but he walked off, shuffling feet taking him away from me.

A bell tinkled quietly, pulling my focus back to reality, to the responsibility I'd assigned myself in my heart.

Phillip, usually happier on Sunday mornings, revealed his inner bear, frustrating both Aaron and I between getting him ready for the day and setting him up for the church service's livestream.

But Aaron hid his annoyance and kept his mouth quiet.

Same as Sofiy hadn't shared her emotions with me.

I wondered how much he internalized or if he honestly owned the strength to ignore his father's hurtful words. An ache to hold Aaron, to comfort him and insist on discourse like I should have done with my wife tore my heart in two—abstaining physically hurt as much as it did my heart, but I couldn't trust myself to reach for him while in the privacy of our home.

Church became less of a joy, almost to the point of discomfort, but I looked forward to leaving the house once we had Phillip settled because I could spend those hours alone with Aaron.

My favorite time of the week because we couldn't get into trouble while in a car or surrounded by godly people.

But that morning, tension strung between Aaron and I in the SUV, his hands in a white-knuckled grip on the steering wheel.

Knowing things couldn't go too far in our situation, I slid my fingers down his bare forearm, and he released his grasp on the wheel. Gave me his hand while letting out a heavy exhale. Laced his fingers through mine atop his thigh.

And we rode in silence the rest of the way, my heart lighter than it should have been, a soft smile on his lips whenever I snuck a peek at his face.

I'd held Aaron's hand countless times when he'd been a kid, but the feel of his calloused palm, his thumb caressing the base of mine was more comforting than anything I'd experienced in my life.

New addiction officially found, I couldn't help but brush my hand against his any chance I got while walking into the church before we made our way through the crowded entryway and slid into our usual seats.

Shoulders touching.

Knees bumping.

And I strangely didn't feel one hint of guilt.

Pastor Jed requested the congregation to stand and pray together—holding the hands of those beside us so that we as a whole could go before the throne of God to beg mercy for a young mother diagnosed with cancer earlier the week before.

Aaron's fingers entwined with mine, sending a jolt clear to my toes, and I slowly exhaled while bowing my head, wishing we could do the same in any public setting, at any time we desired.

I searched my heart rather than listening to the lengthy prayer, shifting through the values I'd held since childhood. My identity early on had been dictated by God-fearing parents and the church, and I'd never once questioned my purpose on earth.

To bring glory to God.

Lead souls to Christ.

Show unconditional acceptance to all of God's creation.

But I couldn't understand the desire to love Aaron I felt deep in the marrow of my bones.

My emotions gyrated around like dirty laundry in a washing machine, filth sloshing about, permeating every thought in my head. The Word of God should have been the cleansing waters, the rinse cycle to rid unholy desire from my mind, but it failed in its responsibility.

Calluses and soft caresses of Aaron's thumb slowly shifted core elements inside my heart. The solid feel of his hand wrapped around mine steadied me. He acted like a ground wire when everything I'd believed in for forty-nine years didn't give me sure footing.

Pastor Jed finished his prayer, but my hand lingered in Aaron's as everyone around us began to take their seats once more. Reluctantly, I released my hold on him and instead focused on how our thighs bumped as we sat.

Shoulder tight against his, I filled my lungs, deciding to accept comfort where and when I could.

Choosing to live a godly life meant avoiding sexuality in our interactions though, so while Pastor Welker began his new series on praising God in dire situations, I settled my heart on staying in line with God's word.

Limits came to mind for Aaron's affection, and I held steadfast to the determination to keep a platonic relationship with the younger man. I would only allow us the culmination of tenderness both our hearts longed for.

Nothing more.

I followed Aaron out into the lobby where other church members mingled, coming to me as they always did on the day of worship. A few hugs and handshakes, their kind and continued words of empathy over the loss of my wife didn't do anything but remind me of my grief I'd found easier to let go than I felt was right.

I'd even gone so far as to leave her crumpled note hidden in the back of my sock drawer that morning so the anguish wouldn't be a constant burn.

Mr. Townson approached with his wife, greeting me with a smile I couldn't find the energy to return. Both Pastor Welker and Pastor Jed ambled close by, joining us.

Aaron brushed against my side, his pinky grazing mine when I stiffened at their nearness.

I fought the need for a quick intake of air, but Mr. Townson's brow flinched, his focus dropping to Aaron's hand that shifted up to grasp my elbow.

So did Pastor Welker's.

"I'll be in the car," Aaron murmured near my ear and walked away, shoulders hunched, hands shoving into his jeans' pockets.

"That boy has an odd affection for you."

My focus jerked back to Pastor Welker. "Pardon?"

"Aaron."

"I've known the boy since he was born," I stated quietly, my stomach tightening, my lips thinning.

"But he's a boy no longer."

As if I needed my pastor to point out the obvious.

"I would advise Aaron to keep his hands to himself before people get the wrong impression, Pastor Ezra." Pastor Welker's tone stayed low, but those in our tight circle heard, itching my feet to flee. "As a man of God, you need to live a life that is blameless not just in the sight of God, but also in the sight of man."

Blameless—something I wasn't. With Sofiy. With my unholy desires for Aaron.

I fought the instinct to slouch beneath his stare, unwavering even though my tongue tied.

"As a missionary, you're held to a higher standard," Pastor Welker continued, his chin tilting up, and I sensed arrogance in his narrowed eyes, a holier-than-thou complex that didn't sit well in my stomach.

Rather than get into a deeper, private conversation about the plank in his own eye, I nodded that I'd heard his words and turned toward Pastor Jed. "How is Jamie?" I asked about the woman he'd prayed for, needing to change the topic of conversation.

"I'm heading over to the hospital this afternoon to visit with her," Pastor Jed replied, his gaze lacking the questioning that the other two men's did.

"I would love to join you," I told him.

"You're still at the Westons'?"

"Yes," I replied, noting Mr. Townson's pursed lips. I imagined he wondered what Aaron and I got up to when Phillip slept.

Curses rose to mind I wanted to spew in his face. My hands fisted.

"I can swing by to pick you up around three."

"I'll see you then." I nodded at Pastor Jed and offered the others a good day through clenched teeth before spinning on my heel to escape the uncomfortable air between us.

Judgmental assholes...but not Pastor Jed. He, I could handle, as he seemed the accepting, loving sort as Christ's church was called to be.

I stepped into the sunlight, inhaling until my lungs ached. Such interactions between me and Aaron at home or in the car might be okay in my mind, but as Pastor Welker pointed out, it wouldn't be with others.

Yet another limit that ought to be set in stone.

My heart ached the slightest bit.

"You can't touch me like that in church," I told Aaron while buckling my seatbelt. "Both Pastor Welker and

Mr. Townson noticed that little *non-innocent* pinkie touch."

"What did he say?" Aaron asked rather than denying my emphasized insinuation.

The truth shouldn't have pleased me as much as it did, but after feeling judged for what could have been taken as an accidental brush of hands, I needed the reminder of his complete acceptance.

"He hinted our relationship appeared to be more than platonic."

Aaron didn't respond right away, and I finally glanced over at him as he pulled out of the church's parking lot. A muscle ticked beneath the scruff lining his jaw.

I inhaled until my lungs hurt, needing to draw the line in the sand as I'd decided while in service. "As a man of God, my life will be scrutinized—and I won't be found a hypocrite."

You already are one.

I slouched in my seat as Sofiy's voice whispered in my head.

"It's hard to keep my hands to myself when people spew shit they think is comforting and all it does is remind you of your loss and bring back your sadness," Aaron finally spoke, his soft tone revealing empathy where others had fallen short.

I tipped my head back against the seat, closing my eyes, some sort of emotion seeping into my chest I absently rubbed at. "How are you so discerning?" I asked, staying in the darkness behind my eyelids.

His hand found my thigh and squeezed—but not in a sexual way that enticed my groin to stir to life. "Is this okay in the privacy of the car?"

I should have said no, but his touch calmed the stomach-churning Pastor Welker's words had stirred up. "Yes," I whispered and sat a few moments in silence, soaking in the warmth of his palm atop my slacks. "How do you so easily put to rest what others hope to with words they probably think the Holy Spirit gives them to say?" I asked quietly.

"Because I know you, Ezra—and I love you. Always have."

My heart stuttered, and I turned my head toward him.

A quick glance my way and Aaron's guileless blue eyes revealed his heart. More than lust, more than a shared past, the young man truly cared about me more than anyone on earth ever had.

I couldn't find the words to properly explain my feelings for him, so I let the matter rest, wondering over the sting in my eyes. My hand found his, and I threaded my fingers through his stronger ones.

Our clasped palms sat atop my thigh where I wanted them more than anything in that moment.

Chapter 12
Aaron

Ezra's fiftieth birthday hovered on the horizon, and I wracked my brain to find ways to make it special. I dreamed about taking him out for a nice dinner, to a club to where no one knew us and we could dance until hot and sweaty. A place where no one would give us the side-eye of hypocritical judgement he'd gotten at church all because I'd touched his pinkie, his elbow, then leaned in to tell him I would wait in the car.

Such utter bullshit.

It'd gotten to the point in my head that I didn't want to attend Dad's old church anymore. I'd been going for the freedom from my responsibilities with him, and had it not been for Ezra sitting beside me in service, the chance to have his body even the slightest bit against mine, I would have ended up in a coffee shop instead.

Long discussions of the sermon with dad could go to hell. I'd never enjoyed them anyway.

And after we exited the sanctuary every Sunday, rather than holding Ezra's hand like I wanted, I kept mine in my pockets where they wouldn't be tempted to wander. At home though, I took advantage of every opportunity afforded to me.

Gentle touches to remind him of my presence while walking past him. Side hugs whenever Ezra seemed in a darker place like when he'd first gotten stateside. Enticing him to lay on the couch with his head on my thigh when he appeared haggard so I could stroke my fingers through his silver-laced hair until he rested and breathed easy.

I'd never felt such contentment in someone's presence, never felt the instinctual need to protect his heart, his mind, and emotions from all his bitch of a wife had inflicted on him. But seeing him relax into my affection did the same for me.

Had he given me the slightest indication he wanted more, I'd have offered him everything—whatever he needed to find peace and joy in his life like he'd had before heading overseas.

Dad and I had lost the Ezra we'd known.

And I was determined to get him back.

The morning he turned fifty, I beat him to the coffee pot and had a cup ready for when he stumbled downstairs. Perfectly sweet and blonde like he preferred.

His half-opened eyes still held sleepiness. "Thanks," he whispered when taking the steaming mug from me. He sipped while standing beside me near the pot, eyelashes fluttering downward.

"Mmm," he hummed and swallowed.

My gaze tracked the bob of his Adam's apple. "Happy birthday," I said, quickly adjusting my morning chub before he opened his eyes.

"Fifty." He shook his head and sipped again, his gaze on his coffee. "I'm old."

Ezra looked damn fine for his age, especially just rolled from bed all rumpled with messed up hair. I expected he'd look even better thoroughly fucked and sated, limbs askew, a soft smile peeking from his whiskers while cum leaked from his flushed hole.

My dick swelled, so I turned away to refill my cup. "I was thinking about heading up to the reservoir today to go fishing like we always used to do for your birthday."

Ezra didn't reply, so I glanced over my shoulder. Softness filled his hazel eyes, and they welled as I held his gaze.

"I'd like that," he said, his tone almost broken.

My fingers itched to pull him into my arms, and I wondered if his bitch wife had ever made his birthday special.

"What about Phillip?" he asked while I tamped down my desire to hold him.

Fishing had been Dad's and my thing, and while the thought of him not being beside me identifying birds while we cast and reeled in stung my heart, I wanted it for Ezra. I could deal with missing my old dad.

"Glenda offered to stay with him," I said, "but I was thinking getting out might be good for him too. Maybe it'll bring back happy memories. Give him something to be jolly about."

"Is the old pavilion still there?" Ezra asked. "It's close enough to the lake for his wheelchair that he shouldn't feel too left out."

"Last I'd been there a couple years ago, yeah."

"Just like old times."

Dick under control from thoughts of Dad, I turned and clinked my mug against his. "Just like old times," I echoed.

His smile damn near took me to my knees, and I grinned, feeling like I could conquer the world.

"I'll pack a lunch," he said.

My smile widened. "I'll dig out the gear."

And two hours later, we worked together to get Dad ready. He complained about having to leave the house, but the minute I got him settled into his wheelchair and overlooking the reservoir, he quieted, the placid appearance of his face seeming truthful for a change.

"Will you be okay up here while we fish?" I asked him, settling a thin blanket over his legs since a slight chill lingered in the late morning air.

"Fine," Dad slurred, and I caught a hint of happiness in his tone.

Thank fuck.

With a quick squeeze to his frail shoulder, I stood and made my way down the slight incline toward where Ezra had taken the rods and old tackle box.

No lines furrowed his brow, and his eyes twinkled while sorting through Dad's fishing lures.

"When's the last time you went fishing?" I asked, allowing a dozen feet or so of space between us just like Dad and I used to do.

"The Friday before I flew to the Ukraine."

My eyebrows shot up. Dad and I had gone together for a few years after Ezra had left. With how Ezra had loved the quiet peace of casting and reeling in, his answer made my eyes widen. "Seriously?"

He shrugged and cast, the plunk sounding before he expounded. "Once on the mission field, I didn't do much of anything but build up the church."

I glanced up at the pavilion to check on Dad. He peered at us without expression, so I grinned and waved, wanting him to feel included.

"What did you do for fun?" I asked, turning back toward the lake.

Ezra took a few minutes before answering that question too. "Sofiy's family were the first people I'd met, the first to befriend me," he finally said, his voice low. "I spent most of my days with them."

He cast again, and I waited, giving him time to decide on what to share. "I didn't do anything for myself those first few years," he finally said. "I'd given all my hours to God, my focus on eternity in glory."

"The mansion of gold promised to His faithful servants," I tacked on what I'd been taught, what he and Dad had used to talk about that had always prompted the decisions they'd made in life.

Ezra nodded, the lines appearing in his brow again. A cool breeze hinting of smoke from a pile of burning leaves or brush fire ruffled his hair.

Sentimentality stirred inside me, and I decided right then that I would take Ezra camping again. Tents and sleeping bags. Dinty Moore beef stew and s'mores cooked over an open fire.

"It makes me happy to see you living again, Ezzie."

He shot me a quick glance, and I didn't hide any of my feelings from my face, same as when I'd told him I loved him. "I'd forgotten how much the little things in life can bring joy," he murmured. "Thank you for reminding me."

One corner of my lips quirked up. "My pleasure." If not for the pink tinge rising to coat his cheeks, I would have thought he'd missed my double meaning.

Ezra checked on Dad, and a half hour later, I took my turn, wondering if he finally felt left out. As I assumed, his mood had soured.

"I'm cold," he muttered, his detached facial expression not matching his tone.

"We can head home," I said, tucking the blanket more tightly around his thin legs.

"Hungry."

"We can pick up some chicken lo mein on the way home for Ezra's birthday."

"KFC."

"Dad." I straightened and glanced down to find Ezra packing up our fishing gear. I guessed he'd noticed Dad's mood earlier and expected it was time to head out. "It's his birthday. Don't you think we should pick up what he likes for all the help he's been giving us? Besides, we just had fried chicken two days ago—Ezra's treat."

Dad made a grunting noise I knew meant he wasn't pleased. "Everything is for Ezra."

One of my eyebrows shot up, and I wondered how much Dad saw, how much he read on my face whenever the three of us shared the same space. "He's our guest," I reminded Dad quietly, hating I even had to do so when fifteen years earlier he'd have been the one to suggest eating whatever Ezra wanted. "And getting him what he likes is the least we can do."

"You take advantage of his kindness," Dad struggled to say, and my heart squeezed in my chest.

Did I?

Yes, I worked a couple of extra hours at the gym because Ezra was home with Dad during the day. I didn't argue whenever he offered to make meals or go to Dad whenever his bell rang.

I glanced down at Ezra again, discomfort shifting my feet. He had enough of his own emotional issues to deal with, and my slacking off in caring for Dad had to add to them.

Dealing with sour moods and negativity wore a man's ass out.

Had I allowed Ezra to burden himself with responsibility that didn't belong to him?

"You're right, Dad," I stated quietly, hating how I'd failed Ezra when I claimed to love him.

Dad gazed up at me, but I couldn't read his thoughts through his watery blue eyes.

Two birds fluttered in the brush beside us, making a racket, but he didn't turn to see what kind they were like he'd have done before his illness. Dad had always carried around a small bird book, trying to identify which chirped and which sang early morning songs while sipping coffee around our campfires.

A caw sounded.

"Blue jay," I said, squeezing his shoulder, needing a topic change before my disappointment in myself weighed my shoulders down even further.

He grunted and finally took his focus off me to peer at Ezra.

"In the spring I'll put a bird feeder outside your bedroom window," I said.

Have I always been this selfish? So caught up in my own thoughts that I didn't think to find small ways to bring joy to Dad's boring existence?

"I'll be dead."

The blunt words didn't bring me sorrow like a good son would have experienced after sharing a great many years up until his diagnosis. Even more shame curled up through my chest over the happiness at the idea of having freedom for good.

To live without constraints.

Perhaps to love.

I ambled back down the hill, feeling like a piece of shit. Ezra crouched in front of the open tackle box reeled me in as easily as he did his fishing line, pulling me from hints of depression. Old jeans hugged his thighs, and the green flannel of Dad's he'd borrowed stretched tight across his shoulders. Sunlight glinted off the silver strands in his hair I wanted to run my fingers through.

Ezra needed to fully live again—and it seemed he'd begun to since his return.

But would he ever be able to love? I caught moments of grief etching his face, but it always eased whenever I made myself known or he became aware of my presence.

At the gym and during our few hours alone every night while watching TV, he seemed a different man than the one Dad saw.

Ezra found life with me, I realized when he glanced up, his smile fixed firmly in place.

"Dad's ready to go," I told him, hating to end our time outside the norm.

Ezra glanced up at the pavilion, and although his lips stayed tilted up, the happiness faded from his face.

"How does chicken lo mein sound for dinner?"

That brought Ezra's attention back on me—and the light in his eyes. "Now that's something I haven't had since…"

"Don't say the day you turned thirty-five."

His smile dissolved.

"Seriously?" I asked that same damn question, my voice raised in disbelief. That had been the week before he'd left us for the Ukraine. "What else have you been missing out on, Ezzie?"

"Too much," he murmured, grabbing up the tackle box and standing.

I grabbed him in one of my side hugs, not giving two shits that Dad looked on. "Well what do you say we go about remedying that, huh?" A quick extra squeeze and I released him to pick up my fishing rod off the ground.

"I appreciate you, Aaron." His voice broke, and I turned again to find his eyes welling even as mine did the same.

Swallowing hard, I nodded, and I wondered if he knew how much those words meant to me, how the sentiment swelled my heart with warmth.

I appreciated *him* more than he would ever know, but I refused to take advantage of his goodness any longer. He deserved to go out and reconnect with other friends he'd left behind, not be housebound with a miserable bastard.

Chapter 13

Ezra

We picked up our Chinese food and KFC on the way home, and although I hadn't been so happy, so content in God knew how long, heaviness weighed on my shoulders.

A few hours after dinner, Phillip's eyes drooped while he sat in the new chair.

I started to stand, but Aaron grasped my forearm, keeping me on the couch. "I'll see to him tonight."

Aaron went over to his dad. "Let's get you into bed."

Phillip grunted and blinked his eyes open. "Ezra."

"What?" Aaron said, still half-bent and ready to assist his move over into his wheelchair.

"Want Ezra," Phillip stated.

Aaron stayed put, studying his dad's face. They seemed to hold a silent conversation, one I couldn't fathom.

"You're *my* responsibility, Dad," Aaron finally insisted quietly.

"Want Ezra tonight."

"Okay," he said as though annoyed, and lips tight, he turned back for the couch. "He's all yours." Aaron shrugged and motioned at his dad before sprawling into the corner of the couch.

"Up you go," I told my oldest and dearest friend while taking his arm to help him shift over and settle into his wheelchair.

Caring for Phillip wasn't my duty, but I gladly gave of myself after having been absent for too many years. But the desire to help care for him also came from love.

Not stacking up those riches in heaven.

After Sofiy's death and the reasons for her taking her life, I refused to put selfish wants before outward expressions of appreciation.

But what if loving how I wanted proved to be the selfish choice?

At what point did I choose godliness and eternal riches over showing and giving His children what they longed for most in their humanity?

Weren't we called to love one another?

Where did people draw the line when others suffered and desperately needed a shoulder to cry on? A hand to hold? Physical affection that fed the starved soul?

Those thoughts had only come to mind after Aaron insisted we go fishing for my birthday. A gift of the greatest sort, from deep thought—he knew what I needed, the way I longed to be loved.

And my mind had stewed ever since.

Phillip stared at me when I knelt in front of him once inside his bedroom, and I pushed the many questions and confusing emotions from my brain. I wondered if he'd asked for me with a purpose or if he'd just become accustomed to me helping him change and settle in for the night.

"Thank you for going to the reservoir with us today for my birthday," I told him, easing off his slippers. "I know you don't like to leave the house very much."

"Stay."

I glanced up from where I crouched in front of his wheelchair. "What do you mean?"

"Spring." His lips worked as though he struggled with the words.

"You want me to spend the winter with you and Aaron?" I asked quietly, studying the pallor of his face, the darkness circling beneath his eyes.

"Yes."

I stood, leaned in, and kissed Phillip's forehead, my throat going tight. Did he sense his end and want me with him when he went on to glory? Loving him as my friend wasn't even a choice. There was no line, no end to what I would give. Answering came easy. "I'll stay," I whispered, and a heavy exhale left his slack mouth.

He'd been a bully since I'd arrived, showing jealousy of the time Aaron and I spent together, but what man in his position wouldn't? Forgiving his words, his anger, wasn't something I needed God's assistance with, and

I gladly helped him stagger to his feet and sit his weight onto the edge of his bed.

"I'm not going anywhere, Phillip," I told him a short time later once we changed him from his favorite black sweats into his pajamas. I pulled his blankets up beneath his chin. "I'll stay."

"To the end." His eyes welled with his whisper, and I nodded, my own stinging over all the time we'd missed out on, all the additional memories we could have shared.

"Until the end, my friend."

Throat tight, I left him, cracking his door open and allowing the hallway light to spill across his prone form. Unmoving. Thin. Wasting away. The man who'd been like my brother for over forty years had no hope of walking on his own again. Casting a line and reeling in a fish like his son did with beautiful finesse.

Grief I hadn't felt for Sofiy grabbed hold of my heart—and I hadn't even lost Phillip yet.

Aaron still sat in the corner of the couch when I returned to the living room. He eyed me as I shuffled forward, and as though he knew my state of my mind, my sorrow, he reached out his hand.

Accepting comfort from one wanting to give it couldn't be wrong in the sight of God.

I went to Aaron willingly, curling on the couch beside him and pressing myself against his side like he'd done to me when he'd been a boy and arrived home from school with red-rimmed eyes and tear tracks lining his dirtied cheeks. He held the back of my head and pulled my face against his chest.

His T-shirt caught my tears, and I clung to him, needing something tangible rather than faith in that moment.

My best friend's impending death hurt more than Sofiy's—and the guilt over that truth burdened my heart ten times over. Would I ever be able to fully forgive myself? Live with the truth of how I'd failed her?

And could I go on creating new memories after burying the friend I never should have left in order to seek riches in glory?

Aaron kissed the top of my head, his hand smoothing down my spine and back up again until I shuddered a final sob and gained control over the sadness swamping my mind, my energy depleted.

I couldn't pull away from his arms and wondered over why I felt I should to begin with.

"Okay?" he whispered against my hair, and a shiver rippled over me.

"I will be." And still I stayed put, allowing his hands on me, his lips on my head.

Definitely inappropriate to some degree, but I couldn't find it in myself to care. His affection, his strength, filled me up more than prayer or faith ever had. Grief faded enough that rest crept in.

Because of Aaron.

I closed my eyes and snuggled in, wishing we could stay that way until we too breathed our last.

Aaron's young heart beat beneath my ear, steady and reassuring, and I inhaled deeply, the scent of dryer sheets and man swirling in my lungs. My groin twinged to life, and I pressed my lips tight, not wanting desire to ruin our perfect moment together.

As though he noted the shift in the air between us, Aaron lifted me away from his torso, his strong hands on my upper arms.

I should have moved to my side of the couch, but I met his gaze and found myself unable to.

Aaron cupped my whiskered cheek in his palm, his focus dropping to my mouth.

Blood rushed to my dick as his thumb slid over my lower lip, tugging enough for my mouth to part open. "Ezzie," he whispered, and I swallowed hard.

Too much, I told myself to say the words we'd agreed upon, but my body disagreed. My voice refused to obey.

And Aaron took my silence as consent, closing the distance between us.

I gasped at the soft brush of his warm lips, my heart pounding in my chest. A sense of comfort welled up, one I couldn't name. Something different. Unholy, perhaps, but in that moment I needed him. His touch. His gentleness that washed my sadness away.

"Let me in," Aaron whispered against my mouth, his other hand finding my face. His tongue flicked over my lower lip and slid inside without resistance on my part.

My mind went blank, a burst of light like fireworks igniting inside me. I realized I clung to his shirt as he seemed to feed off my mouth, every moan, every glide of his tongue along mine causing burning fire to race over my skin.

Wetness seeped from the tip of my dick, and I shuddered, knowing I would come without a single touch if he didn't stop kissing me.

I didn't want him to.

Without taking his lips off mine, Aaron shifted forward —and I laid back willingly, his weight settling over my body a perfect blanket of flesh and bone.

Hardness against my groin, the rocking of his hips brought mine up off the cushion in search of more friction.

"Aaron," I choked out, not sure if I meant the word as a plea for him to stop or to give me more mind-numbing relief.

He tipped my chin up and kissed down my neck, and my eyelids fluttered closed. Hot breath and soft lips caressed along the edge of my T-shirt's collar while his strong hands found my skin beneath.

My stomach contracted at his touch, and I groaned as the backs of his fingertips brushed along my lower abs and under the edge of my sleep pants waistband. He paused.

Blinking myself to reality, I found him peering down at me, pupils blown wide, erasing most of the blue in his eyes. Both of us panted in the tense silence.

His thumb slid down over the front of my pants—along my aching length.

I shuddered, swallowing hard against the whimper wanting to slip passed my lips.

When I didn't tell him to stop, didn't tell him he went too far, Aaron shifted his entire hand inside my pants, his calloused palm and fingers around my throbbing dick.

"Ung." I grunted and grasped at his shirt, my hips rising as I struggled to draw breath into my squeezed lungs.

"Let me," he whispered over my lips, and I didn't bother fighting a war I would never win.

Copious amounts of pre-cum oozed from me, and he palmed over my sensitive head, smearing the slickness clear to the root of my dick, once more causing my hips to jerk up off the couch in search of more.

"Mmm," his voice rumbled, eyes hooded as our gazes stayed locked. I panted, fighting against the eruption begging for release.

The wet sounds of fist fucking hit my ears, but I couldn't be bothered with embarrassment over how I leaked for him, how I moved in opposition to his sensual downward strokes.

He'd asked, I hadn't said no...but his actions weren't selfish. As though he'd known what I needed, same as always, Aaron offered me pleasure, an escape I was desperate for.

It'd been too long since someone other than myself took my dick in hand, and my release tingled in the base of my spine within seconds.

He ground his hard length against my hip, his hushed moans sexier than any feminine noise I'd ever heard.

The image of his forbidden hole grasping at my dick like his hand did—of stroking inside him in time with my thrusts...

"Fuck," I whispered.

"Yes, Ezzie," he groaned against my parted lips.

And I careened over the edge.

Aaron took my mouth in a heated kiss, swallowing my cries as cum shot through my length.

I grasped at his shoulders, keeping his mouth against mine. Curses rang inside my head as I sucked down his haggard exhales, convulsed beneath his body, his strong hand milking every drop of cum from my pulsing balls.

"Mmm," he made that damn rumbling noise again, licking over my lower lip until I shuddered and went lax beneath him.

Completely spent.

Extremities tingling in the aftereffects of euphoria.

Mind gloriously wrecked.

Quiet.

Sated and at ease.

Holding my gaze, he brought his cum-soaked hand to his mouth—and sucked his fingers clean, the hunger in his eyes attempting to bring my dick back to life.

My pulse continued to thunder, and I became aware once again of his erection pressed tight against my thigh. Lust for the taste of him, the feel of his flesh in my hand, between my lips, rushed over me, heating my skin.

I opened my mouth to ask him if I could return the favor, but he kissed me again with the type of hungry passion that emptied my brain of thoughts. I couldn't even be bothered with the fact I tasted myself on his tongue.

He groaned and reached between us.

I tore my lips from his and watched as he shifted his hips, reached into his pants, and freed his hard length. Swallowing a rush of saliva, I stared like a deer in headlights at every peek of his slickened dick head through his fist.

The need to see him ejaculate, to find his own release after caring for me first swept over me, and my hand moved on its own, cupping the warm, drawn-up balls beneath his flushed dick.

"Fuck, yes," Aaron gasped out—and jets of spunk shot from his slit, splattering with mine on my shirt. "Ezzie." He gulped and shuddered with every spurt, collapsing alongside me on the narrow couch once finished.

Hot breath caressed my neck, and he let out the tiniest whimper, the likes of which curled a man's toes and instilled a desire to cause such a noise every day.

Aaron wrapped his arm around me, keeping me against him on the narrow couch. "Okay?" he murmured, but I couldn't align my thoughts to give him an answer.

My flesh wanted more—a hell of a lot more than the sinful things we'd done, but I knew we'd gone too far. Definitely passed over those self-imposed lines I'd insisted on.

I let out a heavy exhale, and as though Aaron noted my rising discomfort, he squeezed me tighter.

"Don't leave me yet." The quietness of his tone, the hint of the insecure little boy in his voice, kept my backside plastered to the couch.

I clasped my palm over his elbow atop my stomach, the backs of my fingers smearing through cooling ejaculate. His or mine? Or was it both of ours combined? I released my hold on his arm and lifted my hand to my lips, the saying about curiosity killing the cat whispering in my mind.

"Do it." The rumble of Aaron's heated words against my ear prompted my action before I fully considered what he suggested.

Saltiness hit my tastebuds at the first flick of my tongue—and I licked again.

"Fuck, Ezzie." Aaron groaned and shifted as though his dick twitched like mine did.

I cleaned the backs of my fingers off, the sudden desire to move down his body and swallow his dick for more of him on my tongue sweeping over me.

Perversion.

My own mind or the Holy Spirit—I couldn't discern, but the whisper carried weight and brought about the proper response.

I pulled away from Aaron, and he let me go. Perhaps he figured I moved in order to visit the sinful thoughts

I'd had, what the cleaning off of my fingers had suggested to him.

But I turned my back on him instead, stumbled up the stairs on shaking legs, and locked myself in my bedroom. In silence, I lay in bed, my mind a jumbled mass of confusion.

Truth and desire.

Eternity and reality.

I didn't know where the lines ought to lie. I didn't *want* limits.

Giving in even further to what we both desired would fulfill our flesh, but what about our souls? Denying Aaron what he offered me unselfishly every day, even beyond the sexual parts, would add to his unhappiness, his lowered self-esteem.

I'd promised Phillip I would stay and see him through to the end..

"What should I do?" I whispered, hoping God would hear.

If he did, he never answered.

I retrieved Sofiy's crumpled note from my drawer and lay back down, fingertip rubbing over the paper while the written words etched in ink echoed through my mind.

A simple note had torn me apart more than the actual loss of my wife who'd cut me off in every way for years. I'd been unable to reach beyond her walls and had eventually shut down as well rather than seeking counsel.

I'd ignored her. Denied her the love she'd needed. I'd put God first in all things and paid the highest price. With her, choosing God had made me a bad person.

A root of bitterness snuck into my soul, burrowing in search of sustenance. God's demands on His children didn't seem to take thought of anything outside eternity, promises of a painless afterlife for obedience —or infinity burning in hell's fires.

What about our years on earth? Humanity, its frailness of mind and heart? How could He allow His faithful servants to suffer negative consequences for choosing Him and His path?

Without a real grasp on an endless existence, it proved hard for a mere man to see beyond his reality.

For the first time since dedicating my life to God, I questioned my faith.

My reason for living.

But I had no answers—and no peace came when I told myself to trust God, same as I'd always done because I didn't know how else to live.

Chapter 14

Aaron

Patience had become one of my strengths after caring for an invalid for three years, but Ezra tested me far beyond what Dad ever had.

He didn't speak a word about what went down on that old couch, going on about daily living as though he hadn't shifted my world off its axis. However, he wasn't subtle in letting me know it'd unsettled him as well.

And not in a good way.

Ezra avoided eye contact. Shied away from my usual touches that hadn't been too much before. And he picked up more hours delivering pizzas on evenings instead of spending them with me.

Rather than lessening his feelings of shame and unworthiness, I'd managed to intensify them. I'd lost him a second time, and I didn't know what to do about it.

Pushing off his offers to help with Dad didn't help matters any, but my little chat with Dad on Ezra's birthday had set my stubbornness on not taking advantage of our friend.

I sat at the dinner table, watching Ezra when I should have been filling my empty stomach. He kept occupied with his food, the clink of silverware on old plates the only noises breaking the silence outside of Dad's occasional annoyed grunts.

Lines furrowed his brow. His lips downturned between bites. Darkness clung to the skin beneath his eyes— and how I longed to pull him against me, to ease whatever renewed grief fucked with his mind.

He'd found comfort in my arms. Rest. And I desired nothing more than to—

Dad dropped his butter knife, jerking my focus off Ezra.

"Need help?" I asked, and his stare brought me up short of reaching to do so.

Watery and normally vacant, his eyes held clarity for a moment—and I knew he'd noticed how I looked at Ezra. Like I wanted to love him. Hold him. Give myself to him in hopes he would find life worth living again.

I shifted my focus off Dad, lips pressed tight while cutting his chicken breast into bite-sized pieces even though he'd said he hadn't needed me to when I'd made up his plate.

"Wrong," Dad muttered.

One word—but it caught my breath, and I felt myself cowering like I'd always done as a kid whenever he'd scolded me.

He didn't speak of how I cut his chicken breast.

Swallowing hard, I finished my task and set his knife back on the table.

"My friend," Dad added.

I opened my mouth to deny his suggestion, but Ezra beat me to forming words.

"What do you need, Phillip?" So calm, seemingly serene—Ezra obviously didn't understand what Dad had meant.

Dad growled with pent up frustration, and I expected he suffered from not being able to express what he wanted with proper words and tone.

"It's okay, Dad." I forced myself to meet his steady gaze. "*Okay*," I repeated, nodding, letting him know I understood the meaning behind his few words. Agreed vocally though I felt no such wrongness. Being with Ezra was the rightest thing I'd experienced in my entire life.

Ezra didn't push the conversation, and I somehow managed to eat a bit of my dinner. He took Dad into the living room once we finished with our silent meal, and I strained my ears, wondering what Dad would say to him while I cleaned up in the kitchen.

The TV turned on almost immediately, so I set about my task while releasing a heavy exhale. There would be no conversation between the two men with the TV on, thank fuck.

Ezra returned and leaned against the counter beside me where I washed dishes.

Considering we hadn't spoken more than necessary in the days since I'd jerked him off and he sucked my cum off his fingers like a starved man, his closeness lifted my spirits—and an eyebrow.

"Everything okay?" I asked, soap bubbles up to my elbows.

"This needs to stop."

"What does?"

Hardness I hadn't seen in years glinted in his hazel eyes as he leaned close to me, giving me a lungful of his rain-drenched leaf scent. "You're my best friend's son. Off limits. Too young."

He didn't say anything about our desire for each other being a sin though.

My lips quirked up.

His gaze narrowed. "Aaron."

"What?" I asked, going for an innocent tone.

Lips pursed, he continued to hold my stare, and where I once would have cowed like I did with Dad, Ezra's attempt at dominance only rushed blood to my dick.

Would he enjoy topping me? Taking what his frigid wife hadn't offered or allowed in years? Would his thick dick even fit inside my hole? Said bit of flesh contracted at the thought.

"Aaron."

I jerked my focus off his mouth—hadn't even realized my attention wandered there.

"He sees that look right there and knows exactly what you're thinking," Ezra murmured, still trying for that admonishing tone.

"And what am I thinking?"

"About putting your lips on mine," he whispered, frowning.

Fuck it. If he wanted honest talk, he would get it.

"Wrong," I whispered, leaning toward him and lowering my voice. "I'm thinking about your dick stretching my ass and stroking deep inside my body. Rubbing my prostate until I come all over my bedsheets because you feel so. Fucking. Good."

Ezra gasped in a lungful of oxygen.

"Pretty picture, isn't it?" I said with a smirk, loving the heat flaring to life in his eyes. "I'll give it to you if you want. No questions, no rules, nothing but you and me quietly and secretly loving on each other in the way we're both desperate for."

His Adam's apple bobbed, but I read the answer in his eyes clear as day.

"If Dad wasn't here," I said quietly, "if it was just you and me in this house alone, would you allow yourself one little taste? Would you let me love you?"

Ezra hesitated long enough I knew he would lie before he did. "No."

Dad's bell rang—and he strode away.

But not before I caught his shuddered exhale.

Liar.

Grinning, I went back to the dishes.

"Aaron!"

My smile dissolved at Ezra's urgent tone, and I grabbed a towel, running to the living room while drying my hands.

Dad clutched the bell in a white-knuckled grasp, his mouth parted. Face pale.

"Call 911," Ezra said and started asking Dad's questions.

My breath seized, heart stuttered. "Dad."

"Call 911!" Ezra barked over his shoulder. "Now, Aaron!"

Adrenaline racing and stomach clenched up tight, I sprinted up the stairs for my cell I'd left on the dresser, wondering what the fuck was going on.

Not good.

My hands shook, and I dropped my cell twice, letting out a few shouted curses before getting a handle on myself.

I realized I wasn't ready for Dad to leave me—not for freedom, not for love.

"Hang in there," I whispered as I finally managed to swipe my screen on.

A tiny stroke—not life-threatening, but being faced with the reality of losing Dad seemed to take years off my own existence. Add in the thought that his finding out I wanted Ezra had caused the stroke brought back that sense of being a piece of shit. I should have hidden the truth of my gayness like I'd done since I was a teen in order to keep our relationship healthy.

Dad got admitted to the hospital after an ambulance ride that would break the bank, but I knew from the previous couple of years, as long as I paid a little every month, there wasn't anything the hospital could do about the piling bills.

I sat beside his bed while he slept quietly, thank fuck, the scent of disinfectant itching my nose. The quiet beeps and occasional overhead speakers in the hallway announcing codes and other such shit kept me alert.

Ezra had settled on the other side of Dad's bed, holding his hand, same as I did. Bags under his eyes hung so damn heavy, I found it surprising they didn't drag down the lower lids and pop his eyeballs from their sockets.

"Go home and get some rest," I said. "It's two in the morning, and it's not your responsibility to act as his guardian angel."

"I told him I would stay," Ezra kept his tone low even though Dad wouldn't be woken up from voices alone with how he'd passed out an hour earlier.

"What are you talking about?"

"On my birthday, Phillip asked me to stay until the end."

"This isn't the end," I reminded Ezra of what the doctor had said, relief and grief alike swirling in my stomach. "Dad will be released in a day or two, and he'll be his usual bastard self—probably even before getting home."

Fuck, I hated how dichotomous my thoughts were concerning Dad's life. I didn't want him dead, and yet a small part of me whispered curses that he still breathed. How awful would he be toward me knowing the secret I kept from him?

"Aaron."

I met Ezra's gaze, wishing I could drown in his hazel eyes that showed more expression than any man I'd known. He hid nothing from me—sadness, wistful longing, affection.

My tongue moved, my brain wishing I could assure him I felt the same. Everything. But Dad lay between us, and I wouldn't take the chance of revealing the connection between Ezra and me in case Dad only had suspicions.

If he found out how far we'd gone beyond platonic, their friendship would be torn apart. Ezra's dead wife had attempted to ruin them by refusing him to visit the states and had damn near succeeded. I wouldn't to be the one responsible.

Such selfishness was the epitome of weakness.

In that moment, I decided I would let Ezra go—until that end he and Dad had spoken of. Which also meant I had to allow him to be his giving self and see to the duties that were mine to shoulder.

"Go, Ezra," I said again, my tone firm, unyielding. "I promise you can look after your friend all you want once we're home."

Ezra studied my face in the dim light a moment longer, and I allowed my eyes to reveal what he looked for. He nodded and quietly exited the room.

"You scare me like this again, Dad, and I'll kick your ass," I whispered, squeezing his hand. "You're a mean bastard some days, but I understand—and I love you still." I kissed his forehead and readied the pullout chair I'd been given to spend the night on.

I didn't sleep worth a shit between hospital noises, nurses making their rounds, and the loud air conditioning kicking on and off, but when the sun rose, I felt rested mentally and emotionally.

Gifted a few more days with Dad, I reminded myself of my responsibility, determined to spend as much time with him as possible. His days were numbered, and I needed to enjoy the moments we three musketeers had left.

Chapter 15
Ezra

After Phillip's return home, Aaron seemed to become more introspective and became the one to avoid physical contact between the two of us. Accepting the space he'd offered, I didn't confront him—but I also didn't like it.

I missed his grounding touches, his gentle warmth, even though I'd hoped, prayed, he would stop since I couldn't seem to avoid temptation.

We fell into a quieter routine with Aaron keeping the bulk of the care of his father. I watched him closely, his resignation for the chore he'd stubbornly designated upon himself.

My offers to help weren't brushed aside or ignored though like they'd been since my birthday.

The only time we spent alone outside church and our quiet car rides was mornings at the gym, and even then, we took separate cars. I'd bought myself a used vehicle since I'd begun working five nights a week.

Delivering pizzas wasted hours away—but allowed too many hours to think. When I should have been listening to Christian podcasts, I drove in silence, contemplating my life, my future.

No inner urging prompted me down a known course, and I felt as though I ambled aimlessly.

Pastor Welker continued to encourage me to work at the church, but services had become more than a discomfort, almost to the point of...a burden. I no longer had a sense of being at home where I'd once flourished.

And shame for the note still in my sock drawer, for enjoying Aaron's shoulder against mine while seated in Simply Grace made for more disquiet in my soul rather than being at peace in a place of worship.

Thoughts heavy over the service the day before, I returned to Pizza Plaza to pick up another round for delivery, the shop's side door squeaking as I pulled it open. My mouth watered at the heated blast of sauce and bubbling cheese scenting the air. For a Monday night, the phones rang off the hook, and I tried to make myself as small as possible amidst the bustling kitchen area.

Two girls manned the counter—both on the phone.

And customers stood three deep in front of them.

"Ezra!" the shop owner called to me from where he tossed dough. He eyed the tickets lined up in front of him. "Grab a two liter of Pepsi and a Mountain Dew— put it with the order for 15 Bashwood Lane."

I hurried around the counter to the soft drink fridge and got both from the bottom shelf. Stepping back to let the door shut again, I bumped into one of the customers.

"Pardon." I turned to offer a smile, and my lips froze as I tipped my head back.

Six feet plus a good six inches of muscled man glanced down over me, his dark eyes like bittersweet chocolate. "No problem." His deep bass slid over my skin like a curious tongue—

I swallowed hard, my face heating, and I fought to keep my gaze on his face rather than taking a slower dance down over his body like he did mine.

Move, Ezra.

"Excuse me," I muttered and hurried on shaking legs back behind the counter. My face, my backside, tingled as though someone stared at me, the same damn feeling that crept down my spine whenever Aaron entered a room.

But yet a little different.

My dick didn't swell to life and my heart rate didn't race, but my insides were...jumbled a bit, my brain off-kilter.

A quick glance over my shoulder and I found the monster man still watching me, a small smirk lifting his lips. Dark eyes twinkling with want and mirth.

Hands shaking, I readied my delivery bags, double-checking to make sure I had everything set.

A deep bass voice placed an order at the counter behind me. "Michael," he replied when one of the girls asked for a name.

Michael. Monster man.

The tingling started back up, but I slipped out into the night, finally able to breathe again.

No man other than Aaron had ever affected me before. Ever. I'd never even looked upon the male form with curiosity or interest.

And I felt like a cheating bastard for reacting in the way I had to Michael. There was no reason for it, no infidelity had taken place because Aaron and I weren't in a relationship beyond friendship.

Shaking my head, I slammed my car's door, lips thinned in a tight press.

What is wrong with me? What are these feelings, these ungodly wants rousing me like this?

I had no answers, and I couldn't go to someone in search of identifying them. Mr. Astbury, one of the church's counselors, had offered his time as an old friend for grief counseling, and while I'd considered meeting with him, fear of Sofiy's note had stopped me.

My strange thoughts and body's workings definitely weren't something I could discuss with him either.

He would give me scripture I already knew. Tell me I needed to denounce Satan and immerse myself in the Word of God. Get on my knees and beg God for strength to overcome my old sinful nature.

Mountain man Michael was gone when I returned to pick up my next orders for delivery, but the thoughts of him remained—long into the night.

When I returned home, Aaron was in the shower, so I stood on the threshold of his bedroom, breathing in the scent of him that lingered. Unlike with Michael, my body stirred to life.

But why? And what was the strangeness that had skittered beneath my skin around the monster man?

I began to wonder about my sexual preferences as a whole. Michael's obvious interest hadn't turned me on in the way Aaron's did, but I didn't hate the attention either.

His focus on me, the blatant lust in his eyes, made me feel...good. Wanted. Sexy.

All things Aaron brought to life in me as well, but on a deeper level due to the connection we'd had for most of his life. Given the chance, I knew Aaron would gladly help me experience those things times ten.

I found myself beside Aaron's bed, his pillow in my hands.

Disappointment in myself had me shaking my head, but I lifted the feather-stuffed case to my nose and breathed him deeply into my lungs.

Longing stirred, and for more than kisses and sexual caresses. I longed to burrow beneath his skin, entwine my soul with his. Become one in a way I'd never felt with my wife.

Shivers licked down my spine, and I swallowed hard while placing Aaron's pillow back against the headboard.

"I'm sorry," I managed to rasp out while hurrying toward the doorway he stood in.

A towel wrapped tight around his hips—low enough the V of muscle and bone teased my senses. Water droplets clung to his torso, his chest, and I had to swallow again.

"Excuse me."

Aaron hesitated until I shifted on my feet. "Why are you in my room, Ezzie?"

"I don't know," I answered truthfully, unable to look in his eyes.

"I think you *do* know."

"Aaron. Please," I choked out the words, desperate to flee, for him to keep offers of release and loving to himself.

He stepped out of my way, and I escaped into the hallway.

I showered the scent of the pizza shop off me and burrowed beneath my blankets, trembling like a child. He'd left his bedroom door cracked open like usual, an invitation I didn't doubt.

But I rejected the gift even while imagining his naked body waiting for me.

Unrest stirred in my bones, making sleep difficult. Dreams of muscle and blue eyes, whimpered moans and caressing hands, roused me in the morning to an aching groin.

A quick jerk off in the bathroom didn't ease the tension riding my mind—and seeing Aaron shirtless in the kitchen pouring coffee dried out my mouth and tempted my dick to swell again.

"Morning," I greeted him, giving him a wide berth so there wouldn't be any accidental touching since I didn't have the ability to resist that morning like I had the night before.

"Hey."

I made my own coffee, my skin alight like I'd stuck a finger in a light socket. "I'm going to drive myself over to the gym," I said without turning toward where I knew he sat at the table. "Running a little late, and I have some things to take care of first."

"Okay." Aaron didn't argue, and I skirted the table, heading back upstairs to put some distance between us.

I sat on the edge of my bed, doing nothing instead of the lies I'd told Aaron, listening as he came up the stairs, made a bit of noise in his bedroom, then descended a few minutes later.

The front door shut, and his SUV came to life in the driveway.

I let out a heavy exhale, slumping where I sat. The tension between us had to relent. Going into his bedroom had been a mistake, one I would never make again.

I eyed the clock, figuring out the next two hours before I would get Phillip up and out of bed for the day like I always did while Aaron stayed at the gym and worked.

With it being a legs day, I knew he wouldn't need a spotter, so I wasted a bit of time before leaving—sniffing his damn pillow even though I told myself I wouldn't—hoping he'd be at least halfway done with the workout so we would be in different areas of the gym.

By the time I arrived, Aaron had already gone on to back squats. Breathing out a sigh of relief, I climbed onto the bike to get my muscles warmed up and ready to lift.

I took my time and kept to myself, careful to focus on what I did rather than his tight backside in his black gym shorts. There was no fun banter between us, no encouraging words across the distance separating us.

And Aaron went into the locker room to ready for work long before I finished my workout for the day.

"Well, if it isn't the sexy silver fox delivery boy."

My muscles seized at the deep voice behind me, and I clanked the barbell onto the rack harder than normal.

Michael.

Sure enough, he offered me that same smirk as the night before, and I paused, torn on showcasing manners or being rude enough he left me alone. While I didn't desire his attention, my pride preened beneath his interested eyes.

"Ezra," I said, sticking out my hand, deciding to not be an ass. Or perhaps I wanted to see if it was only Aaron who'd managed to get beneath my skin.

"Michael," he murmured, not shy about his thoughts toward me. His gaze slid down over my sweaty body, lingering on my groin and then again on my mouth. He licked his lower lip.

And my dick didn't so much as twitch.

I released an exhale of relief, realizing I didn't want to lust for anyone but Aaron.

"You have good form," Michael said. "Maybe you could give me some pointers."

It took me a few seconds to realize he referred to how I'd been lifting—but he definitely included a double meaning. A very quick glance down over his muscle mass, the bulging thighs beneath his tight shorts, and I half-snorted.

"You don't need my help," I said, straightening and tilting up my chin, feeling a bit more composed having put my thoughts about him to rest.

"And if I want it?" One of his eyebrows rose with a suggestion no man could misunderstand.

"I'm not available."

Michael didn't appear put out by my admission, his focus sliding down over me again. "Pity. I'm new here" —he moved to the rack beside the one I'd finished with—"and was hoping to make some friends."

Friends, my ass. Michael, with the swagger and confidence of a dozen Ezras, seemed more bent on finding a hookup rather than a friend. But I wasn't that man—never would be.

"You're welcome at Simply Grace Church," I couldn't help but toss out, grabbing my towel off the mat. "We're always happy to bring new people into God's family. And by the way...it's *Pastor* Ezra."

That shut him down quick as anything, his dark eyes going vacant of lust. He cleared his throat. "I'll check it out, thanks."

I huffed a chuckle beneath my breath while crossing to the other side of the gym to get an ab cash out before heading home for the day.

Chapter 16

Aaron

The. Fuck.

I halted mid-step outside the locker room entrance.

Some massive asshole stood chatting it up with Ezra, giving him more than a once-over. My gaydar clanged in my damn head loud as hell, and a possessive urge to flatten the asshole for talking to my Ezra fisted my hands at my sides.

Not my Ezra.

"Fuck." I clenched my jaw and observed from a distance...watching, reading body language and facial expressions, my entire body tensed and ready to spring at the first sign of trouble.

The dark-haired giant hovering over Ezra looked familiar, but I couldn't place him. Brand new to the gym—I'd never seen him there before—and definitely not someone I would have hooked up with in my past.

I didn't go for intimidating guys who would tower over my almost six feet and make me feel small.

The guy didn't hide his interest. Slow glided gazes over Ezra's body, the knowing look in his eyes when talking to him. And the goddamn smirk on his face—I wanted to bash his fucking head in.

Ezra appeared wary, hands twitchy in the beginning. I couldn't read his face with how he stood with his back toward me, but his shoulders straightened after a few seconds, allowing me to breathe easier and some of the rigidity to leave my spine.

The guy gave Ezra a little space, taking up in front of the rack beside him, and Ezra angled a bit, his mouth moving, words lost to me in the din of music and clanking weights.

The asshole's smirk vanished, his face shutting down completely.

Whatever Ezra had said put the fucker in his place, and I grinned.

Ezra grabbed his towel off the floor and strode to the opposite end of the room with a swagger of his own.

Bravo, Ezzie.

But the asshole continued to watch him from across the gym, his gaze tracking Ezra's movements even after I took up my position behind the counter at the start of my four-hour shift.

"Who's the bear?" I asked Della, my coworker for the morning.

"Godzilla over there?" She motioned with her chin, a flush on her cheeks. "He's hot as fuck. Name's Michael. Just started his three-day trial yesterday."

Michael. I wracked my brain, coming up empty in my attempts to remember how I knew him.

Della continued to check him out, and I wanted to warn her off the man who wouldn't give her a second glance, but revealing I had a gaydar that operated at full-on capacity would out me.

Why do you care?

The question whispered in my head, and I considered an answer, deciding to forget about Michael since he wouldn't be a problem for my Ezzie. Not wanting to disappoint Dad or to bring shame to his name at the church he'd attended his whole life was what had made me hold back from coming out. Being shunned like Levi and Zeke certainly didn't help—but did I even really give a shit about acceptance or being turned away for my sexual orientation?

Fuck knew lusting for dick wasn't a choice like I could make to leave Simply Grace without a backward glance.

Easily.

Happily.

But in a few months, maybe even less, I wouldn't have to worry about Dad's reputation as a godly father. Guilt over a twinge of happiness furrowed my brow. Having a supposed wayward son wouldn't matter when his body rested beneath six feet of dirt.

So why stir up shit in a pot that no one needed to see inside of anyway? What was another year even before taking my freedom and being who I *was*?

Levi had shown some serious balls by standing up for himself and going after what he wanted—but I didn't have his guts, the strength, to stand tall.

I could wait and use that time to wear down Ezra's walls so that when the stars aligned, I could hopefully make him mine.

I sensed Ezra nearing and lifted my focus off the calendar I'd been staring at without noting a damn thing about my schedule.

"Hey, Ezra," Della said.

"Good morning." His rich baritone shifted my insides as it always did, but at least the sleepy rasp from early morning that always stiffened my dick didn't still hold onto his tone.

I caught his gaze as he went to walk past. "Everything okay?" I asked, glancing over at Michael and back to him.

He understood my meaning, his face flushing same as Della's had over the asshole.

No. Fucking. Way.

My lips tightened, and I stared hard, trying like hell to keep possessive jealousy from flaring to life in my eyes.

"Everything's fine," Ezra said.

"Didn't seem *fine* while that asshole was all up in your face," I said, my voice revealing annoyance I'd hoped to hide.

Ezra studied me while using his towel to wipe sweat off the back of his neck. "I can take care of myself, Aaron."

He'd shown that he could—but I didn't want him to. I longed to stand beside him, be his rock, the protector of his emotions, like he'd always been for me.

Guess he didn't desire the same.

Throat swelling, I nodded sharply and went back to the calendar.

Ezra's presence left my senses, and I let out a slow exhale, needing to focus on work.

"The janitor didn't show last night," Della said, "so I'm going to go scrub toilets in the women's locker room."

"Have fun."

She huffed a snort, slapping me with the back of her hand while walking past. "You get the men's later—boss's orders."

Fuck. Nothing worse than cleaning damn bathrooms. That was one chore I'd happily allowed Ezra to keep at home.

"Morning." A deep voice turned me around from where I stocked the protein bars and bottled water. "Can I have a couple of those chocolate peanut butter ones you've got in your hand?"

Michael, I noted with a quick glance, that sense of knowing him once more tingling the back of my mind.

"Della said you're trying the gym out," I said since I had to act professional and shit with my boss's clients.

"Yep." Michael checked me out same as he'd done to Ezra while handing over a ten-dollar bill.

The man did nothing for me, so I ignored his horny ass and bagged up the protein bars, more than ready to send him on his way.

"Here you go." I handed over the bag, and he grasped my hand atop it.

"You're hot as hell, Aaron." His eyes filled with heat. "Up for a hard fuck in the showers?"

I hadn't been so bluntly propositioned in years, and the image his words brought to mind slid like sludge through my guts. "Not interested."

"Shit." He smirked, and I untangled my fingers from his around the bag. "Sorry. I just got back into town and was hoping to hook up to relieve the stress of the move, you know?"

"Grindr is your best bet," I stated without thinking beyond wanting to keep him away from Ezra—and me.

"Your app of choice?"

Fuck.

I shrugged him off, putting the ten into the cash drawer. "Wouldn't know. I'm not interested in hooking up with guys." Three years earlier that'd have been a lie, but a man could change. I'd gone from wanting dicks plural to just one.

"Sure about that?" Michael leaned down on to the counter, arms crossed, his dark eyes studying my face. "'Cuz my cock can spot a hot piece of ass hungry for a good dicking from a mile away."

"I'm not your man," I stated firmly, refusing to give him my attention.

"Don't we know each other, Aaron?"

The hairs raised on the back of my neck over his use of my name—when I didn't wear a name tag—but I shook my head with assurance. "You aren't exactly… forgettable." I offered something to swell his chest about just to keep my rising anger in check.

"Ever been to that gay bar down on Rustle Highway?" he asked, still leaning, still riling my insides up even though I wouldn't focus on him.

"Not interested, Michael."

"I've been reinventing myself and could use a new friend if you know what I mean." He didn't inflect more than his words stated in his voice, and I shot him a quick glance to see if he bullshitted or what the fuck his deal was. "Give me another chance," he said with a slow smirk, one I expected got him laid pretty much by whoever the fuck he wanted. "I might grow on you."

He wouldn't. Fucking ever.

A hand pressed against my back—

Ezra.

Warmth rolled over me as he moved in close, his arm sliding across my waist in a possessive hold.

Well, fuck.

I could feel the tension radiating off him and couldn't help my own grin. If I'd known all it would take was a little jealousy to make Ezra stake his claim, I'd have manipulated some poor son of a bitch into hitting on me in front of him a hell of a lot earlier.

"Hey, baby," I murmured, sinking into Ezra's body while watching Michael's widening eyes.

That's right, shit head. Now get the fuck out of here so I can show Ezra how happy he just made me.

Chapter 17

Ezra

The second I'd seen Michael putting the moves on Aaron, I dropped my gym bag and strode over to the counter, no thought for myself, my reputation—nothing but getting that horny bastard to back off.

It felt like some instinctual animal bared its teeth inside my soul, extended claws, ready to fight.

And I couldn't have stopped myself even if the Holy Spirit suggested it.

Aaron seemed to melt beneath my hand, right up against me as I grasped his hip and pulled him in close.

"Hey, baby."

I shuddered at Aaron's murmur, knowing even if I heard those words from his lips ten times a day they wouldn't grow old.

Michael's calculating gaze flicked between me and Aaron, his eyebrows lifting. "Thought you were a pastor."

Well, hell. I could have left that bit out earlier, but too late. I wasn't exactly a pastor per say, more in limbo with my life, but I lifted my chin, ready to face the fallout for my compulsive actions. "I am ordained."

"Then what the fuck are you doing putting your hands on this hot piece of ass like you're staking a claim?" Michael asked with a hardened tone, his gaze narrowing as he straightened to his full height. All hint of surprise dissolved from his face.

Hot piece of ass—Aaron certainly was that, but to hear it stated so bluntly...and staking a claim?

I didn't know how to answer, and I wasn't sure interacting with the upset man was in either of our best interest. I glanced at Aaron to find him studying Michael's face, a frown deepening in his brow.

His mind worked, and not over the angry words Michael had tossed out.

"What's your last name?" Aaron asked, his voice restrained—wary.

"Bradley. What the fuck is it to you, *Aaron*?" Michael shot back, his tone hard, his eyes holding a glint that raised my hackles as he rounded the counter.

"Bradley...fuck." Aaron's face paled.

"That's right." Michael's mouth broke out into a broad grin, the type that curdled milk as he moved in close, his eyes going hard as flint and just as dangerous. "*Drew* Michael Bradley."

Aaron swallowed and backed up a step, pulling me along with him, his eyes flooding with fear.

"Remember me, *fag boy*?"

I jerked my focus back toward Michael, the puzzle pieces clicking into place. Drew. The youth who'd beaten Aaron up in high school.

Little fucking piece of shit—

"You look at me like I'm a smorgasbord of a meal," I heard myself growl, the disbelief roaring through my head, "and you have the gall to call *him* a fag?"

Michael sneered, taking in my tension-strung body without a hint of the interest he'd shown before. "What's wrong, *Pastor* Ezra? Is your daddy image threatened by my interest in your boy here?"

"The fuck, Drew?" Aaron rasped out, trembling against me. "You outright ask if I want to fuck—knowing who the hell I am and the shit you pulled back in high school?"

Michael crowded Aaron, getting in his face, scuttling *my boy* back against my hand. "I *hated* you because of what you did to me."

"What the fuck did I ever do to you?" Aaron shot back, a bit more spine in his voice—and a whole lot of surprise.

Movement in my periphery let me know Della moved in close, but I held out my hand to stop her.

"My brother caught me jerking off," Michael whispered harshly, leaning close enough I could have clocked him on the jaw, "and I came hard as fuck while groaning *your* name—which he heard."

"What. The. Fuck." Aaron murmured a few more curses.

"So *you* were the fag boy," I said, half-tempted to laugh at the ridiculousness of the entire situation, "and you take out your anger on the object of your obsession?"

"Shut it, old man."

"Are you fucking serious right now?" Aaron asked with a snorted laugh, seeming to find the strength he'd come to hold in his hands since childhood. He straightened a bit, lessening his press against my side. "I can't even... Della, want to go get Martin? Let him know this asshole needs to be escorted off the premises?"

Della scuttled away while Michael—Drew—and Aaron stared one another down. My *boy* straightened to his full height, still short as hell in front of the monster man, but he lifted his chin. Squared his shoulders.

That's it, Aaron. Pride swelled inside me.

"You're a craven piece of shit, Drew," he all but hissed the words. "And to think I let you control my life with fear for four *fucking* years." Aaron shook his head as elation roared through my body.

He didn't need a hero—he was his own in that moment, and I stepped back, letting him own it like his self-esteem desperately needed.

Della returned, Martin, the gym's owner, at her side, but neither rushed the men squared off behind the counter.

"I always thought you were one tough shit," Aaron said, not bothering to keep his voice down. "A bully because you were big enough to intimidate everyone beneath you." Aaron snorted and crossed his arms, a gorgeous display of a man not threatened by the mass of muscle towering over him. "Sure, I thought you were hot"— Aaron surprised the hell out of me by admitting this out loud where anyone could hear—"but rather than get to know the scrawny kid ogling you, you went and beat the shit out of me. Broke my goddamn nose, my arm. Cracked three ribs."

A muscle ticked in Drew's jaw, but Aaron had rendered the asshole speechless.

"Talk about a spineless piece of shit." Aaron snorted.

"Aaron?" Martin asked, shattering the tense silence that had settled over the gym. "What's going on, gentlemen?"

"Michael, here," I spoke up since neither he nor Aaron so much as blinked their focus off one another, "was just leaving. Isn't that right, *Drew*?"

"It's Michael now," he stated through clenched teeth. Drew/Michael, whoever the fuck he thought he was, tore his stare off Aaron and glanced around—as did I.

We'd drawn quite a bit of attention. No one lifted on the floor, and even those on the rowing machines and bikes had paused in their workouts, all eyeing the fiasco behind the front counter.

Doubtless, they'd heard every word. The truth of who Drew was—a bully of the worst sort. He'd obviously come to grips with his sexual orientation but still held hatred in his heart for the guy who'd first turned him on.

"I'm going to have to ask you to leave, Michael, er, Drew," Martin said loudly, letting everyone know where his loyalty lay. "I won't allow trash to harass one of the hardest working employees I've ever had. Your three-day trial is officially terminated, and you're no longer welcome in this gym."

Damn. I grinned at how Aaron's spine stretched even straighter. Regardless of Drew's scowl on his face, Aaron soared—I had no doubt.

"You aren't worth my time, Aaron," Drew hissed, spinning on his heel and barely missing shouldering into Martin who stood in his path.

"Sticks and stones, love," Aaron tossed his way just like that pirate man had in the movie we'd watched the week before. Pink stained his cheeks, and his eyes glinted with a slew of emotions that took my thrumming pulse to thumping beats in my ears.

My groin tightened, and I put more distance between us even though I'd have preferred taking his mouth and staking a real claim on the strong, sexy young man who'd owned who he was without hesitation.

The gym door yanked open and slammed shut behind Drew.

"Care to explain what the hell that was?" Martin asked, his gaze flicking between me and Aaron.

"Just a blip from the past—and a shit ton of answers," Aaron said, shaking his head while planting his hands on his hips. "Un-fucking believable."

"An old boyfriend?" Della asked, the nosey little gossip.

Aaron laughed. "I like my men with a little more spine —you know, less asshole, more the hero type that will stand by you through thick and thin." He turned toward me, sending my heart straight to my toes.

I didn't doubt the need for release that must have thrummed through his cells from the confrontation of a lifetime. One he probably hadn't ever expected and certainly wouldn't have wished for with how Drew had treated him when they'd been children.

Aaron's gaze hooded, a slight smirk on his lips promising me all kinds of deliciousness—if I wanted.

And in that moment, I desired nothing more.

"Is it hot in here or is it me?" Della asked with a breathless giggle, fanning her face in my periphery.

My face warmed as shame rolled in, and I tore my focus off Aaron.

"Let me know if he causes any problems," Martin said.

"Will do, and thanks for the affirmation," Aaron added before his boss walked away. "It meant a lot."

Martin had no clue, but he nodded anyway. "Every word was true, Aaron. You're a good man, and I'd gladly give up that asshole's possible membership ten times over if it keeps you on my payroll. When you're ready for more than three hours a day, just say the word." Martin knocked on the counter and ambled off.

Shivers licked over my skin at the rush of adrenaline still thrumming through my blood. I'd been caught up in the affair—and Phillip was most likely awake and waiting for me to return home.

"Shit." Stretching my hands at my sides, I hurried around Aaron, intent on grabbing my gym bag over by the locker room door.

Heat singed my backside with every step away from Aaron, and I forced myself to meet his gaze while walking past the counter for the door.

"See you at noon," he stated quietly, his eyelids still at half-mast—and full of the promise of what I'd assumed.

A desperate need for release.

My entire body tightened as every drop of my blood pooled in my dick. Fifty and hard as hell in two seconds flat.

I swallowed back a groan and spun to escape before I ejaculated from the heat of his gaze alone.

* * *

Sure enough, Phillip was awake and waiting for me.

"Where were you?" he grumbled, his brow placid as always even though I knew he had to be annoyed at my lateness.

"I got caught up at the gym this morning." Breathless from rushing home and into the house, I helped him settle fully into his wheelchair he'd already managed to seat himself in.

"You spend too much time with my son."

I clenched my jaw as he slurred the words out— guessing the last part of his sentence before it even left his mouth. "No more than we did when he was a kid, Phillip."

He didn't argue, or maybe he didn't have the energy to try for a full-on discussion.

Telling myself it was jealousy and not judgment over our inappropriate relationship that prompted his thoughts, I set about readying him for the day. I wheeled him to the bathroom, thankful he had the pride and spunk enough to care for himself once I got him situated onto the toilet.

I stood outside the bathroom, my head resting against the wall, fighting off the arousal that wouldn't relent.

The heat in Aaron's blue eyes, the intent, the promise…

"I need to leave," I whispered to myself, knowing if I didn't that my world would implode.

Or explode.

And neither would be pleasant.

*But for a time, it could be—*more *than pleasant.*

Groaning again, I pushed away from the wall and paced Phillip's bedroom, flexing and fisting my hands at my sides.

I relived the confrontation a dozen times in my mind, pride over Aaron's strength flooding through me. I'd never seen a sexier sight than the boy become man straightening his shoulders and looking his old bully in the eye. He'd held steady, and it wasn't because of his childhood hero or the fact I'd stood nearby, ready to have his back.

Aaron had faced down his fear.

I expected adrenaline and the need for release still kept him on edge, same as it did me.

A shudder rippled over my body at the thought of being the one to ease his tension.

Freshly showered and cleaning up Phillip's lunch a couple hours later, I still battled the ungodly desire rushing through my limbs. Aaron would arrive home any minute, and my blood sang with excitement.

Anticipation of fulfillment. Dread of choosing wrong.

The door unlocked, and my breath caught in my throat.

"Hey, Dad." Aaron's voice reached me back in the kitchen, and I let out a slow leaked exhale between parted lips, holding the plate and towel tighter so as not to drop them.

Shivers slid down my spine, awareness of Aaron's presence in the kitchen raising the hairs on my neck.

I didn't turn—couldn't. Fear and arousal spiked inside my brain, and I set down the plate, wringing the towel with both hands.

"Ezzie." Aaron pressed against my back, and I whimpered, sagging against his hard chest.

He turned me toward him, his pupil-blown eyes peering at my mouth, the want in them evident. Our groins brushed, and I clenched my teeth to keep from letting out a groan Phillip would without a doubt hear.

Aaron leaned in, a mere inch away from my face. "Ezzie…" he whispered again.

I held still—not saying yes but not saying no.

He read my hesitation as consent and took my mouth in a kiss of pent-up energy, sexual tension, and hunger. One hand on the back of my head, the other on my ass, he yanked me tight against his front.

Fireworks crashed in my ears, exploding behind my closed eyelids as he ate at my mouth, hushed moans mingling between us.

Delicious perfection—and I didn't have the strength to deny completion of what had started between us.

Chapter 18

Aaron

Ezra grasped at my T-shirt, clinging to me even though he rocked my world, and I couldn't get enough of his taste. Silken tongue, whispered moans, hard muscle along my front.

Goddamn, the man could kiss—used his entire body in a way that left me aching and restless.

"Touch me—please fucking touch me," I whispered against his mouth, so damn desperate for release from the showdown of a lifetime, I couldn't think straight.

I'd hoped for a strong grip on my dick, but he rubbed his hands down over my backside, squeezing my ass cheeks.

Fuck, yeah, I can work with that.

"Mmm," I moaned into his mouth—but he didn't take things where I hoped. So I did it for him, grasping his hands and sliding them beneath my shorts over my ass.

"Aaron," Ezra murmured my name, our lips barely brushing as we both panted for breath. His warm hands moved down over my bare cheeks and back up, fingertips gliding through my crack.

"Yes," I hissed, holding onto his face, wanting his heavy exhales deep inside my lungs.

One fingertip grazed my hole, and I dove in for another taste of his mouth to keep noises from escaping my lips. Our tongues dueled—and my hot as fuck silver fox played between my cheeks with his finger, rimming and tapping around my hole until my knees shook.

"I want you inside me, Ezzie," I whispered harshly against his mouth. "So fucking deep I can't breathe."

He shuddered but kept quiet, and I pulled one of his hands off me and shoved his finger into my mouth.

Black pupils ate at the hazel of his eyes as I sucked on him.

Ezra swallowed hard, his focus on my mouth.

I popped off, leaving plenty of saliva along his finger. "Put it in me. Feel how hot I am for you, how greedy my hole is for your dick."

"Fuck." Red blossomed on Ezra's cheeks, his lips parting.

Gazes locked, Ezra slid his fingers back through my crack and pressed against my puckered skin.

I hissed, pushing against him until he breached my body. My eyes crossed at the feel of Ezra's thick finger stretching my ignored hole.

Ezra let out a grunt as though I fingered him. "You're so hot inside," he whispered.

"And fucking desperate for you."

He withdrew his finger and pressed in again, sliding a little deeper.

"Fuck, Ezzie...just like that." I gyrated my hips, trying to help him work all the way in, the sting only making my dick leak for more when I ground over Ezra's hard length.

His knuckles pressed against my skin, filling me as deep as he could with a luscious sting. Fucking perfection...

"So good—I knew it would be." I took Ezra's lips again.

Ears ringing, I ate at his mouth while he fingered my backside in slow glides until the slight bit of pain faded. I lusted for more, dripped for it, an ache spreading through my entire body.

But Dad sat in the next room, no doors and only a thin wall between us.

Me and Ezra would have to wait.

Pulling away from him hurt, but I put distance between us.

Harsh, panted breaths filled the air. Our stares remained locked.

I wanted to be the one to make him lose control. Free the desire in his soul.

"Tonight, Ezzie." I glanced down over his tense body to the massive bulge in his lounge pants. The damp spot where he leaked. I licked my lower lip, and he grabbed hold of the base of his hard dick with a deep groan. I lifted my focus back to his flushed face, his bright eyes, and his swollen lips. "Tonight when Dad is in bed, I'm going to love you."

Without another word, I escaped the kitchen for my bedroom to calm the fuck down.

My agenda for the rest of the day? Shower and prep myself because I *would* have Ezra balls deep inside my body before midnight.

The sexual tension raised to levels I couldn't handle. It was like the air vibrated with need, lifting the hairs on my arms whenever Ezra and I shared a room.

And knowing I'd reached my rope's end, I kept my hands and mouth to myself the rest of the afternoon and early evening. But our gazes clashed, and even though Ezra's face heated to a delicious shade of pink, he didn't avoid my eyes. Didn't shake his head, didn't murmur a single word about it being *too much*.

Dad didn't speak much after dinner where he'd managed to feed himself without the usual mess. He even kept his negativity at a minimum, but Ezra had cooked us dinner. Were it my Shake and Bake pork chops and roasted potatoes on the table, I'd have heard plenty of suggestions on how to make the food less dry and better seasoned.

Ezra sat with Dad in the living room while I cleaned up —took my damn time, thankful the object of my obsession didn't come back in to help me. Dad's close proximity be damned, we'd have ended up on the floor using cooking oil to ease his dick into my ass.

That thought had me heading upstairs for prep of another sort because I didn't plan on wasting one second of getting Ezra inside me.

Once I managed to tuck away my hard-on inside briefs and thicker pants, I went back downstairs and settled on the couch. I ignored Ezra, pretending to watch the movie Dad had chosen for the night and eyeing the old clock on the mantle more than the screen. Damn minutes passed slow as shit. Restlessness about drove me fucking insane, and I wondered where Ezra found the strength to sit still.

I glanced at him, thinking about all the lube I'd put up inside me to ease the passage of his thick dick.

He stared at the TV, his chest barely rising and falling, the pulse thrumming in his neck.

My lips curled upward in a small smirk as satisfaction coursed through me.

He wasn't unmoved.

The movie ended, and I slowly counted to ten before hopping up to take Dad to bed.

I got him settled in his wheelchair, my gaze finally catching Ezra's as I went to wheel Dad past. Excitement buzzed beneath my skin as silent words radiated between us.

Don't go anywhere, I begged with my eyes.

I'll be right here waiting, his seemed to promise.

Dad took forever to do his business in the bathroom, and I paced his bedroom, trying hard as fuck to ignore the relentless ache in my balls and the slickness in my ass waiting to be stroked through. Fucking finally, he finished, and I helped him half-stand and shift onto his mattress.

Once he changed into his pajamas, I tucked him in.

"Goodnight, Dad."

He grunted a reply at my shaky tone, and I forced my feet to go slow while carrying me from his bedroom.

With the light flicked off, I shut his door.

Ezra...

Hands flexing at my sides, I inhaled until my lungs threatened to burst. My legs trembled, and I feared he wouldn't be waiting for me.

But he was, pacing with his back toward me, hands running through his hair—shaking them out at his sides. He spun on his heel to head my way and hesitated upon seeing me.

Face flushed, focus on mine, he attempted a smile that fell.

Don't shut down on me now, Ezzie.

I moved in on him, holding his gaze, and he didn't flee, didn't step back. Wrapping one hand around his neck, I pulled him into me.

He let out a low groan.

"Shh," I hushed him, my lips a breath away from his. We shared air, our bodies coming tightly together. His hard dick pressed along mine, and it was my turn to rumble a noise from my chest.

I slid my cheek along his whiskers, putting my mouth against his ear, my other hand sliding between us to grab his dick. "I want you inside me. Right here, right now," I whispered.

"But Phillip—"

"We'll be quiet," I murmured against his ear. "I'm not waiting any longer, Ezzie."

I stepped back, ripped off my shirt, and shoved down my pants, my dick slapping against my abs.

"Fuck," he cursed quietly, more a breathless exhale, his hands fisted at his sides.

Stepping closer, I pulled his shirt off overhead, our loud breaths the only sound between us. Much more would give us away. While our gazes locked, I slid my hands into his pants and slowly eased them down, dropping to my knees to help him step out of them.

His thick dick stuck straight the fuck out, pre-cum welled at the slit.

A flick of my tongue flooded my taste buds with bitter saltiness, and I closed my mouth over him, ready for more.

Ezra hissed, grasping hold of my head, and I sucked and licked, fighting off the need to verbalize how much I loved his taste.

"Aaron," he whispered harshly, and I backed off.

I stood and pulled him in close again, my lips against his ear. "No one has touched me in over three years, Ezzie," I told him in a hushed murmur, "and I had myself tested a few months ago. I want to feel you inside me. Skin on skin."

He swallowed hard and nodded his consent.

Fuck, yes.

I thought about kneeling on the couch and presenting my ass, but I needed to see Ezra's eyes when he worked himself into my body. As thick as he was, it would be a stinging stretch even though I'd prepared the best I could with my fingers. Fuck knew I had enough lube inside me to ease his way once he breached me.

I tossed a couch pillow on the floor and laid down on the carpet. With a crook of my finger and opened arms, Ezra joined me, letting out a slow exhale while covering me with his body. Our dicks lined up, both hard and leaking.

We kissed and frotted until I couldn't breathe, couldn't think.

"Knees," I gasped out, and Ezra backed off, kneeling between my spread thighs. I raised mine toward my chest, wrapped my arms around my legs, and grabbed my ass cheeks.

Ezra stared, parting his lips and panting as I spread myself open for him. "Aaron." He gulped.

"Shh."

He crowded in close, rubbing the head of his dick over my hole. Sweat broke out on his brow as he sucked in ragged breaths.

I stretched myself wider, and he ran his length through the lube coating me.

Ezra mouthed a curse and held his tip against me. He lifted his focus to my face.

Yes, I mouthed, relaxing my entire body.

He pushed, and holy fucking hell, it felt like a fist trying to penetrate me. I let out a slow exhale and bore down, determined as fuck to take him. My muscles gave way, and he breached my hole.

Teeth clenched, I bit back my curse as he whispered a few of his own.

"So tight... I can't..."

I shifted the pillow beneath my hips and grabbed his hands, placing them on the backs of my thighs. Still grimacing at the stretch, I showed him how to hold my knees higher. He did so and sank in another inch.

"Ung." He pulled out, smearing lube everywhere over my ass, his haggard inhale letting me know he was ready to blow. A few strokes of his hand down over his dick glistened it with lube in the lamp light.

I opened back up my hole with my hands and waited, my pulse thrumming and breaths coming in short pants. Adrenaline rushed through my system at the thought of finally having Ezra inside me. Fully. Making me whole.

With how his dick stuck straight out, he didn't even need to hold his base, just moved closer and watched as he invaded my body again, giving me three or so inches. Enough to make curses spew in my head as stars exploded behind my eyelids.

Hissing, I tapped his inner thigh to keep him from encroaching. He paused and let me breathe—and tried for more.

Our gazes collided. His passion-hazed, lust-filled hazel eyes peered at me, our exhales heavy in the silence. My goddamn heart ached to free him of grief, of the weight of the world...

There wasn't anything I wouldn't do.

I nodded, and he backed away the slightest bit before pushing gently to gain a little more ground. Breathing through the pain, I fought to relax. Full as fuck, and he still had a couple inches to pack inside me.

Stretched like a mother fucker.

A slow, steady exhale eased the tension on my face, and he read my reaction as though we shared thoughts.

He flexed his hips, and I had to tap him again because holy *fuck* he had girth like a goddamn horse.

He swallowed hard while pulling out fully, his harsh pants like lighter fluid to the flames inside my blood.

Still holding my cheeks wide, I nodded, and Ezra sank in.

Goddamn...fucking hell...

Head tipped back, I clenched my teeth, and he spread my legs wider—and claimed that final bit of my body with a snap of his hips.

I gasped, my eyes burning as much as my ass.

He took my mouth, swallowing my groans—of pain, of need for more.

"Move," I murmured against his lips even though I wasn't quite ready for it.

But I wanted to feel Ezra for days. Every time I walked, sat... I wanted the lingering ache to remind me of how perfect we were together.

In case he only gives me this one time.

Chapter 19

Ezra

Exquisite tight heat clenched around my length.

Divine perfection. And looking into Aaron's eyes while being so intimately inside him connected us on a deeper level than anything I'd known with anyone. We truly were one flesh in every sense of the word, and I found no guilt in the moment, only frantic desire I barely managed to restrain.

Every slow drag from his body made my eyes roll back into my head. So slick, so greedy, he pulled me back in until my balls caressed his ass, holding himself open for me.

His dick lay softened on his abs, and I frowned. I imagined taking my dick into his small hole had to be uncomfortable, but I wanted him to enjoy our lovemaking too. He needed the release.

I backed all the way out which earned me a quiet curse from his parted lips, slid down his body, and took the tip of his dick into my mouth. Saltiness from earlier pre-cum coated my tongue, and I swallowed him in deeper, sucking and licking until he firmed enough to gag me.

His hands cradled my face, and he held me gently, allowing me to become acquainted with his length like he'd done with mine.

Silken skin…hardness beneath…bursts of saltiness across my tongue as he whimpered.

So. Damn. Delicious.

I probed at his slit, desperate for more of his taste.

"Ezzie," he groaned quietly, his tone on edge.

I rose back up and shoved his thighs wide. "Hold," I whispered, and he did as told, opening up that sweet little rosebud I ached to taste.

Someday.

I pressed against his puckered skin and took his dick in my hand, determined to have him find the release that had strung him tight all day.

A slower breach—no grimace from him—and I sank in balls-deep.

"Ung." I inhaled through my nose and worked his length in time with my slow thrusts.

Aaron stayed stiff in my hand, gaping as he panted for oxygen.

Our gazes locked, a million words longing to pour from me, but I bit them back, knowing we couldn't utter noises that would betray us.

Harder, he mouthed, and I gave him his request, my hips snapping enough my balls smacked against his ass.

"Mmm." He swallowed hard, focus dropping to where I jerked him. "Oh...ung."

The rumbled noises, the quiet whimpers spilling from him raced shivers over my skin. I wanted to hear his passion, watch as he came undone in my arms.

He gasped—and his ass clamped down on my girth, cum shooting up over his abs and chest.

He breathed harshly as I fought the desire to join him, working his body with every inch I had. Slamming in and out, swiveling my hips for better friction, anything to keep cum dribbling from his slit.

The second he shuddered and went limp, I backed out and licked him clean, my chest rumbling at the delicious taste of him. I owned that bit of him. Took his seed inside my body. Claimed his orgasm.

And I put one foot on the floor, needing to give him mine. Hands on his feet, I lifted his ass off the pillow and plowed into his body. Balls deep.

"Fuck," we both cursed too loud.

Breathing loudly, I held his feet together and kissed them, trying to memorize the feel of his tight clasp around my dick.

My Aaron...blue-eyed gorgeous man...

He peered up at me with more than hero worship etched onto his flushed face, still panting. "Free the desire in your soul, Ezzie," he whispered.

A rush of emotion squeezed my chest, stinging my eyes, and I let go, allowing myself to love him in the way we both wanted.

I rutted into him with abandon, my gasps, my heavy breaths loud as hell in my ears. Every drag of my length from his hot hole, every slam back inside tightened my balls against my body. Jaw clenched, I barely kept from drowning his ears in praise of his strength to take all of me inside him, of appreciation for allowing me to have him.

Thankfulness for loving me enough to offer his body for my pleasure.

My balls seized tight, and my climax hit like a gale wind, ripping a grunt from my lungs.

"Oh..." I gasped, a deep, long groan hot on its heels. Noises continued to spill from me as I backed out and shoved in, pushing to reach farther, to coat him with my seed so deep he'd taste me on the back of his tongue.

I shuddered and pulled out. Goose bumps rose along my skin at how his hole gaped from my girth, trying to wink shut against the white ooze of my ejaculate.

With a growl, I shoved my entire length back into his ass, satisfaction at keeping my cum in his body bringing a smirk to my lips.

"Ezzie." Aaron clasped my neck and drew me down.

I went willingly, melting into his full body embrace.

Legs around my backside, arms draped over my shoulders, calloused hands rubbing my skin.

And the softer lips a contradiction to the hard muscle and bone beneath me.

Heaven.

I felt high, like I'd smoked two potent joints, every inch of my body tingling, my pulse thrumming. Sweat covered my body, and a glorious ache continued to radiate through my emptied balls.

Wrecked—so fucking perfect with Aaron's arms over my back, my hot breath on his ear.

He touched every inch of my skin he could reach while my dick stayed lodged inside him, every shiver that rippled over me revealing how spent I was.

Completely relaxed. Sated like a wet noodle, limp in his arms.

But I still speared Aaron with my thick length that refused to rest.

He squeezed his hole around my girth, and I groaned against his ear.

"Shh," he murmured, his hands clutching at me.

A clank sounded—a sharp inhale.

I tensed as I registered the noise's origin, and Aaron went stiff beneath me.

Our gazes clashed, hearts slamming against shared bone and tissue.

No. God...no.

My eyes welled, and Aaron's hardened, his lips tight as he turned his head.

"Dad—"

Fuck. I backed out of Aaron's body without a sound, and he hissed. I caught a glimpse of cum dribbling from his hole but tore my focus off him to grab my clothes.

I stumbled up to a stand, Aaron covering his groin with his hands in my periphery.

"What are you doing out here, Dad? H-how?"

Phillip struggled to transition fully from his bed to his wheelchair by himself, and I wondered the same damn thing—but I needed my clothes. Lounge pants—on.

"Heard...I *knew*." Phillip turned his placid face toward me, and like a deer caught in headlights, I froze. "Leave."

One ragged, slurred word.

"Dad—"

"No." Phillip cut off Aaron's pleading hiss, hands shaking as he slowly turned his wheelchair around and disappeared back the hallway.

Shirt.

I found it and jerked it up off the floor with trembling hands.

"Shit. Fucking hell." Aaron stumbled in his haste to get his own pants on. He reached for me, but I shied away. "Ezzie!" He grabbed hold of my arm. "Don't go."

My jaw clenched, eyes welling with tears—but I wouldn't meet his gaze. Couldn't. "I don't have a choice, Aaron," I croaked the words, my shoulders rounding beneath the weight of guilt.

"No, Ezzie. We can get through this. I'll talk to Dad—"

"There's nothing you can say to make this wrong right," I whispered, my voice ragged with pain and regret. "It's too much, Aaron. Please."

Please hear me.

Swallowing hard, he dropped his hand from my forearm. "It feels like you're ripping the skin off my body, Ezzie—but fuck, I promised to respect your limits."

And we'd certainly reached one by being caught.

"Too much," I murmured once more, shame like I'd never experienced settling down over me.

"Never enough..." he whispered his disagreement I wanted to latch onto, beg him to repeat over again what I knew to be true.

Pain lanced across my chest, damn near taking me to my knees.

I turned my back on my young lover and slipped up the stairs on weary, heavy legs, my thoughts and emotions shattered like a glass hurtled at a brick wall. Giving in to the desires of our flesh hadn't just ruined a friendship.

Our actions had broken my heart worse than I'd ever felt before.

Chapter 20

Aaron

Dad didn't speak about what he'd walked in on that night. Not. One. Word.

He also didn't mention Ezra's absence the next day when I got him out of his bed and helped him dress in his favorite sweatpants. But I didn't either. In silence, I went about my drudgery of caring for an invalid whose one slurred word had taken away the most precious thing I had from my life. Every step, every time I sat caused my backside to twinge, reminding me of loving the man I wanted—needed.

And no longer had.

Abandoned. Again.

Searching inwardly for anything I might have done to contribute to Ezra's leaving other than loving him proved fruitless. We'd connected, and even though I'd been the one to initiate intimacy and affection time and again, I refused to fault myself. It was Dad's single word that had sent my lover, his best friend, away.

Had Dad not heard us, found a way to drag his ass out of bed, and caught us together, I believe Ezra would have stayed.

Bitterness ate at my guts, but I remained strong and cared for my bastard of a father even though I wanted to rant and rave, scream at him that love was love, that Ezra and I were it for each other.

I didn't doubt that truth.

While he'd been buried inside my body, accepting my love, our souls had intertwined through our eyes. Every push and pull between us had linked more than just our bodies together. His caresses deep inside me had pleased me, comforted me better than any hug or gentle touch.

And fuck, how I missed him.

I'd lost Ezra again when he'd walked out, cowed beneath a weight I didn't know how to lift. I'd gone from high on a mountain to the darkest reaches of the sea, wandering aimlessly. Blind to the pitch black of loneliness and uncertainty.

All within a matter of seconds that painstakingly dragged into minutes. Days.

Weeks of depression.

Months of going through the motions, brokenhearted and wanting to curl in on myself.

But that would be weakness.

Halloween passed without Dad sitting by the front door with his usual bowl of candy. Thanksgiving—Glenda and her husband dined with us, and I couldn't rouse a smile when offering my appreciation of breaking up our monotonous lives. Dad didn't eat a single slice of pumpkin pie when he usually would have asked for seconds.

I had to cut back on my hours at work again and shouldered the house's chores once more. I avoided Ezra's bedroom, fearing his fallen leaves scent would linger on bed linens I hadn't been able to take off and wash. Doing so would mean he was gone for good. Just like all of his personal items from our home.

I gave up pretending I wanted to discuss Pastor's Welker's sermons with Dad on Sunday afternoons. Instead, I found a new place to park my ass while he watched the livestream—in the coffee shop where I should have been going all along. No judgement came from those working behind the counter, no self-righteous bullshit spewed from their smiling lips. No joyous facade that would dissolve once back in the real world of daily living.

I never saw Ezra while out and about. Had I been the one caught fucking my best friend's son while still a newly widowed missionary, my craven ass would probably have fled the country. But I doubted he'd headed back to the Ukraine.

I rested my hope that he'd gone to his sister's in Oklahoma, the only living relative he had left. It didn't take more than a simple search online to find her address, her home phone number.

With how Ezra had left, though, I knew he didn't wish to talk. I gave him his space, all while anxiously waiting for my dad's death. Because the day they lowered his ass in the ground, I would sell everything I owned, pack up my piece of shit SUV, and head west to force a confrontation Ezra and I both needed in order to move on.

Hopefully together, because I couldn't imagine a life without him in it.

By mid-December, depression clung like those goddamn bloodsuckers I'd gotten once while camping, and I didn't even bother pulling out the plastic bin from the attic that held our Christmas decorations. Dad didn't ask for them either. I hadn't expected him to bring in the New Year, but he still breathed like a stubborn ass.

There was no doubt where I'd gotten my tenacity from.

Bundled against the bitter cold of early January, I took advantage of Glenda's goodness for an hour and hit the grocery story on a Thursday night after dinner.

With money tight, I stuck to the basics: meats, rice, potatoes, and in-season veggies and fruits. At least my desire to keep my muscle and health hadn't declined with my mental state—because that would reveal weakness too.

"Aaron!"

I turned to find Pastor Jed with a basket on his arm. "Hey." Not bothering to force a returned smile I didn't feel, I shook the hand he held outstretched while approaching.

"I've missed seeing you at service."

I doubted his words, but his easy smile and eyes didn't lie. "It's best if I don't leave Dad alone these days," I *did* lie, glancing at the groceries in my cart.

"I've been wanting to ask after Zeke and Levi," he said quietly.

My focus shot back to his face. I hadn't spoken to Zeke in a few months, outright ignoring his calls because I didn't want to hear about his happiness with Levi when it would only make me feel even shittier.

"Last I'd heard, they were doing well," I replied, my tone as guarded as my thoughts.

Pastor Jed smile widened, which eased some of the tension in my body. "I'm truly glad to hear it."

I studied his face, again, not sensing a lie. "Why don't you condemn their relationship?" I asked, too damn curious considering his title, his position, at Simply Grace Church.

He glanced around as though checking to make sure none of Pastor Welker's flock lingered close by. "I never was a fan of people bashing all in the name of pointing out sin lest we be tempted ourselves."

My gaydar tingled in the back of my head, but I pushed it away—along with the thought of him being thirty-something and single which was a feat in and of itself considering the women of the church where he worked.

His sexual identity didn't mean jack shit to me.

"So if they were to walk in here holding hands, you wouldn't shun them like the rest of the church has?" I asked.

"We're called to love others," Pastor Jed said, his smile fading, "and unfortunately, many in His church have forgotten what it means to give grace and mercy."

It seemed he and Ezra shared that outlook. Pain rippled over my chest, and I rubbed at my coat, grimacing. "You, uh, haven't heard from Pastor Ezra, have you?"

Pastor Jed studied my face, but I held all emotion deep inside, refusing to show him anything. "Pastor Welker told me he's visiting his sister," he finally replied when I'd thought sure he would ask what had happened to separate Ezra from his best friend.

My assumption on his whereabouts confirmed, I nodded. "Have you heard if he plans to return anytime soon?"

"I don't know, Aaron." Pastor Jed clasped my shoulder like Ezra used to do, and my throat tightened up quick as fuck. "If I hear anything further, I'll definitely keep you informed—if you'd like."

"Yeah," I rasped and cleared my throat. "I'd appreciate it. It's just with Dad not doing well and all..."

Pastor Jed's smile held empathy to the point I wondered how much he'd figured out. He patted my shoulder before stepping away. "I'm sure his heart will lead him back to where he belongs, but in the meantime, if you need anything, Aaron, monetarily or just an ear, I'm here for you."

"Thanks," I said, clasping his hand once more.

With a nod, Pastor Jed moved off while I stared after him baffled. What the hell had he meant about Ezra's heart bringing him back to where he belonged?

Shit.

I let out a slow, steady exhale, not sure I wanted to think too hard or too long on what had just gone down between the pastor and I. Cashier three's lane sat empty, so I angled in and took my time, wasting minutes before heading back to the house that death hovered over in so many ways I appreciated my stubbornness. Drugs and alcohol weren't an option, so patience it had to be.

Even if that fact sucked ass.

Dad slept, and I sat alone as usual, the quiet broken by the TV's din I paid no attention to. The gaping wound cracked clear through my heart remained as fresh and raw as the night Ezra had left, and speaking with Pastor Jed hadn't helped matters any.

The resulting darkness ate at my mind.

I grabbed my cell, thinking myself a masochist, but I needed to talk to someone.

"Aaron!" Levi had answered Zeke's phone, his smile coming clear through his tone.

"Hey, Levi. Your man around?" I asked, my throat tight.

"He's in the shower. Everything okay? He's been trying to get ahold of you for over three months."

"My dad isn't doing well. It's been a sucky winter."

"It's Aaron!" Levi hollered—Zeke must have asked who'd called. "Hold on a second, Aaron...he wants me to put you on speaker."

I slumped on the couch, eyes closed and head tipped back.

"Aaron, the fuck man? Where have you been?" Zeke asked, his voice echoing a little.

"Tell me you aren't naked in your damn bathroom," I muttered.

"He's naked in the bathroom," Levi answered for him with a snicker, and I could imagine him looking my friend over from head to toes.

Zeke was hot, but he wasn't Ezra hot.

"How's your dad?" Zeke asked, ignoring his boyfriend.

"Miserable as ever. Some days are pretty tough," I admitted.

"They were tough before I left." He sounded muffled like he towel-dried his hair or something. "Can't imagine how you're holding up, Aaron."

"Barely."

Someone fumbled with the cell. "What's going on?" Zeke asked, his voice clear like he'd taken me off speaker.

"You still naked?"

"Got a towel wrapped around me—shit...get out of here, Levi," he growled.

Levi chuckled, and a door shut in the distance.

Masochist.

"Aaron."

I let out a slow exhale, pushing aside thoughts of their obvious enjoyment of each other. "You were right about what you said all those months ago, Zeke."

"I'm right about a lot of shit. Which thing?"

I snorted. "I'm gay."

"And?" he didn't hesitate to respond, his tone uncaring.

Of course he wouldn't judge or condemn me with him being bi. I shouldn't have been surprised. "And I'm in love with Ezra—have been since I was a teen. Just didn't realize it until he came home and turned me inside out."

"Talk to me."

I told him. Every damn detail from the minute I laid eyes on Ezra and his graying hair at the airport to the night Dad walked in on us tangled up on the living room floor. The way he'd fled to Oklahoma.

And that depression wanted to suck me down into a pit I feared I wouldn't escape because I'd been abandoned one too many times. I hated the weak part of me that wanted to curl up in a ball and cry like I'd done when Mom then Ezra had first left.

Zeke didn't interrupt me, didn't offer me scripture like he'd have done while being a Christian counselor for Simply Grace the summer before. He simply let me spill, listened, then agreed my circumstances sucked ass.

"It's a waiting game—you've got that right, Aaron," he stated quietly. "This is just a moment in time, and while I understand it's like an eternity has passed since Ezra took off, it'll be a mere blip five years from now when you're visiting your dad's grave."

"I feel so fucking weak." My heart seemed to crack open wider. "Never needed a goddamn hug so bad in my life." I squeezed the bridge of my nose, my jaw clenched to keep tears from rolling down my face.

"I'm coming down there." His voice didn't invite argument.

"The hell you are," I snipped anyway, my eyelids snapping open. "This place is toxic, Zeke—for you and Levi. Too much shit, too many bad memories. I can't let you do it."

"Always the protective one," he said, not unkindly.

"I'm serious, Zeke. Don't fucking come here. You thought the homophobia was bad before you left, but it's ten times worse now that Welker feels he has a legitimate reason to preach against the LGBTQ community. He and his faithful assholes are sick as fuck, and it makes me want to bash a few heads together."

"I take it you aren't attending church there anymore?"

"I quit when Ezra left. Can't fucking handle him not being beside me, his shoulder brushing mine. Knees bumping."

"Fuck, Aaron."

"Yeah." I swallowed hard but felt a tiny bit better having dumped the shit of my life since Ezra had left. "I honestly don't know how Jed Simpson can stand to work there. He asks about you and Levi a lot."

"Pastor Jed?"

"Yeah. I'd bet all seven bucks in my bank account he's gay as fuck."

"I never caught that vibe."

I snorted. "He takes too much interest in how the two of you are doing to make me think otherwise."

"Well, I hope he never gets found out."

"Seriously."

"So, Ezra."

The image of his face flashed in my mind, thickening my throat again. "Yeah—he's it for me, Zeke. No doubt in my head and heart—if it's not him for the rest of my life, then I'll die a lonely as fuck man."

"That Daddy thing does it for you, huh?"

"Fuck off, he's not a Daddy. We're not like that," I grumbled.

"I wouldn't give two fucks if you were, you know that, Aaron."

My lips twitched in the first attempt at a smile in months, and I told myself I wouldn't go so damn long without talking to Zeke again. "How's your man doing?"

"My fiancé?"

"The fuck!" I sat up, my smile breaking through. "Seriously?"

"I asked him the night Malachi and Isaac sang at the Humanity House's opening."

"Shit, man. Congrats and all that good stuff." My chest didn't ache nearly as bad as I'd expected.

"He told his mom, and she actually said she was happy for him."

"I can't imagine his asshole of a father offered any congratulations."

"Asshole doesn't begin to describe the man," Zeke all but growled. "Fucker continues to pretend his son doesn't exist, and while Levi says he's over it, I know he still hurts."

"He's lucky to have you."

"I'm lucky he took a chance on me. Thank you for that, by the way," Zeke said quietly. "He said you're the one who encouraged him to try again with me even though I'd turned him away too many times to count."

"He needed you—you needed him." I shrugged even though Zeke couldn't see me. "It was obvious you two belonged together, and life is too damn short to not take chances."

"That it is, Aaron," Zeke agreed. "But you've got more strength than you give yourself credit for. Hang in there. He'll be worth the wait."

I hinged my hope on Zeke's words being true, and I crawled into bed a few minutes later, feeling lighter than I had for months.

Chapter 21

Ezra

Being away from temptation made it easier for me to focus on what I'd lost while living at the Westons'—my spirituality, a close walk with God. My sister Abby and her husband attended a smaller church than Simply Grace, and the first time I walked in, I felt a rush of warmth come over me. Almost...peace-like.

There were no offers of condolences and pitying glances but smiles and welcomes.

Strangely, I thought of myself as a prodigal son returned home.

But Oklahoma didn't *feel* like home. That kind of rest only came from being with Aaron, hearing his exhales, chatting about anything and everything, and the gentle affection that pebbled my skin.

My body craved him, but with every passing day, the grieving of loss—of both him and his father's friendship—hurt worse than Sofiy's death.

That, I hid from Abby along with my reasons for visiting.

I stood on my sister's back deck not long after the new year, a heavy coat wrapped around me as I watched my niece and nephew play in the snow that had fallen during the night. Cold bit at my nose and made my lungs ache with every inhale, but neither of the kids seemed to notice the bitter wind.

Their giggles and laughter didn't swell happiness inside my heart, and I stared, unsmiling as always regardless of their silly antics.

"Hey." My sister sidled up to me, a steaming mug in her hand.

I took the offering, sipping the sweetened coffee until my tongue burned from its heat. "Thank you."

"Did you sleep any better last night?"

"Not really."

If Abby had any idea of the actions that had brought me halfway across the country and caused insomnia, I felt sure she'd have shunned me for my choice on that fateful night.

To add to my misery, I'd spilled lies about why I'd left Philadelphia, using unfelt grief over Sofiy's death. Restlessness, I'd told Abby, rather than the regret of putting my dick in a man's body—and having been caught.

Aaron. The no-longer-a-boy lover I'd enjoyed for a brief moment in time. My regret came from being found out in the most embarrassing way possible and losing Phillip as a friend. I hadn't repented—*couldn't*—for that hour Aaron and I had spent together in heaven.

He'd shown me greater love than anyone, offering me his body, a selfless act I realized the more I considered every grimace, every frown that had flitted over his brow as I'd slowly worked my entire length into his tight heat.

Clearing my throat, I shifted, trying to focus on the present. Children playing with laughter. My sister at my elbow. Hot coffee in my hand.

"Have you talked to Phillip lately?" she asked, and blood rushed to my cheeks.

"No." I'd claimed to touch base with him the week before, keeping abreast of his illness, but I'd done no such thing.

And Phillip hadn't reached out to me either even though he must've known where I headed when I'd left that fateful night.

I hadn't gone into his room to beg forgiveness before running off like a coward. I hadn't sought out Aaron even though his bedroom door remained cracked open. I hadn't done a damn thing but pack up all my belongings and slip into the night to drive westward in my car.

Fleeing like a craven raccoon who'd been caught with his paws where they didn't belong.

I'd promised to stay to Phillip's end, but after being found balls-deep in his son's body and being told to leave...what choice did I have?

I longed to return to him and keep my word, and my heart broke over betraying him in such a way. Leaving the first time had been for God's will, the second from choices made while living in my sinful nature.

And I was powerless to change the past and space I'd allowed between us.

Phillip must despise me.

"Have you thought about what you want to do?" my sister asked, once more pulling me into the present.

I studied the mug clasped in my hands, considering Abby's question. Ukraine wasn't an option, and while being with my family was better than being alone, I still felt like a fish trapped on dry land. Flopping to find where I belonged and struggling to breathe.

"I'm not sure," I murmured.

"Have you gone for grief counseling?" Abby asked, her tone kind rather than preachy like Mom's would have been.

"There's nothing a pastor can say that I haven't already heard or read for myself, Abs," I replied, lifting my attention to the laughing children once more.

"You don't have to go looking for spiritual guidance or answers. When I miscarried that first time, just sitting down with our pastor's wife and spilling all of my pain into words really helped me."

I'd known as much, how she and Rebecca had become best friends.

"Maybe you just need an ear, Ezra. Sometimes it's good to simply share what's in your heart."

I nodded at the truth of her words, but I had to ignore the suggestion in her voice that led me to believe she offered to be that person. There was no woman, no man, already in my life besides the friend I'd lost that I could unload my heartache to.

And that fact worsened the burden on my shoulders.

Swallowing down the last of my cooled coffee, I considered reaching out to someone who could at least allow me to check in on Phillip and Aaron. Perhaps knowing how they fared would help me in my struggles to find some sense of peace.

I sat on Abby's guest bed, propped against the headboard and two pillows, and let out a slow, steady exhale before dialing Simply Grace Church.

The operator put me through to the only man there I felt I could ask questions to without raising suspicions.

"Pastor Jed speaking," he answered the secretary's transferred call.

Just the kindness in his greeting eased the tension imprisoning my body. "It's Ezra Jamison."

"Pastor Ezra! It's so good to hear from you." His tone stated his truth as much as his words. "How are you, sir?"

I cleared my throat rather than spilling what wanted to escape me. *Horrible. Miserable. In pain. Broken-hearted.* "Steadily plodding through life," I stated instead. "Just trying to find where I belong again."

"I can't begin to imagine your struggles," he said, "but please know that I'm here if you ever need a friend."

"I appreciate it." And I did. More than he probably could imagine. Not sure how to dive right in and ask about the Westons, I hesitated.

"I saw Aaron a few weeks ago," Pastor Jed initiated what I'd hoped for, but his next words brought the hurt back. "He hasn't been to church since last fall, and he looked worn down and more depressed than usual."

My eyelids slammed shut. "Caring for his father isn't easy," I choked out.

"I've asked countless times to visit with Phillip over the previous year, but he refuses company."

"You ought to show up unannounced," I suggested, my tone haggard even though I'd tried for casual. "Phillip would never turn you away no matter how his pride might suffer from having anyone see him in his wheelchair. I'm sure he could use some encouragement—and it sounds as though Aaron could as well."

"Perhaps I will. I can't imagine doing what Aaron does day in and out for Phillip. I've never seen such strength of character."

I made a noise of agreement, guilt prickling my brain over leaving him to deal with the cranky man all by himself. The strain of daily living...alone, without a hand to help. Or hold.

My fist tightened on my lap.

And the thought of not being with Phillip at the end like I'd promised...

An attempt to swallow the thickness from my throat failed.

"You brought such a sense of life to Aaron that he appeared to be lacking," Pastor Jed stated quietly, and my eyes stung. "But he seems lost again now that you've gone."

I rubbed at my chest, trying to ease the ache inside. While not exactly a probe, I could sense Pastor Jed's curiosity in his words. I chose to ignore it, imagining how Aaron's shoulders would stoop beneath the weight of his burdens.

Tears welled in my eyes, the desire rising inside my soul to gather him in close to me, to ease his mind and emotions in ways I knew I could.

But I can't.

"Can I ask what your plans are?" Pastor Jed said while I fought for control and words outside my feelings for Aaron.

Not a subject I wished to discuss or even think on, but I clung to that unease to steady my emotions. "I'm still resting," I lied. "Waiting on the Lord to reveal a door to where he would have me go."

"You aren't interested in heading overseas again, I heard."

"That is correct." I figured Pastor Welker had already shared that bit of information. I couldn't begin to imagine doing so again...there were other ways to gain riches in glory which is why I obeyed the commandment to not forsake the assembling of God's people.

Church didn't interest me, didn't fulfill me in the way Aaron had, but I needed to stay focused on the eternal since our lives were but a blip in time in God's eyes.

"There is a position opening here at the church at the end of the month," Pastor Jed continued, "and I actually had written on my to-do list to track you down today to see if you would be interested in joining our staff."

"What kind of position?" I asked, though working at Simply Grace was far from my first choice.

But I would be able to remain faithful to God's word and be close by for when Phillip's days ended. If he'd allow me to be with him like I'd promised.

Doubtful.

My throat tightened.

"Our missions director is moving to Florida, and quite honestly, you're the first man I thought of who could fill this role," Pastor Jed said. "You've labored for the Lord for fifteen years away from the fold. You've experienced heartache and grief that can draw a man closer to God—but you're also empathetic and sensitive to our humanistic natures."

I hardly knew Pastor Jed, and yet he seemed to have read me correctly.

Aaron no longer went to Simply Grace Church, and keeping my distance would ensure we didn't fall back into what we'd had between us. But being close by would make me available for him—as a friend—when burial day for his father arrived.

"I'll pray on it," I told Pastor Jed.

"I'm so happy to hear that. We need more men like you here, Pastor Ezra." I could hear his smile over the line.

"Just Ezra," I insisted. "Please."

"Shall I tell Pastor Welker that you're considering joining us once again? I know he would give you the position without hesitation."

The opportunity I'd been hoping for. An opened door even though it wasn't ideal.

Perhaps it was time to trust God to see me through since I struggled on my own to find where I belonged.

"Yes," I told him, something settling inside my soul at the simple answer.

A step of faith, a flicker of light lay on the path before me.

God is faithful, I reminded myself, steeling my heart, my mind on going where He led. I would trust Him to see me through to the end of my journey, to glory where He prepared a mansion for me.

I may have found heaven in Aaron's arms, but an eternity of riches and joy awaited those who lived a holy life. Pushing aside thoughts of the other reasons I wished to head back east, I focused on making a plan to return.

And remain steadfast in my faith.

Chapter 22

Aaron

Bitter cold gave way to wet chill and eventually warmer breezes that thawed the ground. Buds sprang to life on tree limbs, the scent of damp soil and rebirth attempting to renew hope in my mind like it did life to the earth.

I called Zeke at least once a week, but he barely helped me keep my head above water.

My heart beat as steadily as Dad's, stubborn in keeping me alive when I'd have been content resting six feet deep. I clung to the truth that Dad wouldn't outlast me, but my patience stretched thin as fuck. Powerless to change my circumstances, I continued to battle darkness in my mind, a sense of helplessness I had no control over that ebbed and flowed depending on Dad's mood and if I'd talked to Zeke that day.

Weak in my emotions but strong in body, I put one foot in front of the other, all my efforts only recognized by Glenda who continued to offer me relief like she'd been doing since Ezra had taken off.

Dad could no longer be on his own for any amount of time—Sundays included. She'd taken over sitting with him during the live service feeds while I escaped for an hour.

She showed up on the first Sunday in April, a smile on her lips and a plate of macaroons in hand.

"You'll never guess who I saw at the store up near my sister's place yesterday," she said, breezing into the kitchen where Dad and I ate breakfast. "Ezra!"

Dad and I both stopped eating, our gazes clashing. His eyes remained passive as always while a riot erupted inside my entire body. Adrenaline rushed, and my breath hitched.

Ezra had come back east.

But he hadn't stopped by to check on Dad—or me.

Bitterness wanted to choke out my joy over his being in Philly again, but I loved the man, needed him too damn much to hate him for leaving me alone.

I swallowed hard, putting down my fork and the pile of egg whites I'd scrambled. "Did you talk to him?"

"Quite a bit, actually." Glenda said, setting the plate of goodies on the countertop. "He's been working at Simply Grace since late January. I'm surprised he hasn't come by."

"Yeah," I muttered.

Glenda turned, and I could feel her gaze, but I shoveled food into my mouth. She'd never been nosey or the gossiping type, so I didn't offer information. When Ezra had split nearly seven months earlier, she'd mentioned his absence, and I said he'd gone to his sister's in Oklahoma. As a new neighbor since Ezra had left for the Ukraine, she hadn't known the relationship he and Dad had shared prior to his going on the mission field and didn't question his leaving.

Dad's hand shook in my periphery as he lifted his toast to his mouth. No longer able to use a spoon or fork on his own, he opted for foods he could feed himself—and suffered physically because of it. He wasted away to skin and bones, a mere shell of the man he'd been prior to him kicking Ezra out all because he refused to let someone else lift a spoon or fork to his lips.

"How are you, Phillip?" Glenda asked while pouring herself a cup of coffee, the topic of Ezra shelved—for a time, I expected, considering the inquisitive tone she'd had and the stare I'd felt. "Are you looking forward to Pastor Welker's sermon today?" She prattled on even though Dad rarely replied most days.

Sitting down beside him, Glenda launched into a recap of what Pastor Welker had shared the week before, and my mind shut off to any thought except Ezra.

My heart ached while I attempted to swallow down tasteless food, mere sustenance when what I craved —*who* I craved—finally lay close by. Burning desire to see his face, breathe in his exhales, taste him again flooded me to the point of bursting into flame.

Only half-finished with my breakfast, I stood, needing to ease the restlessness plaguing my legs.

"Did Ezra happen to say where he's living?" I rasped out at the first pause in Glenda's chatting about church while I rinsed my plate off.

"He's renting an apartment north of the church in those new buildings up by Spindler's Pond that had been in the news two years ago."

I remembered hearing about the court fiasco between two families and a developer who'd gotten his hands onto acreage through shady means. I'd never caught the whole story and couldn't be bothered with it even then. All I cared about was that Ezra had chosen to live a half-hour from the church—in the opposite direction from where we did.

Almost an hour away, without a doubt intentional considering plenty of housing sat available nearer to our home.

I washed my plate and flatware, knowing what I would do even though Ezra obviously had no wish to see me or Dad.

"He told me he lucked out with a first-floor apartment on the corner overlooking the pond," she continued, prattling on as though discussing what was common knowledge.

She had no clue Ezra had taken off without word, that we hadn't heard from him in months.

"When should I be home, Glenda?" I asked, my back still toward her and Dad.

"I have no plans today," she said. "You take as much time as you need, honey."

I nodded and headed for the stairs.

"No." Dad's grunted word hit my back, and while I caught his meaning, I continued on as though his word escaped my ears.

While I wanted to take my time in the shower, prepare properly in the event I got lucky, I rushed through a scrub, didn't bother shaving, and yanked on the first pair of clean sweats and T-shirt I found.

The TV sounded from the living room when I hurried back downstairs, and Glenda moved into the hallway where I grabbed my keys off their hook by the door.

"There's no need to rush back, Aaron." Her warm brown eyes peered up at me, and lips tight, I nodded. "The hubs doesn't expect me home until dinner time, and Ezra appeared as though he could use a friend."

"Did he...ask about Dad?"

"He did, but that was it." She offered a sad smile.

I nodded, realizing she must have seen more than I thought.

"Thanks," I managed to force through my tight throat.

"Number one-fifteen," she whispered as I pulled open the door. "I got that much from him for you. Good luck, Aaron."

I escaped into the spring morning, breathing fresh air into my lungs that wanted to collapse, wondering what all else Glenda had taken note of while Ezra had lived with us.

Sunday morning meant he would be at Simply Grace Church where he unbelievably had chosen to work. Knowing the church's stance on homosexuality, the way Welker had preached against two men loving one another, yet Ezra still chose to labor beneath him...

Without doubt, Ezra had turned his focus back on God, those riches in glory he'd sought after for so many years.

I had zero expectations of changing his mind from the path he'd chosen, but I knew his heart belonged to me.

Resting my confidence in that truth, I headed north on the familiar route I'd driven every Sunday up until Ezra had left me.

Adrenaline leaked into my bloodstream, causing my hands to shake and insides to quiver. I exhaled to the count of eight in attempts to slow my pulse while pulling into the parking lot, but my arteries continued to throb heavy thumps in my ears.

Ezra's car sat in the staff area, and I found a spot a little ways back where I could watch the side door, my windows opened to let in the spring air hinting at a new start.

I'd considered entering the building and sneaking into a seat near the back, but the idea of listening to Welker in the pulpit made my skin crawl. Any belief I'd carried around in my head and heart since childhood had dissolved, leaving reality to rule where faith used to grip a strong hold on my mind.

I didn't grieve the loss of my dad's religion in my life. I'd found my own peace in facts proven time and again by science that blinded people chose to ignore in clinging to their truth.

What mattered to me was living to the fullest while we had our few moments and accepting those around us. Because what did I care who people were attracted to? What was it to me which sex organs hid beneath clothing?

How other humans identified held no bearing on my thoughts.

Every single being breathing in oxygen deserved to love and be loved in the way they desired.

I pushed against the seeds of bitterness wanting to sprout up whenever I considered Simply Grace, those of staunch faith who lifted their noses when the Jesus of their Bible commanded them to love and do unto others as they would appreciate being treated.

The side door opened, and people began to spill out into the bright sunshine, jerking my thoughts to the present—and soon seeing Ezra.

My heart sped up again with another shot of adrenaline, and I forced my hands to rest on my thighs rather than reaching for the door handle.

I couldn't approach him in the parking lot, but I could be a total creep and follow him home and eventually find the balls to knock and beg entry into his life again.

Every time the church's side door opened, my heart sputtered, only to be disappointed when someone other than my sexy silver fox walked into the sunshine.

My gaze flitted to the right, taking in those flocking from the main doors and rounding the building to the side where I'd parked.

The Atwaters and Townsons moved as a party of four across the lot, and I slouched down a bit in my seat, scowling.

How Levi's father could continue to pretend he didn't exist baffled me. I wanted to grab the asshole by the neck and shake him until he went limp and begged forgiveness, promised to love his son no matter what as any good Christian would do.

The door pushed outward, snapping my focus forward once more.

Ezra.

My breath left in a rush as he stepped over the threshold and moved back to hold the door for those leaving behind him. I didn't bother watching the people passing him but studied the man I longed to wrap in my arms.

I'd expected haggard. More lines on his face, a deep groove in his forehead. The appearance of feeling as lost as I'd been without him.

But he seemed...peaceful in a starched light blue dress shirt and yellow tie, spring-like colors as though he'd dressed to match the new beginning he'd chosen.

Ezra turned toward a blonde woman who looked close to his age and had waited off to the side as the others meandered away. He offered his arm, and she took it while smiling sweetly up at him.

I blinked.

Refocused on her hand clutching his forearm as he led her toward his car.

He lowered his head as though to better hear whatever she said and lifted once more to laugh, the baritone chuckle reaching me through my car's windows.

Pain arced through my chest, deepening as he opened his passenger door and she slid in.

I swallowed hard and stared at his steady stride around the front of his car.

He climbed in to join the woman, and the two of them drove off. Together.

Fuck.

Fighting to breathe, I sat long after the parking lot emptied around me, reliving every step, every move Ezra had made before leaving the church. There'd been no hesitation in his actions, the offer of his arm, his smiles and laughter.

He'd looked good.

Happy.

Like he'd moved on.

I clutched my steering wheel, trying like fuck to ignore the sting in my eyes, the longing to curl up in a ball and disappear.

Chapter 23

Ezra

For over two months, I managed to avoid Aaron like I'd planned when returning east. Choosing to rent in an area far north of where he lived and worked made it easier. By appearance, I'd started over with my life, but my heart refused to contemplate matching the facade I placed on my face every morning.

I'd chosen servitude, working where God had led me. If only He'd given me a sense of home, of peace, at Simply Grace. With every passing day, I hoped my faithfulness would fill me with happiness, of knowing I accomplished what God set out for me to do.

And every day, I groveled at the throne of God because all I experienced was heartache and grief.

Sofiy's note had once more became my constant companion, and I clung to the memory of my shame lest I fall once more into temptation from being so needy. I allowed her to haunt my present even though everything about her except for my sense of being at fault for her death lay in my past.

A good reminder of my failings and how I refused to be responsible for someone else's downfall.

But I agreed after a few weeks of persistence from Pastor Welker to try dating again. He assured me "getting out there" would help with what he assumed was lingering sorrow—but he didn't know *who* my heart missed. No woman would fill the hole I'd created in my soul by leaving Aaron.

I put on a merry face to the rest of the world, pretending to move on from becoming a widow while still dying inside.

And Monica Soper, one of the day school's secretaries who bubbled with life and energy, agreed to dine with me after service. I should have been celebrating the spring's warmth, a chance to fully start over on in a godly way.

I couldn't.

Monica chatted all through our meal at the small Italian bistro we'd decided on, sharing stories about the kids at the day school, her own late husband, and their son who would finish up his first year of Bible college in a matter of weeks.

She smelled as sweet as the spring flowers that bloomed beneath the warm sun shining through the window beside us, her twinkling laughter like a bell. Beautiful blonde hair, bright blue eyes...and all soft curves when I longed for hard muscle and a scruffy jawline.

A puckered hole glistening with lube, dripping my cum, masculine heavy breaths in my ears.

I cleared my throat and forced a smile over the table, fighting to focus on the woman's face and her sweet voice, but I couldn't imagine having her beneath my body.

She would feel...wrong.

No comforting scent of dryer sheets and soap, no calloused palms rubbing over my skin while we both panted for breath. No tight heat clamped around my girth, freely given in love.

Too much.

Never enough.

"Ezra?"

I blinked Monica's face back into focus.

She offered a kind smile, her head tipped to the side—but her eyes stated the truth clearly. "This isn't going to work, is it?"

Swallowing hard, I considered lying, but doing so would only prolong the inevitable. "No," I managed to say past my tightening throat.

"Is it too soon, or is it me?"

"B-both, I think." My smile wobbled, and she clasped my hand atop the table.

"You're going to make someone very happy someday, Ezra. I'm sorry that it can't be me."

I nodded, half-tempted to spew the truth of who and what I was, the man I desired more than breath.

No.

My path had been set before me, and I wouldn't deviate.

So why didn't the Lord give me joy in my choice? Why hadn't peace come over me upon returning to the ministry? Two plus months, and I struggled to continue on.

"Life *does* get easier," Monica promised quietly. Having been widowed for five years longer than me, I expected she spoke truth.

But not mine. Finding a life outside Sofiy emotionally had come easy. Too easy thanks to someone who'd always held a piece of my heart, and the loss of him ate at my insides and my mind.

"I hope it will," I agreed, a little more in control of my emotions.

She smiled brightly again. "Let's skip dessert and you can just take me home, okay?"

"I'm sorry, Monica."

"So am I, Ezra." She patted my hand and sat back. "So am I."

On the way to her house, we talked lightly about the sermon earlier that day, the conversation more stilted than it had been over our luncheon. Uncomfortable, for both of us knew we only spoke to pass the time until we could say goodbye.

I breathed a heavy sigh of relief when I once more closed myself into my car. Alone.

There would never be another woman. No more dates where perfume flooded my car's interior and my nose.

My body, my heart ached for one person only, the man I couldn't have. Arms that had comforted, hands and fingertips that had steadied me. Lit me up and made me feel alive.

Temptation to drive south toward Philly rose inside my head, and my heart swelled at the thought of seeing my Aaron again. Just a peek at his perfectly formed body, those stooped shoulders. His blue-eyed gaze he never sheltered his emotions from when looking at me.

I wanted to lose myself in his hooded eyes while sinking deep into his body, feel the clasp of him around me...welcoming me to partake. Loving me. Cradling my face in his hands, my soul within his own.

But eternity...

"Goddamnit." Teeth clenched, I drove away from the curb in front of Monica's and drove north.

Toward home where no one and nothing but heavy silence awaited me.

Chapter 24
Aaron

I woke Monday morning feeling like I'd been run over by a train. For the first time ever, zero desire to head to the gym pulled me from bed as 4:45 a.m. shone red on my clock in the darkness. Staring at the ceiling, I contemplated the day ahead of me.

Work out hard as fuck for an hour.

Clock in and man the desk at the gym for the next three hours.

Come back home at nine-fifteen and get Dad ready for a day of sitting around the house.

Maybe sneak out for a fast run while Dad napped in front of the TV.

And every second of every *fucking* minute think about what I'd seen the day before and deal with the ache still radiating through my chest. I'd told myself countless times while driving home from Simply Grace that Ezra had simply been giving the blonde woman a ride.

But she'd held his arm—they had appeared too comfy in my opinion to be mere friends.

I hated it, fucking loathed it more than I did Drew Michael Bradley who hadn't shown his face at the gym since the day Martin had tossed his ass out.

I imagined Ezra dating a woman. Spending time with her, sharing laughs and kisses. Sticking his thick dick into a warm, wet pussy...I saw red.

Couldn't.

Fucking.

Handle it.

"Fuck." I tossed off my covers and shot out of bed, needing answers more than unleashing some aggression with dumbbells and barbells. I brushed my teeth, threw on some gym clothes, bypassed the coffee pot, and headed straight out the door after sneaking a peek in on Dad who still slept like usual.

Four hours: one to drive to Ezra's condo, one to drive back...that left two to get answers and settle shit between us.

I texted Glenda, asking her to check in on Dad if I didn't get home by my usual time, just in case. I also told her where I headed.

Morning traffic should have been minimal, but a half-hour into my drive, a screech of tires and explosion of metal and plastic erupted on the road ahead of me. The accident stranded me stranded, SUV's bumper too close to the car in front of me, another vehicle damn near up my ass.

A fucking head-on collision a mere hundred or so yards away on the road blocked passage northward.

People hopped out of their vehicles around me while I sat clutching my steering wheel and cursing. The guy behind me already had his cell to his ear while rushing past my driver door, so I didn't bother dialing 911. The fucker in front of me climbed from his car too, joining in the circus.

Not having training to deal with injuries and seeing as how plenty of people already flocked to the scene, I didn't bother.

I swiped my cell to life and brought up a map, searching another route since the accident literally five seconds ahead of me spread over the two-lane road. Thank fuck for catching the tail end of that red light coming out onto the main road back at home or it could have been my vehicle mangled to shit.

I hoped no one lost their life—I wasn't that much an asshole—but I needed to get the fuck out of there.

A nice little jaunt through the neighborhood to my right would put me past the collision site, but I couldn't get my fucking SUV out of the squeeze around me.

"Fucking hell." I hopped out, double-checked the few inches between me and the vehicles bracketing me, and glared up the road where smoke and voices rose.

Sirens sounded in the distance, and I stood powerless, unable to get to Ezra.

What seemed like hours ticked away while I waited for the good Samaritans to return to their cars so I could move on with my life. Forty fucking minutes later—with

Glenda's texted reply wishing me luck—I escaped that neighborhood and roared up the road, pulling into the apartment building's parking lot later than I'd expected.

I still had an hour and twenty before needing to head back home.

Hopefully, it would be enough time.

I thought about guessing at Ezra's apartment, but considering two corners faced the pond, I didn't want to disrupt anyone's sleep by knocking on the sliding glass doors leading to their patios.

I got lucky as hell, gaining entry to the building as someone left for work. No need to buzz Ezra and give him the chance to turn me away.

115—golden numbers on a white door announced I'd found him.

Resting my forehead against the cool wood, I counted to ten, trying to slow my racing heart.

Please don't turn me away. Please.

I knocked and shoved my hands into my pockets to keep them from shaking.

No noise sounded from inside, and I stared at the peephole, wondering if he saw me, stepped back, and considered pretending he wasn't home.

But I'd noted his car in his assigned spot. 115—same as the door read.

Ezra Jamison stood or lay beyond the wooden enclosure separating us, and I wasn't leaving until I got to drink in his face.

Six-forty-three, I noted on my watch. I knocked again, knowing he had to be awake and sipping sweet, blonde coffee.

The bolt slid, jolting my heart beneath bone, and I held my breath.

A swish, and the door pulled inward.

Sleepy hazel eyes peered at me as the scent of wet leaves after a rain storm swept through my senses.

I whimpered and stepped forward without thought, drawn toward the man who owned my body and soul.

"Aaron," he whispered, standing like a statue, unyielding...seemingly unwelcoming.

Or stunned.

My feet propelled me forward in hopes of the latter, and I wrapped my arms around his waist, burying my face in his neck.

Sleepy warmth, the scent of his skin...*home*.

Fucking perfect even if he stayed stiff in my hug.

The door clicked shut behind me as though closing on its own—and Ezra's hands found my head, pulling me back to face him.

Our gazes clashed, heat erupted in that pregnant silence, and I stole his mouth before he could deny me. A bruising kiss, hungry and angry. Demanding and full of hurt for what he'd put us through.

And fuck, how he melted into me. He gave as good as he got, groaning at the first lash of my tongue, his fingers ripping at my hair, my shirt—grabbing my ass.

"Fuck...Ezra." I bit his lower lip and suckled the swelling skin into my mouth. "Why did you leave me? Why?" But I didn't offer him time to answer, spearing my tongue into his mouth again, needing to taste every inch of silken warmth, to swallow his exhales.

Our groins crushed together, hard and hot as fuck. Desperate for a release after seven months.

I tore my mouth from his and dropped to my knees, taking his sleep pants to the floor with me with one swift jerk.

"Aaron..." His voice held warning, but I ignored him and sucked his dick down deep, glorying in how he stretched my lips and gagged me. "Oh God," he moaned.

"Let me," I croaked the second I popped off and swallowed him again.

"Fuck."

I tipped my head and caught his gaze, those hazel eyes hooded and pupils blown with lust.

Let me.

He did, kicking off his pants and cradling my face in his hands while gently thrusting into my throat, his thumbs rubbing the corners of where my lips wrapped around his girth.

Saltiness coated my tongue, but I needed more.

I fondled his tight sack, rubbed his taint—and slid my finger upward to feather over his puckered asshole.

"Aaron," he gasped, his stance widening, lips parted as he peered down at me worshiping him.

I tapped his hole.

"Yes," he whispered with a rumbled groan.

The single word I wanted to hear…

I popped off his dick, sucked on my fingers, and returned them to his crack, smearing saliva where I lusted to penetrate his body. Holding his gaze, I took that gorgeous cock sticking straight out at me as deep as I could—and slid the tip of my finger into his ass.

"Oh…God, Aaron…yes." Ezra swallowed hard and shoved into my throat, gagging me. "Ung." He gasped as I pushed into his tight heat, rubbing deep inside him.

My own hole clenched as pre-cum dribbled from my slit along with his on my tongue. I wanted him balls deep inside my body, destroying my ass. I wanted to be bruised by his hands, his mouth.

And I wanted to do the same to him.

His balls seized up after a few slow thrusts of my finger, and I pulled away, hopping to my feet. A quick shove of my sweats slapped my dick against my abs, and I moved in with enough force Ezra slammed against the entry's wall, our dicks in perfect alignment.

I grasped us both the best I could considering his girth and smeared our pre-cum and my saliva along our lengths.

"Ezzie," I whispered his name, our foreheads together, our exhales shared between lips hovering mere centimeters from each other. Three harsh strokes accompanied our panted breaths—and we both erupted, our dicks jerking in my hold. Wet heat covered my hand, oozing and dripping between my fingers.

But his deep groan of release sounded like fucking music to my ears. I soaked that shit up, took his mouth, and swallowed each and every whimper he gave me.

My Ezzie.

Mine.

There was no denying the pull, the connection I felt rippling between us as we came down, panted breaths over each other's lips.

He sagged against the wall, and I kept him there with my body, my lips lazing over his neck, his ear, while still lightly holding our softening lengths in my hand.

A sticky, beautiful mess.

Ezra grasped my wrist, tugging.

I gave him a few inches, allowed him some space. Satiated bliss hazed his eyes, his slack mouth.

Fucking hot as hell.

He slid down the wall, and I planted my forearm where his head had been as he licked up my flagging dick.

A deep rumble of appreciation rose to my ears, his whispered "Delicious" attempting to stir life back to my dick. Ezra suckled and cleaned every last trace of cum from me.

Fucking Ezzie...

I groaned, thunking my head against the wall. Could the man be any more perfect?

He sank his teeth into the inside of my thigh, and my eyes jerked open. "The fuck?"

"Aaron." Ezra let out a heavy sigh and pressed his cheek where he'd bitten, his eyes closing, hands clasping the back of my thighs.

Not a hug we'd shared before, but my clean hand found his hair anyway, soothing against his scalp as our breaths leveled out.

I wanted to spout off a million questions, demand answers, but couldn't open my mouth in that moment of sweet tenderness, his breath hot on my groin, his thumbs rubbing my skin in small, circular motions.

Seconds ticked past while I rested peacefully, my heart light for the first time in months.

Eventually, he groaned and pushed upright, putting us on an even level with one another.

"Ezzie," I choked out his name, my eyes stinging.

He lifted my sticky hand and used his tongue to clean that as well, his eyes holding my gaze and causing heat to tingle in my groin. Once finished, he laced his fingers through mine and tugged.

I quickly kicked off my sneakers and shorts, stumbling in my haste to follow him back through the hallway.

Chapter 25

Ezra

I didn't think—just acted on my desires.

The sight of Aaron through the peephole had taught my heart how to thrum again, and I'd pulled open the door without hesitation, no thought for sin or eternity.

And he'd come at me, a man starved.

For me.

For affection.

For life.

Our needs aligned, and I almost wept with gratitude for his strength to seek me out when I hadn't been able to do the same.

The initial lusts sated, I gloried in the lack of regret or shame, simply living in that moment. My nose pressed against his groin as I breathed in his musky scent, the luscious taste of his salty spend lingering on my tongue.

It seemed I had a cum addiction.

But I also longed to feel his skin, every inch of his body hugging mine.

I led Aaron to my bedroom where the blinds still shut out the rising sun and blankets and pillows lay rumpled from my troubled sleep. Turning, I pulled my shirt off—and he did the same, nothing but heightening breaths shared between us as our eyes once more locked on one another.

Heat still reigned in his gaze, but a deeper meaning wrapped in the unseen tendrils of tangible *something* between us. And I wanted nothing more than to be tied up tight in everything Aaron, where nothing but him and I existed in our own little world.

Hidden away.

Made whole.

Aaron placed his hand on my chest and gently pushed, following me down as I laid back on the bed behind me.

Our tongues met first, then lips, our moans finally filling the silence.

"Missed you so damn much," he whispered into my mouth before breaking away to my whiskered jaw and the shell of my ear which caused shivers to lick over my skin.

"I'm sorry."

"Shh," he tried to silence me, but he needed to hear my words.

"So damn sorry, Aaron." I grabbed hold of his head and met his gaze. "I shouldn't have taken off like that, shouldn't have left you alone without a word. I couldn't bear the thought of facing my best friend after what I'd done, couldn't imagine the heartache loving you had caused."

"I forgive you."

Three simple words, but I'd never been so set free in my life. "I don't deserve it."

Aaron brushed his lips over mine. "Nothing you ever do will change how desperately I want you, how much I adore you, Ezzie."

Tears coursed down my cheeks as he made love to my mouth, and he swallowed the whimpers I emitted while touching every inch of his skin I could reach.

Crouching atop my hips, he ground his thickening dick against my flaccid length, those soft lips of his finding their way down my neck to my collar bone.

He sucked hard, pulling a gasp from me. I would bruise...and that knowledge brought a flicker of life back to my groin and lifted my hips off the mattress in search of more friction.

Aaron loved my body with his tongue and teeth, leaving bruises across my chest, our gazes clashing whenever I groaned at the stinging pain he inflicted.

He explored every inch along my torso, even dipping his tongue into my belly button. Until he reached my groin where I'd recovered enough my semi greeted his greedy mouth.

Again, he swallowed me down, sucking until I swelled fully on his tongue.

"Aaron," I rasped his name, licked my lips, and tried again to find words. "Want to taste you too."

"Fuck, yes." Aaron lifted off me and spun around, his knees above my head, his hard length at my lips.

My dick jerked at the thought of the sight we must make—and he lowered his hips, filling my opened mouth at the same time he took me as deep as he could.

Wet heat surrounded my girth, his tongue lathing, incredible suction pulling groans from my chest as I attempted to pleasure him in the same way he did me.

Spine-tingling perfection.

He tasted of salt and musk to my fumbling attempts at a blowjob...all Aaron.

My newest, most delicious addiction hinted in a burst of pre-cum on my taste buds. I wanted every spurt down my throat, in my belly. I wanted his sweat dripping onto my skin, soaking beneath the surface, both bodily fluids becoming a part of me, same as he owned a piece of my heart.

His fingertips found my ass again, and he gathered up his saliva dribbling over my taint and into my crack to press a finger deep inside me.

I groaned around his length, lifting my hips, my hands holding tight to his thighs as he rutted into my mouth.

He twisted that finger...reaching and probing...and rubbed over my prostate.

I choked on a cry, cum erupting from me without warning, gagging Aaron. He moaned his pleasure, rubbing and sucking until every last bit of cum oozed from my slit. And still he shoved his tongue in as though desperate for more while I attempted to breathe around his length sliding in a slow rhythm between my lips.

But he rolled off me before filling my mouth, settling on his knees between my thighs.

I spread wide, watching as he studied my ass, his hand lazily stroking his hard dick. Lips parted, he panted, my saliva and his pre-cum making for one beautiful-sounding fist fuck.

No words came to mind, but I grabbed hold of the backs of my thighs, lifting my knees to my chest.

Offering myself to him as he'd done for me all those months ago.

I grasped my cheeks and spread myself, studying how Aaron's pulse thrummed in his neck, how he sucked in a lungful of air through those parted lips.

"Love me, Aaron," I whispered on a ragged exhale, needing him so badly I didn't care how much it would hurt. Our hearts had connected years earlier, but I wanted him inside me, showing me things I'd never felt. I wanted to set him free like he'd done for me seven months earlier.

"Oh, Ezzie." Aaron shuddered and moved forward, rubbing the slick tip of his dick over my hole. Back and forth, up and down. Slight presses but not breaching, once more sliding up over my taint.

He finally lifted his focus off my ass and found my eyes.

I held my breath at the heat, the love overflowing from his pupil-blown blue orbs. "Yes," I choked out the word that had always set him into action before.

"You're not ready for me, Ezzie," he said, positioning my legs around his hips before giving me his full weight.

His lips feathered over mine as he rutted against my spent dick instead of taking what I'd offered.

"Soon, Ezzie," he whispered—and moved with sensual gyrations of his hips, thrusts short and long, teasing both of us.

I imagined him gliding inside me, the sultry noises he made against my mouth in tune with how his body moved over me. A provocative dance of skin, slickened by sweat and pre-cum my mouth watered to taste.

Adrenaline coursed through me, tingles awakening in my fingertips that grazed over his back, but I'd drained my balls dry. That didn't keep me from loving him with my tongue, my hands—my legs clamped firmly against his hard thighs.

His mouth found my neck, and he shuddered. "Ezzie." Warmth erupted between our stomachs, his deep groan curling my toes.

I clutched at him, my eyes closing in the absolute bliss of feeling Aaron fall apart in my arms. Moans and whimpers with every jerking thrust spilling more cum onto my belly filled my ears and heart.

Aaron shivered and slowly pushed up onto his hands, our groins pressed tightly together. He peered down at me, the blue of his eyes more beautiful than a summer sky, his soft smile sending butterflies alight in my stomach.

He opened his mouth—and a cell rang from the hallway.

"Ignore it," I told him, rubbing my thumb over his plump lower lip.

Aaron bit the pad of my finger, his focus still on my eyes.

The ringing stopped, and he bent his head, offering a languid kiss that matched the peaceful laziness settling into my bones. I'd never known kissing could be so consuming—

My cell rang on the bed stand beside us, but we ignored that call as well while our tongues danced a slow waltz.

His phone took up again.

"Shit," he muttered, pushing up into a plank.

"Go," I encouraged, releasing my hold on his body, staring after his flexing ass as he hurried from the room.

I grabbed my cell as his rumbled, "Hello?" sounded out from where we'd dropped our pants.

Glenda had tried calling, I noted while glancing down at my phone's screen, but she hadn't left a message.

"What?" Aaron's voice rose. With a curse, I climbed off the bed, snatching up my chinos I'd worn the afternoon before. "Did you call 911?" he asked who must be Glenda, a hint of panic lacing his tone.

Phillip.

I swallowed hard, my ears ringing while I yanked a clean shirt and socks from my dresser.

"Shit... Goddamnit. I'm on my way."

A thump sounded.

"Ezzie!" Aaron choked out, and I picked up his shirt off the floor and hurried into the hallway to find him struggling to tug on his sweats. "Dad—another stroke."

My lips tight and heart racing, I helped him dress. I grabbed my own keys and followed him out into the hallway, almost forgetting to slide on my old loafers I kept by the door.

"I'll drive," I told him, my tone firm and unyielding. His hands shook, and I couldn't allow him behind the wheel.

Aaron handed over his keys without argument and led me to his SUV.

"What happened?" I asked, my own heart racing with concern for my dearest friend.

"Glenda went to check on Dad and found him unresponsive." Aaron's voice shook as hard as his hands running through his hair. "But he had a pulse. She called 911 then called me."

"She rang my cell when you didn't answer."

"I told Glenda where I headed this morning in case I didn't make it back in time. Fucking hell." Aaron's voice broke.

"Thank God she went over to the house," I said, turning southward.

Aaron didn't reply but gazed out the passenger window as I forced myself to stay just five over the speed limit when I'd have preferred blowing past everyone on the road ahead of me.

"I've wished him dead a thousand times," Aaron murmured, his tone already full of grief. "My greatest secret, my deepest shame." A heavy sigh sagged him into the seat, and he tipped his head back.

My fingers itched to reach over and clasp hold of his hand, but I kept them steady on the steering wheel. I knew releasing those words out loud hadn't come easy...I still held both *my* secret and shame tight to my heart, that damn note I'd left in my chino's pocket the night before once more burning through to my skin.

"No one who understands your situation would judge those feelings," I told him, expecting the words would sound empty in his current headspace, but I needed to say them to assure myself someone, somewhere would understand mine as well.

We drove in silence for a good forty minutes, and I could feel the worry radiating off his slumped body. The gears of his mind shifted into overdrive, speeding along, I didn't doubt.

"What am I going to do?" he half-whispered, but he wasn't asking me.

"One moment at a time, Aaron." I clasped his shoulder briefly, needing the physical link between us, hoping to give him strength, to ground him like he always did for me. "And I'll be there by your side."

Aaron grabbed my hand and kissed my fingers. "Don't ever leave me again, Ezzie."

"I won't," I choked out my promise, knowing even as I did so that I condemned my life to hell.

Chapter 26
Aaron

The stubborn ass refused to die—and I found myself relieved when he finally opened his eyes. But the stroke had done serious damage, rendering him damn near helpless.

I wouldn't be able to care for him at home, his needs surpassing what I had the strength for.

Anxiety over looming medical bills kept me bleary eyed and wide awake while sitting beside him forty-eight hours after he'd been admitted to the hospital. Ezra perched across from me, sharing in the silence broken by quiet beeps and the din of voices through the door shutting us off from the hospital corridor behind me.

Dad slept.

"What am I going to do?" I whispered the same question that had been ransacking my mind for what seemed an eternity.

"You're going to let me help you."

I eyed Ezra and the slash of his thinned lips. I'd denied his offer countless times already, but he'd proven to be just as stubborn as Dad. "I won't take your money, Ezzie."

"Phillip is my dearest friend—"

"Who kicked you out of his house."

"—and there's nothing I wouldn't do for him. Even if he hates me for what he saw that night."

Our gazes stayed locked.

Dad hadn't spoken a single word to Ezra, only turning his focus on his oldest friend for a few brief seconds after waking. He'd ignored Ezra ever since but hardly replied to any conversation I initiated too.

His speech slurred worse than before, a single sentence taking him minutes to release from a mouth that didn't want to work. Growls were the only sign of frustration from his frozen face and useless body.

"You're going to have your freedom now, Aaron," Ezra finally broke the silence that had grown thick between us.

"But only because I don't have the strength to care for him anymore."

"Strength has nothing to do with it," Ezra snipped, his hazel eyes growing stormy. "You don't have the necessary training to nurse someone like he needs twenty-four hours a day. That takes years of schooling, and you can't fault yourself for knowledge and abilities beyond your capabilities."

He spoke the truth from a technical aspect, but I still felt weak as fuck.

Ezra clasped his hand over mine that held Dad's. "You're one of the strongest men I know, Aaron Weston. Physically, mentally...even emotionally. Many would have caved months ago under the stress you've been burdened with."

My eyes stung, and I swallowed hard, releasing Dad's hand to thread my fingers through Ezra's. "I love—"

The door opened behind me, and Ezra moved away from me, sitting back into his chair. "Pastor Jed," he greeted our visitor quietly, a hint of red rising to his cheeks.

"Ezra."

I turned to find Pastor Jed smiling.

"How are you holding up, Aaron?" He offered me his hand without hesitation, and I shook it with a quick nod.

"Not too bad all things considered. Thanks for stopping by." I gave him my chair, and he sat beside Dad, studying his slack face.

I'd already spoken to Pastor Jed who'd called the day before, but his unannounced appearance even though I'd invited him to visit left my feet skittish.

Had he seen Ezra's and my fingers entwined? Did he note how Ezra had lurched back as though embarrassed—guilty—of doing something supposedly wrong?

My stomach twisted over the thought.

Ezra shifted on his chair, glancing up at me, and the love in his eyes assured me he didn't, thank fuck.

Perhaps he just needed time to settle his mind on the truth of us.

I rounded the foot of the bed to stand beside him, keeping my hands to myself when I wanted to clasp his shoulder to offer my love and support for whatever raced through his head.

Pastor Jed lifted his focus off Dad and eyed the two of us. No trace of judgement hinted in his eyes, no frown or pursed lips.

I let out an exhale I hadn't realized I'd held.

Ezra did the same.

"The two of you look like you're ready to fall over," Pastor Jed stated quietly. "Why don't you both go home and get some rest. I can sit with Phillip for a few hours."

The exhaustion he spoke of hit me hard at his observance. "Are you sure?"

"Of course. I'll give you a call if anything changes."

I let out another heavy exhale and nodded. "Thanks, Pastor Jed."

"Jed. Please," he insisted.

Ezra stood, and my hand found his lower back without thought or intent.

Jed took notice, but his smile remained, no words of condemnation leaving his mouth.

"Thank you," I stated again with deeper meaning.

He nodded and motioned toward the door with his head. "Go. Rest."

So we did.

I woke two hours later, my limbs entwined with Ezra's, my nose in his neck. We hadn't done anything more than strip down and fall into my bed when we'd arrived home, but our bodies had drawn close, offering physical comfort.

And we'd stayed that way, unmoving while sleeping.

Peacefulness from my rest remained when I woke. Ezra snored lightly, his leg between my thighs, his arm hung over my torso, and his hand pressed against my lower back in a possessive hold. His pinkie finger at the top of my ass crack twitched, stirring my dick to life.

Absolute fucking heaven—and sheer fucking torture being so tightly pressed against his body. I wanted to pause time and love him until we passed out again.

Choosing to lay still, I let him sleep and studied his unlined face, the slight dark smudges beneath his eyes. Slack mouth parted for escaping breaths that still smelled like the coffee from earlier in the day.

I soaked in his warmth even though a light sheen of sweat already covered my skin.

Slowly filling my lungs, I caught a whiff of my arm pit and realized I hadn't showered since Monday morning.

Fuck, I stink.

I eased from Ezra's hold and climbed from my bed. He sprawled beneath my blue quilt that frayed from overuse, unmoved but quiet.

My hot as fuck silver fox—in my bed where he belonged.

Smiling over that thought, I ambled into the bathroom and set about scrubbing my body from head-to-toenails, but I only soaped up my hair before Ezra stumbled into the bathroom, the lines of his sexy body visible through the barely-steamed shower door.

"Mind if I use the toilet?" he mumbled, his voice husky from sleep.

"Not at all."

He relieved himself while I watched like a perv, and when he turned to leave, I decided I wasn't about to let him escape me.

"Get your fine ass in here, Ezzie."

Smirking, his cheeks flushing, he did as told, shutting himself into the shower with me.

He stood quietly as I washed him with gentle affection, keeping things on a platonic level even though my dick wanted more. Ezra in turn did the same for me, and it wasn't until I toweled him dry a good ten minutes later that I initiated a kiss.

A soft swipe of lips, nothing of the frantic hunger we'd shared the morning of Dad's stroke two days earlier.

He pulled me into his arms, our naked bodies still damp, and I surrendered to his hug with a sigh.

"You're going to let me help you, Aaron."

My throat tightened, but I nodded where I'd buried my face once more in his neck.

"And you're going to start by allowing me go relieve Jed. Alone."

"I don't think Dad wants you there."

Ezra pulled back, keeping me at arm's length. "It's time for Phillip and me to have a talk." A hint of fear fluttered through his eyes, but he held my gaze with firm intent. "He needs to hear words I have to say—my own secrets to share, and I'll be patient in listening to him speak even if it takes until midnight to clear the air between us."

"You've been nothing but a good friend to him."

Ezra kissed my forehead, his exhale bathing my face. "I missed out on so much, allowing Sofiy to create a chasm between us."

Clasping his hands holding my face, I held him close, ready to reveal something else even though it might hurt.

"I wasn't sorry she passed, Ezzie," I choked out, knowing he might hate me for the cold, hard truth that I couldn't keep from him a moment longer.

He nodded, dropping his gaze and his hands from me.

Coolness slid over my body, but he clasped my shoulder, connecting us once more. "Neither am I," he whispered before turning and walking away.

I let him go without another word, without explanations or voicing a why.

His reason for admitting his feelings was easily guessed at, same as mine. But I felt sure that suicide note I'd seen all those months ago while doing his wash had a say in his emotions too.

I wondered if he would ever be free enough to share that burden with me. Even if he didn't, I would love him until my last inhale.

Chapter 27

Ezra

Fourteen years of childless marriage, countless hours of serving the Lord and chasing heavenly riches together in the Ukraine...and Sofiy swallowed a few too many sleeping pills.

The pathologist had called her actions an accidental overdose, but the note she'd left behind, the one I'd found after crying over her cold, lifeless body, stated otherwise.

Horrified, ashamed by the truth of her unhappiness I hadn't noticed because of my striving to please God, I'd hid the note—from the authorities and her family.

Sofiy, I whispered her name in my head like a prayer while watching Phillip sleep on his hospital bed.

The blonde-haired woman whose innocent face and inner beauty had stolen my heart and tons of memories I could have made with Phillip and Aaron. She'd owned me in every sense to the point I had bowed to her every whim. But as the years had gone by, she'd stopped sharing her thoughts and feelings. As though she'd hidden herself behind a brick wall, my wife had shut me out. Emotionally, verbally, and physically.

And rather than poke or prod, force her to discuss what bothered her, I'd assured her God had a will, that she needed to trust Him in all things. I'd focused on our ministry, on eternity rather than reality, thinking about all the golden crowns I would be awarded in heaven while she'd spiraled into a hole of depression.

And my resulting inadequacy to help her and bitterness over her not allowing me to had widowed me at age forty-nine.

I'd never known loneliness like I had living with the woman I'd pledged my life to, the one who'd been nothing more than a roommate for close to a decade.

I'd gone from a Bible-loving, Jesus-preaching man of God who got fired up by His truth to a man broken and straining beneath the weight of falling short in his humanity.

Perhaps some of my inner anger toward her that hindered our relationship had finally come to fruition over that fact as well. But I had no one to blame but myself for that either. I'd allowed Sofiy to dictate a lot of my choices.

And nothing I'd done had been good enough.

Wasted years where she'd kept me from my friends and family...or had they been?

I'd learned the meaning of faithfulness during that time, learned how stoic dogmatism could rip people's lives to shreds. I also came to understand heartache and shame. Guilt and despair.

But because of it all, I'd returned home and found a greater love than I'd ever expected.

I hadn't lied when admitting to Aaron about not being sorry Sofiy had passed. It'd been her hand, not mine, that fed her those pills and gave me a freedom I hadn't realized I'd wanted.

My heavy exhale caused Phillip's eyelids to twitch, and seconds later, they blinked open.

Recognition took a bit, but I couldn't discern any other emotion in his eyes. His mouth worked as though he wished to speak.

"I'm not leaving." I lifted his hospital bed a bit and held his glass of ice water close, putting the straw between his lips. "You're going to down a few sips and then you're going to let your old friend unload all the shit of his past so we can settle things between us."

Phillip drank then grunted when I set the cup aside.

"Yes, I'm totally taking advantage of the fact you can't get up and walk away from me right now," I told him. "Do you need anything other than just wanting me to leave?"

He stared and finally muttered a "No."

And I talked. About the Ukraine, how driven I'd been to become a rich man in glory. Falling in love with Sofiy came next.

How I failed her.

The note burned through the sweatpants I'd borrowed from Aaron, and I pulled it from its hiding spot with trembling hands. For the first time, I read her words out loud, putting into the atmosphere my greatest shame, the secret burden I'd carried for far too long—because I knew Phillip wouldn't ever uncover my sins no matter how much he disliked that I'd made love to his son.

I crumpled Sofiy's note in my palm, dropping my fist to the hospital bed. Tears rolled down my cheeks, my vision of Phillip wavered by wetness.

He covered my hand with his own and squeezed. "No... guilt." Phillip swallowed and tried again, his vocal cords agreeing to work with his mind. "Her choice."

I nodded, knowing he spoke the truth, but it was the sharing that lightened the burden sitting on my shoulders for almost a year just like Abby had promised.

"About Aaron," I started, expecting Phillip to pull away, but he squeezed my hand.

"You...love him."

Not sure if he asked a question, I nodded anyway. "Very much. Aaron is...home to my heart. Peace for my soul."

Phillip stared at me, his watery blue eyes intent. "You were mine."

I blinked at the words slurred from his mouth, sure I misunderstood. "What are you saying, Phillip?"

"I always loved...you."

Thickness clenched my throat, and I released Sofiy's note to the mattress in order to clasp my best friend's palm to mine. "You loved me."

"Still."

I swallowed hard, searching Phillip's placid face, wondering how I had missed that fact for all those years we'd lived together. He'd never made a pass, never initiated more than bro-type back slaps, the kind of affection two brothers might share.

"I didn't know," I whispered.

"I'd thought my feelings were...wrong." Phillip let out a sigh, and I sat patiently, allowing him to finish with slow speech. "Wasted those years."

"They weren't wasted," I assured him, placing my other hand atop our entwined ones. "Think of all the memories we built, Phillip. All the good times we spent together. The late-night movies. Sneaking a few beers we both felt guilty about drinking because we'd been taught alcohol was only for sinners. Smoking that one joint on the Fourth of July. Fishing every weekend during the summer. Camping up north and talking late into the night."

As I spoke the last one, I imagined going again—with Aaron...

But I focused on the present, sharing my own recollection of Phillip's and my trips together before I'd left for the Ukraine, only pausing when the nurse came in to check his vitals.

A few times, Phillip's lips twitched as though he wished to smile. He prompted a few memories of his own which I then shared my view of them.

And through it all, I held his hand between mine, offering him the only love I had available to give.

Finally, silence fell, sleepiness dragging at his eyelids.

"Why don't you rest now," I suggested, straightening his blankets over his thin chest.

"I clung to God."

Phillip's whisper stilled my hands, and I relaxed in the chair again. His eyes remained closed, but he slowly worked out words.

"Instead of allowing myself to love you...I should have chosen differently."

Stunned, I stared. Phillip had regrets, and I couldn't begin to believe them with how staunch he'd been in his faith. Aside from those beers, that single joint, and the occasional curse, he'd never strayed from the straight and narrow.

"I lived the second half of my life without love." He dragged open his eyelids, his gaze finding mine while I waited for his near-frozen lips to allow words passage. "I don't want that for you," he whispered.

My eyes welled.

"You have...my blessing."

Tears dripped from my cheeks onto Phillip's face as I leaned over him to kiss his forehead. "Thank you, my friend."

My heart and mind tumbled with the knowledge I'd gained, so many truths I couldn't begin to align them in my brain as our gazes locked.

My best friend had been in love with me and hid his desires because of his commitment to God. I imagined the angst within his soul had been a hundred times what I'd dealt with since returning to the states and recognizing my feelings toward his son.

And nearing his end, Phillip regretted not taking a chance. I hoped to not face the same when death hovered near. I wanted to live. Grab life by the balls and enjoy the present.

Because we weren't promised tomorrow.

Plans lit inside my brain, and I knew I had some things to sort. My emotions rumbled like a storm over the sea, tossing thoughts haphazardly, but the calm would come in time.

"Go home...to my son," Phillip finally broke the heavy silence over us. "Live like I wished I had. Eternity... pointless without love."

My throat tightened, and I squeezed his hand.

The door swished open behind me.

"Phillip," Pastor Welker's voice sounded, and I swallowed hard, straightening my shoulders. "Am I interrupting?" he asked, rounding into my line of sight.

"No. I was actually just leaving." I stood and bent to kiss my friend's forehead once more. "I'll see you tomorrow."

Pastor Welker took my seat, and I escaped to the cafeteria and sipped a bitter coffee before calling Aaron to let him know that his father and I had made our peace and spent the afternoon reminiscing.

I didn't share what I'd learned, expecting I ought to just take Phillip's own secret to the grave. Pushing aside his declarations of love, I focused on the future: his going into hospice and me whisking Aaron away on a much-needed vacation.

"Up to Lake Wallenpaupak?" Aaron asked when I suggested the idea of a weekend of camping once Phillip moved into the nursing home. A hint of excitement lit his tone, bringing a smile to my mouth.

"Just like old times," I told him. "Tents and sleeping bags. Dinty Moore beef stew and s'mores cooked over an open fire."

"I'm taking your old quilt."

My blood warmed over the memory of being wrapped in his arms beneath its weight the night before. "But this time you're going to share it when snuggling beneath the stars."

"Shit, Ezzie...you're making me hard."

I chuckled over the cell, glancing around at the people in the cafeteria with me even though they couldn't have heard his words. My own dick had thickened, but I forced all thoughts of affection and sex from my mind. We had enough to deal with before escaping for a few stolen moments of freedom.

We discussed work the rest of the week and his father's stay in the hospital and transfer in the morning.

Going away for the weekend would be flirting with sin, hell, the *promise* of a fall from grace, but I couldn't bring myself to care. It would be hard enough to get through the final two days at the church when all I could think about was having Aaron beneath me again.

I wanted to live as Phillip had encouraged me to do, because I felt sure when I lay on my deathbed, I would regret not making the most of my time on earth.

With Aaron.

"I'm going to head home to the apartment tonight," I told him.

"I was hoping you'd stay here with me."

I longed to—hell, I desired nothing more, but if we shared a bed, we'd wouldn't leave it for quite some time. "Let's finish out the work week and see to Phillip being settled in his new home. Then we can focus on us."

"Us. *Fuck*, I like the sound of that, Ezzie." His ragged tone ignited lust in my groin.

"I'll reserve us a camping spot up north for Friday night through Monday if you can get off work."

"Martin loves me, so that shouldn't be a problem, but it's kinda cold for a tent this early in April."

"Then we'll just have to share some body heat," I suggested, my dick fully on board.

"Shit." He groaned, and I imagined his hand on his leaking length. "Now you're talking."

I had to wait for my erection to relent so I could stand and walk out of the cafeteria. Ten minutes later, I left the hospital and headed north rather than into the arms of the man I loved wholeheartedly. Excitement for the weekend ahead heightened my senses like a kid headed to a carnival.

Nothing pulled me from the high—no thoughts of shame, no guilty conscious, and no Holy Spirit's whisper.

Chapter 28
Aaron

We got Dad and a few of his personal items into the nursing home on Friday, and I took off work the following Monday.

So did Ezra.

We headed north in my SUV Friday late in the day after spending a few hours with Dad at the nursing home. Whatever he and Ezra had shared together, the air had cleared between them.

But still, Dad didn't speak of what he'd seen, and I chose to keep my lips closed on the topic as well. All that mattered to me was that Dad didn't ignore Ezra when we'd visited together.

I left the windows on my SUV down, both Ezra and I in sweatshirts while cruising up the highway, destination Lake Wallenpaupack, same as we'd done dozens of times in years past. But rather than the three musketeers, it was just the two of us.

Alone for three days.

"I talked to your dad about your money situation last night."

I whipped my head Ezra's way, my old unease rising to the surface. While I hadn't yet figured out my finances, I'd decided to set those worries aside to enjoy my weekend away from the shit of my life. "Not exactly what I wanted to think about today, Ezzie," I muttered, turning my focus back on the road.

"I know." He laced his fingers through mine and placed our clasped hands on my thigh. "But he and I came to a conclusion, and it's going to happen whether you want it to or not."

"I don't like to be handled," I said, my annoyance bleeding through.

"You like it when *I* handle you," Ezra replied, a smirk in his voice.

I shot him a quick glance—and he fucking winked at me. My dick twitched, but I scowled without a lick of anger in my eyes. "What's the conclusion you came to without my input?"

"I'm breaking my lease on the apartment and moving into your house. It was Phillip's idea."

"Dad suggested you live with me after seeing your dick lodged up my ass?" I asked, my voice high and giving away my surprise.

Ezra let out a rumbled groan and shifted, squeezing my fingers. "The way you talk."

"You love it," I all but purred at him. "Now tell me how the fuck he got over that sight so damn quickly."

"He has regrets of not trying for love again, Aaron."

Well, shit. "And he longs for you to be happy."

"He knows—he's seen—how you brought me back to life."

My throat tightened in renewed grief for Dad with how he'd dealt with loneliness for so many years.

"He wants us to live, Aaron, and for me, that's you."

I lifted our clasped hands and kissed the back of his. "I feel the same."

"Did you bring two tents?"

"Fuck no," I said with a chuckle. "I even have the old-style sleeping bags we can zip together to make one cozy bed."

"That's my boy."

I glanced over, eyebrow raised. Pink fused his cheeks. "I'm not into that daddy shit if that's what you're hinting at, Ezzie."

"You're all man in my eyes, Aaron Weston."

And those hazel orbs of his promised a hell of a lot more. My asshole clenched as I turned back toward the road, my lips stretched in a wide grin. "*Your* man."

"Mmm, I like the sound of that."

I planned on liking a lot of sounds over the weekend—couldn't fucking wait.

We'd decided to camp even though storms had been predicted to clip just south of the lake. A water shield stretched over top the tent I set up while Ezra built a fire and heated dinner, but it wouldn't stop a downpour from drenching us. Worst case, we could sack out in the back of the SUV if need be.

On my knees, I zipped the two sleeping bags together, eyeing our double bed. With how we'd been tangled on my mattress back at home on Monday night, I expected we'd have no problems sharing the small space.

I backed out of the tent into the fading daylight, zipping it closed behind me.

Ezra sat on his folding chair and hunched forward with a large spoon in his hand, his focus on me.

Flames licked upward from the fire pit in front of him, glinting gold and red off his eyes. An old pot perched atop the grate, steaming and filling the chilly air with the scent of canned beef stew I hadn't eaten for fifteen years.

A grin spread over my face as I moved around the fire and planted a solid, lingering kiss on his upturned lips. "Supper smells good."

Ezra grimaced as his attention went back to the pot, and he gave the contents a stir. "I'm hoping it tastes as good as I remember because to *me* it smells like day-old dog poop."

Chuckling, I grabbed two plastic bowls and settled onto the chair beside him. "I'm starved, so I'll be the guinea pig and take the first bite."

We ended up cleaning out the pot and heating up a second can as thunder began to rumble in the distance.

Out came the s'mores makings, and once we'd eaten our fill, night had fallen and bouts of lightning flashed across the sky, booms of thunder following only a few seconds behind.

"Think we're going to get lucky?" Ezra asked, eyeing the darkness overhead.

I knew I was getting lucky one way or another, but a couple rain drops fell. "Maybe we ought to hang in the back of the SUV just in case?"

Ezra's attention went to the tent that rippled with a sudden gust of wind. "How waterproof is that thing?" he asked as lightning lit the sky.

"Not very." A too-loud boom answered after I mentally counted one-Mississippi.

"Well, I don't want this trip ruined our first night out here."

We shoved our food bins beneath the picnic table, grabbed the sleeping bag and pillows from the tent, and ended up hightailing it to the back of the SUV as the skies opened up.

That forecasted storm had headed a little more north than the weatherman thought.

Cramped and laughing in the light of a single flashlight, I laid down the back seats and got our sleeping bag somewhat spread out. We managed to kick off our boots, strip down to our briefs while sitting in the front seats, and climb into the bed in back—the old quilt on top of us.

Chilled fingers and feet sought out warmth from one another, and we both cursed a few times while laughing and snuggling close in the darkness.

Flashes of lightning brought vision, and I found Ezra's eyes opened, same as mine until sudden darkness blinded me again.

I pressed a gentle kiss to his mouth. Being in his arms would be enough if that's all he wanted for the night, but my body definitely had hopes for more regardless of the cold and the storm outside our cocoon that smelled like Ezra's fresh scent and woodsmoke.

His dick thickened against mine, and he slid his hand to my backside while slipping his tongue between my lips.

All the consent I needed.

I rolled Ezra beneath me, settling between his thighs where I could frot against him with the sensual rolls of my hips I knew he loved. The sweetness of chocolate and marshmallows lingered on his tongue, and I ate that shit up, pulling a moan from his chest.

"You taste so good, Ezzie," I murmured against his mouth before sucking on his lower lip.

His hips lifted, his hands once more finding my ass.

Thunder boomed, and cold rain pinged harshly on the roof of my vehicle, but I ignored both, losing myself in the man beneath me. Pre-cum smeared between our groins, making for one hell of a messy grinding dance of seduction. Heated breaths escaped us, without a doubt fogging every damn window.

"You told me to free the desire in my soul when I buried in your body." Ezra breathed out the words, and I let out a moan at the memory of his thick dick stretching my hole. "I want you to do the same, Aaron," he went on before I could reply, stilling me atop him. "I want you inside me. Loving me."

I lifted onto my elbows, wishing I'd left the flashlight on.

"I-I've been preparing myself all week," he added while I stared stupidly in the dark.

"Fuck, Ezzie." I tipped my forehead against his, fighting off the sudden need to bust a goddamn nut as his hot breath caressed my mouth. "Seriously?"

"Yes."

With a groan, I pulled myself away, crawling up over his body to reach for the packets of lube I'd stashed in the jeans I'd left on the driver seat.

Ezra put to good use how I moved in our cramped space. He grabbed hold of the backs of my thighs bracketing his head and licked up my tight balls to my dripping tip. "Mmm," he groaned his approval of my taste before taking the head of my dick into his mouth.

"Ah, fuck." I clutched my driver's seat headrest, caught and delayed by his actions.

He licked and sucked, untrained, but his hot mouth took me to the edge fast as fuck. A harsh boom of thunder startled me and kept me from erupting. "Better stop or I'm going to blow my load down your throat."

"I love the taste of your cum. Want it on my tongue." Ezra dug his fingertips into my ass and pulled me closer. Gagged. Groaned again, sucking harder as I tried to back off.

"Thought you wanted my dick in your ass?" I stated through clenched teeth.

He popped off. "You're young and we've got all night. Give me a mouthful, Aaron." Wet heat closed over my tip again.

Well, alright then. I thrust a few times and obeyed, a fucking boatload since I hadn't jacked off for a few days.

He gagged again but swallowed down every pulse shooting into his throat.

"Fuck, Ezzie…" I clutched the headrest but grabbed hold of his hair with my other hand, emptying myself until I shuddered, the sound of rain overhead muffled in my ringing ears.

His tongue licked me clean, and he let out a satisfied hum and something that sounded a lot like *definitely addicted*.

He wouldn't hear any arguments from me.

I fumbled in the dark to grab the lube packets in my jeans pocket before crawling back down over his body, panting, my dick semi hard, not enough to fuck him like he wanted.

But he spoke the truth…it wouldn't take me long to be ready to go again.

Chapter 29

Ezra

Aaron yanked down the sleeping bag's zipper, exposing my body to the warmed air of his SUV's interior. The taste of his saltiness lingered on my tongue, leaving me wanting more, but my length throbbed and ached, almost making me wish I'd let him have me first.

He moved around a bit, settling on his haunches between my spread thighs. "Scoot up a bit," he told me, and I shifted on my back, giving him room in our tiny little world of two where we hid from reality.

Blessed lightning shot across the sky beyond our small enclosure, allowing me a glimpse of how he stared at my jutting dick and exposed hole.

With a groan, he shoved his face in my crack, breathing in heavily before licking clear up through over my taint.

I grunted and grasped his head, lifting my knees to give him better access.

Aaron grabbed hold of my backside and dove back in, rimming and suckling. I'd never known such intimacy—and no embarrassment eased my need for him. My balls continued to ache, my dick leaking copious amounts of pre-cum.

"God, Aaron." I moaned, my head tipped back as release hovered on a knife's edge.

"Mmm hmm," he seemed to agree, shoving his tongue into my hole.

"Yes." I groaned low and long as he fucked in and out of me, driving his tongue in like he couldn't go deep enough. "More."

He backed off and used a fingertip to play with my puckered skin, teasing with slight presses but not breaching.

"Aaron." My voice hinted at the adrenaline thrumming through my blood. "Please give me more. I promise I can take it."

And I could. I hadn't lied about preparing myself for him. I'd found my asshole enjoyed the hell out a little penetration since first feeling his touch and deciding I didn't just want his finger inside my body.

"Where's the fucking lube?" he grumbled, movement rustling over the sleeping bag.

I smoothed my hands in search along our makeshift bed as well, but he found it before I did. Waiting caused goosebumps to shiver over my skin even though the chill had fled from the SUV's interior. I grabbed hold of my ass cheeks and stretched myself open like he'd done for me.

One of his hands closed over mine, the other's slickened fingers running up through my crack.

"Ung." I shifted, lifting my ass higher, my hole clenching at the feathered touch.

"Bear down," he told me and gently pushed against my hole. His finger slipped in like butter exactly as I'd expected, and he let out a curse. "Fuck, you're tight."

I hissed when he pulled out and pressed back in, my ass clamping down on him. "More."

"Patience." His murmur revealed a smirk, and he slowly fucked his finger in and out of me. "We can't rush this."

He closed his other hand around my dick. Wetness leaked from the slit, and he smeared the natural lube all over his palm before sliding his grasp down to my root.

God. "Oh..." I swallowed hard at the delicious sensations rushing through my groin and ass, curses ringing in my head. "Aaron..."

"Shh." He fingered my hole while slowly jacking my length.

My hips shot up when he rubbed over my prostate. "Oh...fuck...do that again."

"Mmm." He worked in a second finger without much resistance and gently reached deep.

A low groan rumbled through the vehicle as he rubbed inside me, causing more wetness to leak from my dick.

His scissoring fingers opened me up until I begged for another. "Please, Aaron... Tell me you're hard and ready for me because I need—"

He slid his fingers free with a squelching sound, and I hissed again, my hole clenching shut.

The wet sound of him stroking lube over his length filled the SUV's small interior along with our heavy breaths.

The storm had passed us by, leaving us in complete darkness, and I closed my eyes. "Please..." I whispered, and the blunt end of Aaron's dick rubbed over my hole.

"Let me in, Ezzie...let me love you."

My breath caught, but I forced myself to relax, wanting exactly what Aaron requested.

He breached the ring of muscle without much difficulty but stilled, giving me time to breathe through the sting.

I released a slowly leaked exhale, shifting beneath him enough so he sank in a little deeper.

"Fuck, are you tight," he stated as though through gritted teeth.

"Give me more." I reached for him and found his forearm as he bent forward over my body.

A flex of his hips stuffed me to the point I hissed again, but he leaned down and took my mouth in a gentle kiss, the soft pillow of his lips giving me something delicious to focus on rather than the obscene stretch of my ass.

I ran my palm up over the short hair on the back of his head, angling my own to deepen our kiss. Our tongues tangled, and Aaron rotated his hips in that provocative way he'd rutted on me, slowly sinking into my body until his balls rested against mine.

Fully joined, one body—and one spirit.

"Ezzie," he whispered before peppering kisses over my eyelids, my nose, and my whiskered cheeks.

The ache eased as I relaxed beneath him, and he began moving inside me as though he'd read my thought to ask for more. Long, slick withdraws and deep presses back in caused us both to groan as we shared breath in the inches between our faces.

There was no need for silence, no reason to hush the vocal appreciation of the other while Aaron showed me an act of physical love I hadn't known was possible.

Consuming in his sensual movements over me.

All thought obliterated—more so than when topping, more addictive than the taste of his cum.

Offering Aaron my body for his pleasure, allowing him to own me in the most intimate way brought new meaning to my life. Any need I'd had, he filled. Any healing my soul had longed for, he soothed.

He gave me the love I'd been desperate for, the kind I hadn't even realized I'd wanted.

Sacrificing all I'd been, all I'd lived my life for up until that moment came easy. I surrendered everything to Aaron, choosing him over and over again with every slow, deep thrust into my body.

"I love you," I claimed without further thought while holding him tight, the truth resonating in my soul.

Aaron cradled my face in his hands, his hips still slowly working to drive me insane. "Love you too, Ezzie—always have." His lips found mine in the darkness, and the way he moved over me, in me, slid hard muscle and pre-cum over my length trapped between us.

Elation swelled in my heart, tightening my throat.

My balls seized up tight as tears squeezed from beneath my closed eyelids—and I came, crying out my release against his mouth. My body convulsed beneath his weight in its desperation to spurt wetness between our stomachs.

He groaned, wrapped his arms completely around me, and thrust hard, jabbing harshly into me, hitting my prostate and prolonging my climax.

"Ezzie." Aaron grunted and buried deep before I felt his ejaculate fill me. "Oh fuck...Ezzie." He kissed my mouth, panting against my lips, every twitch of his length inside me causing him to jerk in my hold.

I clung to him, euphoria rushing over my skin, through my arteries. His heart pounded against my chest, both of us gasping for air, and I wanted the moment to never end.

We relaxed as one, sweaty and cum-slickened.

Aaron kissed my closed eyelids again and lapped at the tear tracks on my face. "You cried," he whispered but didn't pull away.

"Happy tears," I whispered and angled my head as he made his way along my jaw toward my ear.

"I love you." His deep words shivered my skin as much as his tongue flicking over my lobe. He pressed a kiss to my neck. "I love you," he repeated, trailing his lips lower. "Love you." His mouth settled over my collar bone, and he sucked hard enough I groaned, my ass clenching around his softening dick.

"Hell." Aaron pressed his hips against me. "Wish I was still hard as granite so I could fuck you for real."

"That felt pretty damn real to me," I said with a smile, smoothing my hands down his spine to ease the growly voice he'd uttered.

"Mmm." He kissed my mouth once...twice...and backed away from my body.

My ass stung as he left me empty, but he curled right up against my side, his hand sliding down to cup my backside. Warm wetness leaked from my hole, and he lazed his fingers through it, gently pushing it back inside me.

The possessive action filled me with a sense of satisfaction beyond being satiated, and another heavy sigh shuddered through me.

I didn't care that his softened, wet length pressed against my thigh. I didn't care lube still coated my crack, mixing with the cum he finally allowed to seep from my body onto the sleeping bag.

And I didn't care we both smelled of sweat and spunk.

I rolled to my side and curled against him.

Right where I belonged.

Chapter 30

Aaron

Best. Vacation. Ever.

We snuggled beneath the quilt by the fire the other nights, making out like teenagers before stumbling into our tent to enjoy the hell out of each other. The one hike we took along the lake's edge ended with him fucking me over a fallen tree. Even the campground's heated bathroom saw some action while we showered in lukewarm water.

When not fucking around or eating, we fished.

But we didn't carry on any heavy discussions, nothing deep that would possibly ruin the peaceful solitude of our escape from the world waiting for us at home.

Ezra knew my emotions toward him—I hadn't held anything back—and I rested in the fact he carried the same emotions toward me.

Where that left us once we returned to Philly, I wasn't sure.

I didn't ask how he was feeling about what we'd done to each other's bodies countless times over the weekend. We didn't discuss him moving into Dad's house with me like he'd mentioned on Friday. And I sure as fuck didn't bring up the fact he worked at Simply Grace and fucked a man in secret.

Eventually, we would have to talk about the future, but I chose to live in the moment and just enjoy the fuck out of my Ezzie.

Life—and death—would sort itself out soon enough.

I dropped him off at his apartment and helped him carry his things in—and my ass ached when I drove home an hour later.

Alone.

But I realized something in my time away that lay everything else to rest in my mind.

It was okay to take things for yourself, regardless of what others might think. It was okay to seek out happiness, and it was sure as fuck okay to *be* happy even when others around you didn't understand.

I sat down beside Dad's bed. He peered at me with that bland expression I'd come to hate. "Hey, Dad." I smoothed hair off his forehead. "Is this place treating you well?"

"Yes," he mumbled.

Ezra had told Dad we were going camping for the weekend when we'd visited with him on Friday afternoon. He hadn't questioned us or made any comment, but since the stroke, he hadn't spoken much at all.

Not to me, anyway.

"Weekend?" he asked, surprising the hell out of me.

Wondering if he felt jealous, I wasn't sure what all to share with him. "We had a good time." I decided on some truth. "Didn't catch a single fish, though."

He grunted, but I didn't pick up on any negativity.

"Ezra said you want him to move into our house."

A noise of agreement sounded in his throat.

"You're really okay with that?" I asked, searching his face for any evidence of emotion—good or bad.

Dad inhaled deeply, and I steeled myself for whatever words he prepared his body to allow out into the atmosphere.

"You sacrificed...your life...for me."

I swallowed hard at his drawn-out sentence but didn't nod or verbalize an agreement.

"I ask one...last thing." His words slurred, quieter than usual, and I leaned forward, taking his hand.

"Anything, Dad. You know that."

"Make my Ezra happy again," he whispered, wetness filling his eyes.

Blinking, I considered his words radiating through my head.

His Ezra.

I remembered what Ezra said about Dad regretting not seeking out love again, and I considered the possibility of what Dad had meant, what my suspicions suggested.

"You…love him?" Dad asked before I made up my mind if I wanted the truth or not.

"I do." I didn't hesitate to finally admit to being gay and loving his best friend, even though my voice rasped from the sudden tightness in my chest.

"Live your life."

No condemnation. No pulling away or abandoning me emotionally. I couldn't find a fucking word to utter with how my throat swelled shut.

Dad took another deep breath. "My God…never yours."

He spoke the truth, and I waited patiently, knowing he wasn't done speaking. Not that I could talk anyway with how overwhelmed I'd become by his declaration.

"He gave me you…so thankful. Loyal…merciful son."

A tear slid down my cheek, and I squeezed his hand, the vision of him hazing.

"I was jealous. Angry." Dad swallowed, his mouth working. "But I want you to…love him for me."

For me.

My heart cracked right the fuck open, my mind blown. Dad affirmed my thoughts, and I couldn't begin to fathom all I'd not seen, the emotions I'd missed years earlier.

With how Ezra responded to my touch, his own fumbling explorations of my body, I highly doubted they'd had an affair, which led me to another bit of truth.

Dad had loved Ezra in secret.

I'd always wondered why he'd never dated after Mom left, why he never made any attempt to find another woman.

"I'm going to love him, Dad," I swore a vow, barely able to speak, "even if his convictions turn him away from me, until I breathe my last breath. Promise."

Dad let out a heavy sigh and closed his eyes. "Sorry," he slurred.

"For what?" I swiped my arm over my wet eyes.

"Grumpy bastard."

I barked a laugh even though my chest still ached. "It's okay, Dad. It's really okay."

He squeezed my fingers, and I swore a smile tilted his lips too.

Chapter 31

Ezra

My entire body ached from a weekend sleeping in a vehicle and on the hard ground with nothing more than a sleeping bag covered in dry cum and sweat.

But I'd never felt better.

After a brief conversation with Aaron on Monday night after he visited with his dad, I climbed into my own bed, sighing at the softness, the scent of dryer sheets instead of woodsmoke and spunk.

But I missed the hard body entangled around mine. Missed Aaron's roughened hands, his feathered kisses over my face, and the murmurs of how much he loved me.

Still, I smiled against my pillow.

Even though work at Simply Grace loomed with the sure sunrise, I slept like a baby, and when morning came, I stretched, my lips once more curling upward at my body's reminder of the weekend.

A hot shower loosened me up a bit, two cups of coffee bringing life back to my foggy brain.

Aaron and I hadn't discussed our options for the future, but I'd already packed up all my meager belongings the previous afternoon once he'd left my apartment to head south.

I studied my reflection in the mirror while tying my tie around my neck, readying for work. It seemed fewer signs of aging lined my face, and even though we hadn't gotten much sleep over the weekend, no dark smudges bruised beneath my eyes.

Plenty of other types of bruising littered skin hidden by my suit pants and starched button-down shirt.

Love bites.

Hickeys.

My groin tightened over memories of Aaron's groans while marking me.

Caveman. I bit back a grin, my eyes twinkling at the memory of his fingers pushing his cum back inside my body.

I loved it. Loved everything about Aaron Weston.

"And now it's time to figure out how to move forward," I told the image of myself peering back at me from the mirror while straightening my shoulders.

My lips tightened, that same sense of firmness portraying in my eyes. A nod of assurance at myself, and I left for work.

A half-hour later, I opened my office door and stumbled to a stop. Pastor Welker sat behind my desk —and the entire board of elders and other staff along with Pastor Jed—waited inside for me on folding chairs in the small space.

The blood drained from my face, and I cleared my throat, forcing my feet forward. "Good morning," I offered as though their being crammed in my office wasn't an unusual occurrence. My heart attempted to beat its way clear through my breastbone, but I nodded at each of them, taking in stern stares, some uncomfortable...Pastor Jed's full of compassion.

Pastor Welker nodded when our gazes met, his lips flatlined. He motioned to the only empty chair in the room—across my desk from him. "Have a seat."

Had they learned about my affair, or was this some sort of intervention they felt I needed?

I crossed the room on shaking legs and settled into the indicated chair, setting my bagged lunch and water bottle at my feet as silence reigned over us. Another clearing of my throat took place so I could speak and get whatever ball they held rolling. "To what do I owe the pleasure, gentlemen?"

Pastor Welker pulled a rumpled piece of paper from the inside of his suit coat—

Sofiy's note.

Blood rushed from my head, leaving me swaying in my chair.

I hadn't thought about my greatest shame since telling Phillip about my time in the Ukraine...I'd dropped her note to his hospital bed.

And Welker had come in after I'd forgotten about it during Phillip's and my reminiscing.

I scrubbed a hand down over my face, blinking at the crumpled paper he spread out on my desk, not bothering to ask where he found it or what he made of her scrawled accusations. The evidence of that answer lay with the witnesses around us.

I didn't doubt they would judge me for my failings, for withholding evidence from the authorities and her family—their faces claimed as such.

Except for Jedidiah Simpson. I gave him my attention while steeling myself for the sure ruination of the self-esteem Aaron had begun to help me rebuild. "We're taught the church comes first—and I clung to that truth," I rasped out, still focused on Jed.

No pity shone in his dark eyes, but he dipped his head in agreement.

Pastor Welker shifted in my periphery. "Pastor Ezra."

Hell, I hated having to focus on his disproving face, but I did so, my chin lifting slightly, ready to face him as God's appointed authority in my life. I'd chosen his church, to submit myself to his teachings.

Even though I'd turned my back on both over the best weekend of my entire life.

"God graciously gave you a faithful wife," he said.

And I failed her.

"And according to her accusations, you didn't love her as Christ loves the church," Welker stated what I expected. "You ignored her needs—"

She never shared them with me until it was too late.

"—because you were *too caught up in serving the Lord*." Welker shook his head at the exact words he read from her note. He lifted his attention to my face again, a very pregnant pause thickening the tension in the room.

The shroud of shame fixed heavily over my shoulders.

"Rather than support your walk down God's path He set before you," he continued, "she chose selfishness and lived in her emotions instead of trusting Him."

I stared, sure I hadn't heard Pastor Welker right. Where were his words of condemnation for *me*?

"God always comes first in a faithful man's life," Pastor Welker added while settling back in my chair as though it were his throne.

A blink didn't help clear up the truth of what I read on his face.

"While I know you loved Sofiy, she chose death over the life God had gifted her." His lips thinned a brief moment. "You cannot allow guilt, the bitterness in this note, to keep you from moving forward in the light. Striving toward fulfilling His purpose for you. Crowns of gold await you, Pastor Ezra." His chin lifted in that look of arrogance I'd seen once before.

And same as then, my stomach twisted, but still I stared, without words.

"You were merciful in keeping the truth of her sins from her family." Welker ripped Sofiy's note in half. Ripped it into fours. Eighths. Demolished her final attempts at manipulation as thoroughly as he'd done her character in front of his staff.

I stood once more on the edge of the unknown, a heavy silence in my ears as disappointment in the church replaced the shroud of shame hanging over me.

Live in fear or be courageous? Embrace change or retreat?

I'd done enough retreating...

It's time to stand up.

I realized I'd looked to Jed when he nodded as though he knew the conclusion I'd come to in my mind. He was my sole supporter in that room, I had no doubt by the compassion and regret in his eyes, a true Christian in every sense of the word. It was clear the shit Pastor Welker had spewed didn't set well in his heart either.

I turned back toward the man I'd submitted myself to and straightened my shoulders.

The joy the church used to bring me was no longer viable, and although I still believed God was one of love, a lot of His children got it wrong. The man in front of me especially.

"Christ laid down his life for the church," I stated quietly, holding Pastor Welker's steady gaze. He nodded as though he was an authority on the topic, but I wasn't done reminding him of the truth he'd claimed to *know*. "He sacrificed the one He loved for those who'd cursed His name. Nailed Him to a tree."

"And He rose victorious three days later."

I ignored Pastor Welker's interruption and the amens that sounded around the room.

"And I couldn't take the time, rouse up the energy or balls, to seek out the medical help my wife desperately needed." I raised my voice until they quieted. "By staying faithful to my greediness for riches in glory, I failed her—God's gift to me, one of His children. I didn't force those pills down Sofiy's throat, but I *am* guilty of not loving her as the Bible commanded to do —just like she wrote in that note."

A pin could have dropped and clanged in the sudden silence.

"Loving one another *should* come first—above the church—and I'm ashamed for not recognizing that until it was too late." I stood, all my nervousness gone, my heart and mind lighter than it had been in years. "While I'm here confessing what most of you would see as nothing worth airing to the world, I'll mention my disappointment in how you've chosen to judge my deceased wife—and offer my two weeks' notice as well."

"Pastor Ezra—"

"I'll be going by Ezra now." I cut Pastor Welker off. "I'm simply a man who has fallen in love again, and he will always come first in my life. If that means I'm no longer welcome in a pulpit and God no longer hears my prayers, then so be it. But I won't stop praying for others—just in case my words reach a throne of grace I can't believe would judge me for choosing the man who loves me unconditionally."

I grabbed my bagged lunch and water bottle, ready to spin on my heel.

"Man?" Welker rasped out, and I found myself smiling. *That* word, at least, had been heard.

Others shifted around the room, Mr. Townson's sniff of disdain from beside me not the only one to sound out in disgust.

"Man." I offered confirmation with a firm nod.

Welker stood to his feet, looming over the desk I had zero desire to sit behind ever again. Red flushed over his face. "Perversion," he all but hissed the word.

"Perhaps in your eyes, but my heart says its love."

"Get. Out."

"Gladly." I cast one last glimpse at Jed whose face had paled. The rest of the men I spared a passing glance. "May God have more mercy on your souls than you show the ones who don't conform to your thinking."

I closed the door softly behind me and escaped the clutches of a church I expected God was sorely disappointed in.

Chapter 32

Aaron

It felt good to be back at the gym giving my muscles a workout even though I'd had a few hours of excellent cardio over the weekend.

Telling Martin I would be available for longer shifts pumped me up even more, especially seeing there was a light at the end of the financial trouble tunnel. I grinned, flying high as a fucking kite knowing I didn't have to rush home at nine to care for Dad too.

I did call the nursing home to check in on him before clocking in, and the nurse told me he'd slept peacefully through the night. I wondered how gracious she would sound once he woke and they readied him for the day ahead. Zero pity rested in my heart for whoever worked the morning shift there at the nursing home.

But I would visit with him around dinner time. Maybe sneak him some KFC.

"Aaron?"

That voice...

My head jerked up from where I stood behind the desk, scrolling aimlessly on my cell.

"The fuck do you want, *Drew*?" I scowled. "The gym's owner said you weren't welcome here."

My old tormentor didn't bother correcting the name usage, and I noted his shifting gaze and how he moved from foot to foot.

One of my eyebrows shot up over his obvious discomfort—something I'd never once seen Drew wear.

"I...wanted to say I was sorry."

I choked on a snort of laughter. "Get the fuck out."

"I'm serious, Aaron." He finally held my gaze, and I read that truth in his dark eyes. "I was an asshole to you when we were kids because I was confused as fuck. Taking it out on you was wrong in so many ways—"

"Got that fucking right." I crossed my arms, squaring off a bit and lifting my chin.

"—and while I'd originally come on to you last fall because that hatred still ate my insides, I've since recognized the problem is mine."

"How many hours of therapy did it take for you to sort that shit in your brain?"

A wry grin, and he turned his focus off me again. "A lot." He let out a heavy exhale. "I've been messed up for a few years...came home to clean up, get my act together."

"And how's that going for you?" I asked, finding I really didn't harbor any more bitterness toward him.

"Good." He smiled, seemingly more relaxed. "It's taken over seven months, but I think my therapist has finally helped me remove my head from my ass."

I eyed him for a few seconds, contemplating— considering giving him another chance at a new life he attempted to build. With all the regrets, the shame, and the secrets I'd dealt with since Ezra's return home, I only had one option.

"We're running a spring special," I told Drew, grabbing one of the flyers I'd printed out a few minutes earlier. "One month for twenty bucks."

He studied me, slowly reaching for the flyer. "That's it? I mean, you're willing to leave our shit in the past?"

"Every man should have the opportunity to live their best life, and you've made good choices in finding your way."

Drew's slow smile lit up his face. "I'm going to go out on a stupid limb, but I gotta ask about that sexy as fuck pastor."

Rather than seethe with jealousy like I'd have done a few months earlier, I barked out a laugh. "Marked and claimed, Michael."

"Well shit." He offered a sheepish grin. "If you boys ever want to spice things up a bit in your relationship, let me know."

"I don't share."

"He's a lucky man."

"So am I," I didn't hesitate to point out.

Michael nodded—and I signed him up as the newest member at Martin's gym, listing his first name exactly how he wished.

Talk about another fucking high...

Then Ezra walked in at nine-forty, tie askew, face flushed, his eyes twinkling when he caught my gaze. He strode toward me while I took in his suit pants, shiny shoes, and the starched shirt stretched over his shoulders.

"Done with work for the day already?" I asked.

He crowded me behind the counter and laid his mouth on mine, wiping my damn head clear of thought. No tongue, no heated groin presses or thrusts against me, but hunger lay on his lips, the kind that roused my blood to boiling and dick ready to grind in the blink of an eye.

"The hell was that for?" I asked, breathless when he pulled away.

"Done with work for good." A sexy-as-fuck fire lit his eyes. It looked like...rebellion...and he wore it damn well. "I told Pastor Welker I'd fallen in love with a man, and I left Simply Grace without a backward glance."

"You what?" I gasped the words out with disbelief.

Ezra laughed, his baritone chuckle lighting bubbles inside me that ended up erupting along with his.

"I gotta hear this story," I said between laughs.

He caressed my forearm but didn't pull me back against him like I'd have preferred. "How long are you here for today?"

"A full eight hours, believe it or not."

Ezra kissed me quickly once more. "I'll see you at home for dinner."

"Home?"

The happiness shining on his face melted my damn heart. "I'm moving back. Today. And we're celebrating with a roast, mashed potatoes, and carrots."

"I'm starved already." I hooded my gaze, letting him know I meant for more than food.

He shuddered beneath my stare. "Dinner first?"

"If you're *un*lucky." I slapped his ass as he turned for the door.

He shot a glare over his shoulder, and I blew him a kiss.

Fucking Ezzie…

So damn perfect for me.

Ezra left me hard and aching, and I spent the rest of the day hiding my tented shorts behind the desk while fantasizing about my man meeting me naked at the door.

When I finally got home, he stood in *our* kitchen making dinner. He still wore his work clothes instead of how I'd hoped to find him, but he'd ditched the dress shoes and went barefoot.

I crowded up against his back so he would feel how hard he'd made me, my lips finding his neck. "I've never been so happy to come to this house in my life," I said against his skin that carried his luscious scent into my lungs and tightened my groin even more.

Ezra set aside the serving spoon he'd held and turned, finding my hips to tug me closer.

I cradled his face in one hand, my focus dropping to his mouth.

He licked his lower lip as my thumb caressed over his whiskered jawline. "As much as I want your hands and mouth on me—"

"Don't forget my dick in you," I tacked on, shutting off his planned letdown.

"Damnit, Aaron." He let out a huff.

I laughed and nipped his lower lip before soothing it with a kiss. "Continue, please. I'll dick you down so good you'll forget your own name after whatever it is you want done first."

"I have a story to tell you, remember?"

"Oh yeah. That. I got so caught up thinking about sinking into your body..." I kissed his nose and stepped back, giving him space as he released another frustrated groan.

"You're insatiable," he muttered, adjusting his bulge.

"I'm not the only one." I nodded toward his groin. "But go ahead and tell me about your morning, then I get to tell you about mine."

His smile damn near melted my heart. "Over dinner?"

"Roast?"

"As promised."

I rubbed my hands together and went to sit my ass down at the table he'd set—with fucking candles and everything.

"Wash up first."

Rolling my eyes, I went to do as told. "Yes, daddy."

"Don't start," he muttered, slapping my ass with the serving spoon he'd picked back up. "You hate that shit, remember?"

I grinned like a goddamn idiot long after I sat down, but my lips flatlined as Ezra shared over our dinner the reason for that note from Sofiy in his laundry.

"I found out that secret last year, Ezzie," I stated quietly. "You left it in your dirty laundry once, but nothing you've done or said in the past will ever change how I see you. You're a hero to me—always will be even if we don't see eye-to-eye at times. You're also my lover." I smiled while leaning forward, hoping to ease the wetness welling in his eyes. "The best I've ever had."

Ezra smiled through his tears. "Thank you for believing in me, Aaron, for giving me the benefit of the doubt. For forgiving me and allowing me a second chance to be a part of your life."

"Easily done. Now, what went down at the church." I shoved more food into my mouth.

To hear the resulting shit from Welker having found Sofiy's suicide note and how the men in his office had treated him...

"What the actual fuck?" I sat back, fork still in hand, staring across the table. "Could he be any more of an asshole?" Welker had torn down the memory of a woman I couldn't stand, but his words were uncalled for. Unjust and unnecessary. "Tell me you told him to fuck off."

"I did something even better." Ezra bit back a smirk, the heavy emotions of discussing his wife past for the time being. "I fed him the words he'd often shared from the pulpit, backed by scripture."

I huffed with laughter as he recounted what he'd stated—right up to admitting he'd fallen in love again.

With a man.

"Holy fucking shit...you came right out? Just like that?"

"Just like that."

Not one ounce of regret or shame filled his eyes and smiling face.

"You're one hell of a man, Ezra Jamison." I shook my head, fucking blown away by his strength, his character. "What you did, that choice you made..." My throat tightened right the fuck up, and Ezra reached over the table.

I gave him my hand, and we both squeezed.

"I appreciate you, Aaron, more than you could fathom," he stated quietly. "You've shown me how to live again, how to love in a way I didn't know was possible. And how you selflessly cared for your dad..." His voice trailed off too, and we both sniffed, our eyes going glassy.

"I love you so fucking much, Ezzie," I rasped out.

"I love you too, Aaron. So, so much."

"Tell me the rest of dinner can wait," I begged, entwining my fingers through his.

"Dinner can wait—but what about your story?"

"Drew came into the gym, apologized, I forgave him. End of."

He chuckled at my rushed words. "Well, shit."

"Yeah." I stood, rounded the table, and pulled Ezra up out of his chair. "Want my dick here in the kitchen or upstairs?"

"I was feeling like the king of the world earlier today… and fantasized about topping you." Ezra's spewed second half of his statement caused a groan to rumble in my chest and clenched my hole.

"I get first dibs," I grabbed hold of his thick dick with a firm grip. "But if you can hold off from shooting your spunk while I'm enjoying the hell out of your tight hole, you can have mine after."

"Is that a promise?" His murmur drew my focus to his lips.

"Fuck yeah."

He smiled, sending butterflies to flight in my stomach. "I'm about to show you the benefits of being an old man, Aaron Weston." He headed toward the stairs, and I willingly followed along without him tugging on my hand.

I had the thought my asshole would bear the consequences of egging Ezra on, but I grinned, knowing the ache his girth always inflicted would remind me the whole next day at work how much he loved me.

Chapter 33

Ezra - Four weeks later...

I held Aaron's hand tight in mine as we watched the casket lowered into the ground. Songbirds tweeted in the warm breeze caressing my face, and I smiled, thinking of how much Phillip had loved birds.

Aaron and I had set up a feeder outside his window at the nursing home, and we'd enjoyed hours of identifying them from the tattered book I'd taken from the house.

I found it fitting that God's creations would lift their tiny voices in song that morning since no churchgoers stood alongside us as Simply Grace members used to do when saying goodbye to an old, faithful friend.

Had Welker's flock been anything like my sister's in Oklahoma, I knew things would have been different.

I came out to Abby over the phone the day after leaving my job at Simply Grace. She accepted and loved me regardless of our thoughts and beliefs having strayed from one another's. Like Pastor Jed, she embodied the true spirit of a Christian.

If only more of God's children plucked the plank from their own eye before judging others, there would be less hatred, less racism—without a doubt, less depression and suicide. If only people chose love…

A heavy exhale left me as I forced myself in that moment to do so toward my enemies.

Focusing on the future rather than allowing bitterness to grow in my heart, I squeezed Aaron's hand and lifted my attention off Phillip's casket to the two young men alongside Glenda and her husband standing across from us.

Zeke and Levi had driven down from Boston, their palms firmly clasped, rings on both their left hands drawing my gaze. They'd married the week before, and jealousy turned my stomach an ugly shade of green.

I never thought I would want to be a husband ever again, but my love for the man beside me and seeing Zeke and Levi together had changed my mind.

Although I knew Aaron belonged to me and I was his for as long as I breathed oxygen into my lungs, I wanted a physical display of our love to tell the world how much he meant to me. Unbroken rings given as a reminder of the commitment we'd already made to one another.

I'd also promised Phillip in our final private moments together that I would love and cherish his son forever. Even though he'd slipped into a coma a few days earlier, I rested in the truth he'd heard in my quiet words. I'd held his hand, watching his chest rise and fall twice more after my vow before stilling for eternity.

Aaron didn't regret not being by his dad's side when his spirit left us—and I'd been glad to have Phillip to myself to assure him I would carry the memory of him deep inside my heart along with my love for his son.

A jay's caw sounded in the distance, bringing my focus back on the two young men standing across from us. Levi leaned into Zeke, his head tipped onto his shoulder, and Zeke wrapped an arm around his waist, holding him close.

Aaron let out a shuddered sigh beside me, and I did as Zeke had done, pulling my lover against me.

The night before, Zeke had introduced us to his friend's hit on the pop charts from the previous summer, and as Malachi and Isaac had sensually crooned together through Aaron's stereo speakers, I found myself echoing their words in my heart.

Beautifully us, worth the sacrifice. I would choose you all over again.

My light.

My life.

My love.

Aaron was all that to me and more. My best choice, the shoulder I could count on when I needed his strength. The unselfish one who gave affection until my soul flooded with contentment.

I embraced all I'd become, all he offered, knowing in my heart that no God of love could possibly see us as wrong. While I no longer read the Bible or attended church, I chose to believe in a higher being, sure that man had misconstrued those teachings in the far past.

My heart full, I turned my focus back to Phillip's final resting place. His body might be enclosed inside metal, wood, and soft cushions of white, but I believed the essence of him stood in glory, whole and smiling down at us.

Aaron wiped his suit coat sleeve over his eyes, and I squeezed him against me, kissing him on the temple. There weren't any words necessary over his dad's grave. We'd shared everything—and I mean everything in the previous couple of weeks as Phillip's health steadily declined.

There were no secrets between us.

He admitted to jerking off in my silk boxers while doing laundry.

And I admitted to sneaking into his room a few times to sniff his pillow.

Now we shared one more often than not while falling asleep wrapped in each other's warm embrace—and we jerked *each other* off.

I shouldn't have grinned at the thought, shouldn't have even had that thought while walking away from Phillip's grave. Zeke and Levi followed behind us chatting with Glenda and her husband, but my best friend had wanted us to live.

And I had no plans to do otherwise.

Sliding my thumb over Aaron's fourth finger, I decided on another plan: putting a ring on it, because a lifetime with him?

Never enough.

THE END

About the Author

USA Today Bestselling author Lynn Burke is a CrossFit and coffee addict. Her three spawn and two fur babies dictate how often she can be found hunched over her Mac, typing as fast as her fickle muse cooks up hot stories.

You can find more about Lynn at her website: www.authorlynnburke.com

Also By Lynn Burke

Abel's Obsession

Divulging Secrets

Healing Storms

In Between

Reluctant Lumberjack

Resisting his Mate

Billion Dollar Love Anthology

Blood Born Series

Bonds of Worship Series

Dark Leopards MC

Darkest Desires Series

Devil's Outlaws MC

Elite Escort Series

Elite Escorts MM Series

Fallen Gliders MC

Forbidden Obsession Duet

Found by Fate Series

Midnight Sun Series

Missing Link Series

Risso Family Series

Sandy Ridge Series

Sinful Nature Series

Vicious Vipers MC

9 781955 635332